God Loved Her
With High Heels

God Loved Her With High Heels

VARSHA PRATAP

PARTRIDGE
A Penguin Random House Company

ISBN:	Hardcover	978-1-4828-2307-3
	Softcover	978-1-4828-2306-6
	eBook	978-1-4828-2305-9

Print information available on the last page.

To order additional copies of this book, contact
Partridge India
000 800 10062 62
orders.india@partridgepublishing.com

www.partridgepublishing.com/india

DEDICATION

I dedicate this book to my loving father, Late Pratapeshwar Singh and to Aghoreshwar Bhagwan Shree Sambhav Ram Ji.

Acknowledgment

To mark the beginning of my acknowledgment I extend my humble gratitude to His Holy Highness Shree Gurupad Sambhav Ram ji for his unending blessings and guidance without which my book wouldn't have been possible.

I am grateful to my husband Vikas Kumar Singh for his encouragement and love.

I extend my sincere thanks to my mother Mridula Singh and to my sister Vansla Singh for their love & support.

My heartfelt gratitude to my brother Vikram Pratap for reading my writings and giving constant feedbacks to me.

My special thanks to my brother's staff, Sandeep and Satender without whose timely help, my writing would have been incomplete. I am also thankful to Pradeep Raul for helping me with computer work in times needful.

Last but not the least my humble love and many a thanks to the resourceful team at Partridge publishers without whom this book wouldn't have seen the light of the day.

CONTENTS

INTRODUCTION

Every race has a human every
human has a soul and every soul has a life
beyond worldly wisdom.

"We need happiness to be happy and not people," these are the wise words of a woman contemporary, soothingly beautiful and loving in all her ways. Born with the audacity to make life fail in failing with style, that was as much original, as, was inherited. Her faith in God was as permanent as was her passion to live life king size. A brand ambassadress of hope and patience, she dared to dream with her eyes open and willingly paid the price of living her dream. There were some things she always had in abundance; care for needy, strong drive for luxury and a very positive attitude towards life and people. Her sufferings improved her, and glamour even in the

1

extreme suited her, for she always knew, where to draw the line and which horizon to chase. All through her life she gave people two options to choose from; either they loved her or, they loved her a lot. Such was her divine mysticism and her charisma that led to successful transformation of every soul she touched, helping each of them to evolve and live their dreams, as blissfully, as she lived her own.

The villa spread in an area of six acres with dainty coconut trees lined around its boundary, magnifying it's glorious appeal and watching over it for ages, that passed from one generation to another was the home of a happy couple.

Today the lady of this sprawling villa, was lying on her bed praying that her baby joins the world in good health. She was surrounded by some women she knew very well and an old nurse, who were together pacifying her.

Outside this room with large windows was her husband, unraveling a new story out of his experience, with his friends as he was pacing up and down the entrance anxiously, in anticipation of the birth of his first born.

First the delay in labor and now the labor itself, were hiking up their anxiety making this new father to be turn into an oscillating pendulum, with two coveted questions on his mind. 'Will my woman deliver a girl or was she going to deliver, a boy?'

In the mean while the unborn child and the much awaited newborn to be, was taking it's own time to rest their anticipation, for destiny, they say, takes own time in bringing new souls into the universe physically. This happens when the stars of the universe signal her of their perfect placement, to embrace the birth of a new born. It's only then that a soul enters the universe, as a baby does it's parent as an living enigma, to the world.

'Every soul in a body is a story teller, says my woman,' said Anand, 'and I can't wait for the story this soul is to reveal.'

'Oh! Women say many a line. But since this one comes from your wife . . . it ought to be believed,' said one of his friends.

Keeping his hand on his shoulders, the man of the villa replied, 'Oh yes! I need some lessons in patience.'

'Calm down my friend . . . I can tell you lots about patience . . . but then, we can take a horse to a pond, we can not make him drink water,' his friend replied.

'I agree. But my friend today I am a happy man, free of guilt and all social barriers.'

They smiled to each other as their pacing continued.

'I wish Aseem were with us . . .' the man reminisced.

'Is that what you confess,' asked another gentleman friend of his, from amidst his group.

'You bet,' said the man and his eyes had a sheen. 'His honesty lingers on in me that reflected through his happy smile.'

'You see, life is humbling,' said the yet another friend of his looking in the distance as though he could see his dead friend, Aseem, coming alive. And just then came a news to them cutting all their conversation in between, as they rushed towards the door of the room.

It was in this afternoon that she, as a healthy baby girl weighing ten pounds, was born in Chennai to Anand, the non conformist Brahmin businessman as well as the man of the villa and his wife Andrea, a pretty looking devout Christian, German woman. They as a couple, were known to be in love with love and in love

3

with each other with a tenacity that was, beyond the realm of this life.

Inspired by the leading lady of the legendary love story of the bygone era, they choose the name, Laila, for their much anticipated baby girl.

Laila was born with her father's thoughtful deep brown eyes and his smooth black hair, and her mother's porcelain pink skin and her beautiful smile, that dimpled on the corner of the lips. This baby girl was born out of love, to love.

Nervously taking his daughter from the nurse's arms, Anand held the weeping Laila in the safety and the warmth of his arms, now for the first time as the baby's official father, in his mind. And so came the time for the official information to go on records which the nurse did with delight.

Full of dramatic pride of becoming a father, he said aloud to his friends, 'she's my angel. Oh . . . she feels like a soft ball of cotton wrapped in a cloth. So blissful and loving that my heart can sing a thousand songs on her birth.' His friends lowered their heads to take a look at her, in his arms, alike adult birds looking over a nest full of eggs; naively feeling in charge.

Then Anand held her close and closer to his heart and she trembled, breaking into a gesture that appeared like a smile. Seeing her smile, he felt like standing on a victory podium with showers of unfelt happiness and a elated feeling of victory that superseded all his previous achievements as a man, as a professional and as a husband.

Thankless to the universe though thoughtful of his beautiful wife, for the joy she had brought to him, he gladly said to his friends, 'My angel is prettier than her mother . . . she is my dream come true and beyond, I shall give her a life full of joy,' and he swung the baby in his arms with happiness, like holding a trophy loosely to an audience.

The victory of his fatherhood was visibly apparent to the eyes and hearts of all. His friends embraced the lovely baby, whose large eyes looked at them with equality and purity. She brought to every heart, that witnessed her birth in the villa, an ambience full of love.

This day marked the beginning of her divinity and charisma. With her was born the unheard glory which she was to unleash into the world, so full of the crisis of the soul, that tears apart lives, and the unending war between greed and ego, where miseries never seem to end and where material is blasphemy, yet so full of attraction which leads a man far-far away from his existence and from the realms of his soul.

'Into this loud world came this girl bringing with her, the secrets of divine master, within every soul' thought her mother as she closed her eyes, as though she doesn't desire to live any more. And on the outside, men began to start a new day with loud laughter and sipping cold coffee.

It was the evening of the same day; Anand had his villa decorated with streams of lights converting his Indo Portuguese style villa into a place no less than a marriage set of a film. Visitors poured in from all corners of Chennai to congratulate the couple and to bless their new born daughter.

Time moved on, winter receded, spring moved in and summer took over.

——◈——

In the first summer of the child, her parents were raising her in the womb of affluence and affection. Needs being needs they were catering to it all, even before their baby learnt to make a mention of it. Toys, clothes, footwear, perambulators, baby cot, aprons, feeders and Governess—came to her from varied parts of the world.

'My baby is a fulfilled child,' thought Andrea,' and may this fulfillment last her a life time. "But nothing lasts for ever", goes the old saying. And just then she heard Anand's voice.

'She has a happy face, that made me sing a thousand songs. She touched my soul . . . as deep as . . .' remarked Anand with mysticism while he was stepping up to the stairs of the terrace with Andrea next to him.

'So, finally you have a soul,' said Andrea holding his hand gently and supporting Laila's tender body in with her other arm.

'Oh! Sorry my love,' snapped Anand happily, 'm' supposed to be soulless except for when I married you and became an out caste . . . something you forget to cherish.'

'OH! That was Brilliant piece of art Anand,' responded Andrea, "my marriage to you and also the sequel . . . that being your father's emotional divorce from you.' Both of them chuckled as a happy couple in love. 'What say Anand!'

'Anything for you,' said Anand with a pause, 'I presume you still find me as strikingly handsome as you narrated to your father. "Ruthlessly handsome," that's how you described me, now that was quite a thing from your silent mouth.'

She looked away with her thoughtful eyes and said, 'He was too rich to talk of your innocence and love, so I spoke of your non existent jaw line.' She chuckled with a face as if love were in the air, and she was having her fill. 'God what a hard time we had getting married. It's a thing about marriage. Nothing remains fancy either before or after it. Somehow something creeps in. Some get married and suffer while some suffer like us before marriage.' Saying so she was overwhelmed and kissed him gently on his cheeks to which he tended shyly. 'But that's what makes it special Anand.'

'Don't worry my love, Laila will avenge. He made me reckless and took me away from my soul,' said Anand delighted by her gesture. 'I will not hold her in her arms, I will make her walk very soon so that she goes and troubles that old man, the father of yours.' And he played with Laila's tiny first finger holding it with his first finger and thumb exhibiting anxiety. 'That wicked BASTARD!'

'That's an old line Anand,' she responded.' Post that she didn't reply and then her man's conversation drifted to food. As his conversation drifted, she mentioning him that today his favourite Rasam and rice was being cooked. He was pleased taking away Laila from Andrea's arms.

From the crawling infant, Laila became a toddler who could sit for a few minutes and would roll backward as her tender spine gave way. When she mastered sitting, she began to stand up and then learnt to walk. Oh! What a splendid joy it was to her parents who kept a record of all the new development in her colourful baby book.

Then she, wearing a pink and white baby frock with frills and a big bow was tied to her hair, marking her first birthday. This day was clicked with her cutting a three tiered cake before the dinner was served to the huge crowd that had gathered in the lush green lawn of her home. Confetti and flower petals fell on her and on the little one around her, like blessings from above. The guest clapped and sang for her, her birthday song, as the cameras fluttered continuously and gifts were poured in.

But, this was not all to it.

From this year on, on her birthday, every year her father, on Andrea's humble request, took a day off from his busy schedule to hold his daughter in his arms, like a bouquet of flowers; pretty and delicate.

It was Andrea's wise idea to make her daughter, present when the lunch was distributed among the poor outside the neighborhood temple, along with simple but thoughtful gifts for them.

Anand's domestic help made the alms seekers stand in two different lines, one of males and other of females, to distribute the gifts, post the lunch to mark the splendor of day.

If we fill any date in our life, ordinary or otherwise, with genuine and soulful love for ourselves and for others, then occasions tend to have a different pleasure to it. Needless to say, it becomes an outstanding memory that lasts a life time, cheering us up, in hard times.

Time trotted, Laila was growing up playing endlessly, with the children not only with the elites of her neighborhood, but also with the children of her domestic help who lived in the backyard of the sprawling villa.

Andrea saw to it that those children were served the same meal as Laila, if they were around during her meal time. This was her way of teaching her child, to share her privileges with other thus remaining sensitive to the desires of the needy as long as life permits, because for her, every child, rich or poor, had desires for the usual things one liked as a child; a candy, a birthday dress or a plate with cartoon characters peeping from behind the sumptuous meal or just a pair of neat slippers. And Andrea believed that, every soul satiated in ways small or big, was a way to serve God, especially when done selflessly.

It also nurtured a sense of gratitude alongside. This she inculcated in her child by teaching her relentlessly to thank the Almighty, for keeping them privileged enough to be able to cater not only to their needs, but of those as well, who couldn't cater their own.

A needy for the wise Andrea was God's ways of keeping her humble, for she took it as a reminder that being needy was a way of life irrespective of our financial class. She believed that all of us turn into a needy at one point of time or another and if we share our care (privileges) with others who are in greater need than we then God and His universe, will multiply and return our help back to us, in times least expected and most desired.

'Grace is the least of the mercy the universe brings forth to its children, young and old,' this Andrea believed. And as life unfolded, there were lots to teach her wisdom to her child.

'You are a cow, and ugly owl.' babbled Laila at her male helper, who stood behind her until she finished her glass of milk which she resented fully.

Her father heard her and came forward from reading newspaper. He knelt down at the level of her tiny table and said firmly, 'Baby, only a cow can be a cow and not him. Right?' There was no response, she was still angry.

'And owls are not ugly. They can't be. Nobody can be ugly because God makes only beautiful creatures,' said Andrea.

God makes every creature beautiful because His beauty is unexhausting and supreme.

'Yes.' She replied with affectionate voice. She did understand this one and also what her father said next.

'He is older than you, as he was born, before you. And good girls always respect their seniors. So please, no rudeness towards Rajaji, from next time. We respect our seniors always. And if my lovely Laila is angry, she will talk to her papa about it. No abusing anybody. Right Laila?' He said politely as Andrea was watching over. Correcting her, he gave a peck on each of her cheeks and got a simple affirmative nod, in turn from her. For him, no mistake of her's was a mistake big enough to blow it out of proportion or to make it a public disgrace for making such a thing damages the children's confidence in themselves and dent the tenderness of childhood, converting them into snappy and fault finding angry adults, of which Andrea had made him aware.

Privileges, ideally blended with humble parenting was going, to make a well bred child. During the period when parents were obsessed with crowning their children with knowledge, Laila's mother taught her wisdom intentionally, as education can go wrong and can under go change but wisdom is free of these both. 'And once,' she believed,' this foundation is laid deep and strong in a child, the edifice of their life, builds over with the unchallenged convictions, mercy and faith. And then nobody can stop his/her achieving any mark.'

Today there was excitement in Laila's voice as Laila went to school, tenderly enjoying her days until the report card day came up.

Today was Laila's report card day and seated in one of the classrooms of the primary section of the school were, Laila, Anand, Andrea and Mrs. Marvor,; Laila's old class teacher.

'Ah! Laila, the naughty one, you are bright,' remarked her class teacher. 'Come to me, my child.'

By five years of age, she was disciplined to the order of a cadet and also was turning bright as a child, a development that pleased Anand immensely.

'Oh Laila, my little one, the good head that you wear on your narrow shoulders, will one day make us very proud.' He said hugging his daughter before Mrs. Marvor as she praised her.

'Bright children are nice but it's kind children who lead a much happier life,' responded Andrea wisely, as she sat next to him in one of the two chairs placed opposite her child's class teacher.

'There you are right,' spoke the old woman to Andrea. 'Your child is kind as well. So congrats on that note, my lovely lady. Sorry I didn't get your name.'

'Andrea.' She said with a smile. 'I . . .'

'You see, Mrs. Marvor,' interrupted Anand avoiding Mrs. Marvor in her eyes, 'my wife and I fell in love for our similarities and now we realize that the only similarity between us was indifference to each other.'

The old Mrs. Marvor smiled with her old teeth shining from her mouth, 'she has given you Laila. Isn't that one good reason to look over your differences. You see Andrea,' she turned her head slowly as she spoke, to look at her, 'I know this boy since he was that little,' she spoke pointing to Anand, 'and ever since then, nothing could satisfy him. Nothing . . . nobody. So, don't take his words to your heart, my dear.'

'Oh, Mrs. Marvor, now I am a changed man, 'Anand replied to her.

'When we repeat a lie too many times we begin to believe it to be a truth,' said Mrs. Marvor. 'You agree?' She asked him and the pretty Andrea.

'Mrs. Marvor, kindly do not waste your precious time on interrogating my husband's soul,' said Andrea softly to her. 'It next to never replies a wise knock.'

The old woman, Mrs. Marvor nodded, 'I agree,' her voice quavered, 'but I believe, it's better late than never. What do you say Alok? Tell me my son.'

'Anand!' he replied snobbishly. "I am Anand, Mrs. Marvor'

'Oh! Pardon me. My memory is receding partially . . . ,' she replied.

'Alike his soul,' added Andrea.

'Yes,' replied Mrs. Marvor, 'perhaps.'

'Mrs. Marvor, there is no such thing as a soul . . . it's a myth.' Agitated, said Anand patting Laila's tiny hand on his palm. 'And by the way, why are we talking about soul and life beyond death . . . it's far from what we are here for, isn't it Mrs. Marvor. How is your health these days'?

'It's about our soul's voice Anand, you should understand my boy,' she smiled with her lips shaking, as she spoke. 'Those who deny the Self are born again for the ones blind to the self are enveloped in unending darkness.'

'Sorry to interrupt you Mrs. Marvor,' said Andrea wisely, 'my husband is very sensitive about such topics. The topics that keep him away from his soul are the one's that he relishes much more. So, Mrs. Marvor let my husband be. Ignorance is a bliss for him.'

'Yeah! I am a devil.' Said Anand. 'Happy?'

'You are not a devil Anand. The devil is your lack of satisfaction with life.' Mrs. Marvor replied in her wise and feeble voice from across the table. 'Life is happy and so is each day for we never know when our worst starts.'

'One should never be satisfied, Mrs. Marvor,' said Anand tiredly.

'This Mrs Marvor is the secret of his soaring expectations from his tiny daughter,' said Andrea.

The old woman smiled feebly. 'You got lucky with such a wise wife Anand.'

'Women are always wise for they remain idle all day and thus can dive into spiritual enquiry and keep up their quest for wisdom. Whereas we men, Mrs. Marvor, we work our backs off in real so we remain unwise and cruel.' He replied.

She smiled looking away. 'You may mock me . . . but that's the truth.' Staring at the crayon's scratching by tiny tots on the woods of her table, she said, 'Anand, my wise father told me once . . . that, the biggest liar can man meet is, he himself. And this liar is difficult to escape. One can't escape until one decided to be honest to themselves. 'Laila listened attentively and looked at her father.' And being elder to you, I would tell you Anand, that the soul seeking spiritual path has nothing to do with having free time. Our soul,' she paused, 'finds time for the God within us irrespective of tightest of days. Don't confuse idleness,' she paused again to catch a breath,' with meditative calmness. One is about lack of work and the other is about realizing futility of it before God's name. It's dissatisfaction which leads to greed. It's like, me calling you Alok instead of Anand . . . confusion. Keep away from such confusions my boy. Keep away.' To this wisdom, Andrea gave one her most beautiful and satisfied smile to her, whereas, Anand got up from his chair.

Politely he thanked Mrs. Marvor and dashed out of the room, to his car giving in to his ego. Andrea, followed suit but only after she gave a peck on Mrs. Marvor's cheek and handed her the cake the one she baked on her mother's instruction and with her own kind love for the old woman, who taught simple wisdom, to her grand child, Laila.

And the little Laila, held her mother's finger. 'Laila, baby say bye to Mrs. Marvor.'

Mrs. Marvor, kissed Andrea on her forehead and said, 'God bless you. May the earth have more generous and loving women like you. Thank you for this.'

Andrea said, 'you're welcome.'

'You make me believe in humanity being alive in this day. You are indeed very graceful and soulful,' replied Mrs. Marvor. 'I wish my child would have given the same love to me.'

'When Anand was a kid, you taught him to love. He then learnt to love and we met. So, I am here because of your guidance. And I'm not out of love, as yet, despite his everyday tantrums.' Said Andrea.

'God bless you my child,' she said as a reply. 'And to you too my little one,' she said to Laila who then waved goodbye to her, and her life's journey ended the next day filling the city with shock.

'She left a spiritual message,' said Andrea,' that one should be happy and enjoy life everyday for one never knows God's timing for us.'

Poor Anand, he felt week in the stomach when he heard about her death for now he couldn't ever apologize to her for his rudeness towards her and more so because his impulse was proving to be an impediment for him, as his firing one staff took the peace of one of his factory. Lost in his success and worldliness he missed out on absorbing the messages, which his lovely wife understood quietly when she put Laila in Christ's Montessori school, so that Mrs. Marvor could see her grandchild with her own eyes.

Andrea continued with her line of wise thoughts, adding grace to Laila, spiritual as well as physical, which was molding the child into a pretty ballerina with the mind of the oriental monk. Anand on the other hand remained wordily and confused carrying grudges with himself and the world in his head and heart. Grudging was his way of relaxing for it is easy for our head to absorb and release tons negativity to the universe while Laila toed his mother's footsteps believing her father was kind in not forcing his ways as he did to his mother all the time . . . not knowing her future.

It was from her mother that Laila acquired her love for animals because for the wise Andrea pets were a way to teach her child selfless love and care. She had realized that animals love us unconditionally, giving us solace from the cynicism of the world and the corruption that enters our system while living the journey, called life.

Animals purify our energies through their pure love. And in doing so, they not only give us company and love even in the brightest of hours, they also adore us equally, when we return home, on a days when everything goes against us. Our dejections, our grudges, our disappointments and our hurt, all gets diluted by our pets with their magical sensitivity and love.

'What a better way to be loved than to be loved, just the way we are, shattered or successful,' were Andrea's thoughts as she built more kennels and barns for more animals to share their unconditional love with her daughter.

With this wisdom in her mind she along with her adoring husband, got Laila a fleet of pets of six dogs, two stray puppies, picked up injured from the street on two different occasions and four thorough breds. A turtle name Johnny and two cows, Heera and Panna and two rabbits, Annie and Louie. There were a couple of hens in their backyard and a place to feed the pigeons every morning and afternoon.

As a baby girl, her familiarity with her pets, was as good as her comfort with people. At times, she would lose the pace of the day to such an extent that it required coaxing to wean her away from the company of her pets who enjoyed having her around as much as she enjoyed their company. The girls, on her own had developed a habit of being lost in a fantasy land, where, she was the ruling queen a her kingdom with her pets, the one's she ruled with her kindness. In her kingdom chocolates grew on the trees and candies on the ground. There were swings all around the land and no school to go to. 'Laila doesn't attend school. She has no time for it with so much to look after. Who will manage all her work and her animals for her.' She would think justifying to her own mind ignoring the pace of the world around her. Right, she was in her thoughts regarding school, and ironically animals never go to school yet they love us immensely, for love needs no education, like Alaska wouldn't require refrigerators for its snow.

Given her high intelligence quotient at school and love for animals, Catherine, her watchful Irish governess, was becoming sure in her mind that, someday this child would become a Vetinary doctor.

She did her part of encouragement as dutiful Governess to the child and began addressing her as, 'Baby, Doctor Laila'. To this highly regarded reference, that some what pleased her father, Laila would smile proudly ear to ear displaying her tiny milk teeth, as though it was her mock doctor's kit that actually worked towards the recovery of her pets. She would swell with pride to see the animals recover, as if, it was her fake injections and fraudulent medicines, the jaggrey balls, that Catherine would hand her, with a serious face and gentle care, that seemed to the girl as wonder drugs.

It certainly wasn't the medicines she gave them life, but it was her tender love and attention, that healed the animal as pure love has a supernatural power to heal disease of body and mind. Kindness was gradually becoming the girl's essence.

'Baby Doctor Laila,' was in indeed meant to go places for words have vibrations and vibrations give way to the real manifestation of the meanings implied by the words we speak.

Laila who was now a teenager; tall, wise and shy from boys was also a girl who enjoyed the most in life; her friends, sports and being kind, which was most important of all to her.

Being a little detached from the world at a tender age was becoming her habit. She could enjoy being with people as well as spending time in her own company. For the latter tendency was responsible for her right interpretation of the bickering that earlier use to leave her feeling some what low and dejected when she saw or heard the tussle between her parent's which mostly over shadowed her mother's thoughts and emotions.

'Everybody has something or the other missing in life, for me this is the time to see love between my parents, being eclipsed,' thought Laila as she opened her closet to put back her hair clips. Then she drank her milk and kissed her father as she dashed out in her sporty outfit. 'I will take it positively as God's message for me to spend more time in my own company.' Said the girl wisely.

'We need to talk,' said her father firmly to her, when she got back home on that Sunday, after a round of basketball game in her courtyard with her staffs' children.

'Umm . . . can we please do it later I am very tired,' she replied holding the ball in her hand.

'Sit down,' he said cutting the call of her body. 'This is more important.' He spoke like a tyrant.

She looked around hankering for her mother. 'Ok,' she said tiredly dumping the ball on the floor and tapped it a few times.

'That's not the way to behave with your elders Laila,' he said firmly. She didn't reply. 'You are going to study general medicine and chuck all his child's play.' He said looking at her face half way.

'I understand father,' she replied. 'But . . . that's . . .'

'There is no arguing with me. You are far from the adult world. So, leave it up to me to decide the life you shall lead.' He replied.

She looked in his eyes with denial and childlike stubbornness. 'But . . .' A thought crossed in her mind of her mother being her savior, but she wasn't home on that evening. This Laila took as God's way of teaching her to stand for herself.

'I have considered putting you in a reputed medical school,' he said drumming his fingers on the back of his other palm. 'Get your act together.'

'Medical school,' she spoke with the energy of a half-mast flag on the death of a celebrity. 'O.K.'

Laila did study medicine and instead of animals, she stood by her father's request to apply for general medicine, for human beings.

On the day, he was filling her application form for the entrance exam, her wise mother, had in a glance, visualized her lovely daughter's state of mind, her life and her future as Laila lifelessly stared at the carpet. It felt as though her child was moaning her own death, deeply. She was moved by her child's plight and chewed her lower lips as though she was apologizing on Anand's behalf. Where as Anand was happy and took pride in what he was doing.

'Everybody gets that one moment to be happy. I shall wait for mine.' Said Laila to her father, unaware that her mother was around.'

Her father was shocked mildly and then the reply came from her mother. 'Nobody shall stop you from reaching that day of your life provided you are with your soul.' Laila raised her head gently to look at her and her eyes saw the faith she wanted to see in that moment. She smiled and Andrea smiled back. Where as her father went back to reading her forms. She felt low but she consoled herself saying, 'that's the way wordily people are. Life for them is always outward and visually decorated.'

Was this love or murder of it? Was that a phony wisdom of the unwise or injustice by a mighty? Was it a bright new beginning or just another death, of a joyful life led by his daughter? This only time or a psychic could answer, as for Laila, she left on time.

Saturn connived with her stars and she bid goodbye to all the innocent happiness that she enjoyed at home. Her life draped a black garb and gave her a serious face to wear, for a starting. Play and fun took a rigorous academic turn, as she was forced to hold on and live by her father's will.

Sometimes in our lives, we adhere to our elders out of respect and out of our love for them. This love like any other form of love, becomes a pain to us when our adherence to their demands and pressures, takes us away from our own soul. Then we can't be who we are created to be. This is equivalent to defying God's creativity. Such respect is extracted from us out of compulsion and compulsions, then conceive twins; sufferings and disgust. A natural rebel is thus conceived.

From here on the cherubic lovely child began to suffer in silence and wept at the thorny path, on which she has to walk alone because the one who stopped giving her company was her own soul. And when soul turns it's back away from us, sufferings are not only more painful, it's meaningless too. Meaningless, because we suffer without a purpose like a pot of water kept to boil endlessly, until water evaporates and burns the vessel like burning away essence of humanity from a person.

The child in Laila was dying and she found no answers as to why was the world not letting her be, who she wanted to be.

As a medical student, she tried to ape others and thus gradually her soul started to take leave of her. Her original identity was loosing grounds. Moreover, her creativity was taking away with it's self what we call original charm of a person. Whereas Laila's soul was planning a long holiday or may be wanted to be marked absent in her for forever, thus dwindling her life energy.

So. what she was left to do was ape others, which then made it compulsory for her to be lost in piles of thick books, slogging her way in and out of the lectures and the laboratory of her college, St. John's, Bangalore.

The sporty and easy going child gradually became a book worm. Though there were teachers to teach, who are entirely different from preachers like Andrea who taught her truth of her existence. This hampered her sense of asking questions from and of the universe, which went beyond the thickest of books. And since life can't be lived out of books, a void began to grow within her.

Besides, just teaching teaches us submission, inevitably and preaching teaches us love and assertive life. Any student can be a good student who can be taught but only a soulful disciple can be preached. And the one who has soul has to have success because in soul resides God and when there is God, He ensures we get the best of life. He gives meaning to our sufferings and a reason to go through the pain as seeker of God.

But here, Laila was a student, the one who was being rigorously taught materials from one chapter to another. The noticeable result of it was submission again, like she did to her father's will.

And as everything has something unique to it, so did this rigorous rote learning. It was assassinating her happiness and made pain, an unfamiliar word, to her become, a familiar one. Cunningly it lead her to the doors of regrets, as one by one, she failed to justify her doings in life to herself.

A couple of months down the line, there came a time when she looked dark and depressed. She was unable to trace the real cause of her misery. She couldn't understand, what was happening to her so the mess she created, lingered on.

But then, like most of the mess in our life, this one didn't happen to her in a day. It required unconscious and persistent running away from her soul. Since she didn't know the cause, she was far from addressing the effect as well. As a result of her self created miseries, Laila became cranky and ill tempered.

She began creating nuisance at home and said bitter words to people or suddenly would shut herself away yelling, 'get the hell out of here. Can't you see I have to study.' Or a mere, 'just leave me alone,' indicating a lack of sensitivity.

'Hi!' said her classmate entering her room on one occasion.

"I am sleepy.' Replied Laila, 'so byeeeh,'

'They are ganging up against us,' she responded like a hi-end detective.

'So shall we. What's there to think about. By the way you are looking fresh in your purple stole on blue salwar suit (Indian two piece upper and lower garment).

'Thanks!' replied the girl feeling happy.

Mockingly laughing said Laila. 'Don't mess it. It's a lovely piece. It's like the next wonder of the world. I wonder how you chose this combination. Great! Lovely. Go get some sleep.'

'Don't laugh so much, you will tire,' said the mate of her's.

'I already am . . . God knows what you have in your collection . . . I mean your wardrobe.' Said Laila. 'It must be a stand up comedy with doors open. Allah! I can't believe, it's true!' She whispered quietly to herself.' Now get lost,' she said still laughing. 'And I am Alexander, I can fight any one,' And suddenly five girls entered her room.

'What's going on?' said a girl staring out of the group, throwing a challenging look in Laila eyes.

'Was thinking about you,' she replied looking at the bunch of girls. 'And now get out of my room.' And just then suddenly her mood changed and she gave a fighter's looks through her eyes. Same girl, who's only way to live life was through mercy and with peace was being aggressive to a small time invaders. Now this was that stage life when somebody uninvolved pushes us to be like them.

A fat tall girl from the group held her t-shirt's neck line that sat on the nape of her neck. 'We eat first and then you chicks. Understand you fucking Anglo. Don't play against us.'

'Leave me!' said Laila and jolted her hand away from her. 'You girls need something special. May be a dose from my . . . . father.' and as she was about to grab her by her collar, the warden came by and gave a good blasting to the group of encroachers in Laila's room.

Laila gave a piece of abuse which dragged to the next day.

Then the leader of the group brought up the issue in the college canteen and a verbal fight started between them and again the warden who was having a plate of rajma rice there, stood up from her chair and scolded them and took two girls to the principal.

'How does it feel being here,' the principal asked them both.

'She started to abuse me threatening me to get me screwed by the rich father,' said the leader of the opposite group.

There standing before the principal there was a little bit of bickering from Laila's side but suddenly there was a brief moment when Laila realized what her mother told her once, 'when all words fail open the door of your soul and heed it precisely then you wouldn't go wrong.'

'I apologize.' Said Laila out of no where. 'I sincerely apologize for my behavior. Forgive me mam.'

And the verbal tussle ended right as the other girl couldn't trap her before the principal using her skill of being aggressive and smart verbally.

'Restricated, don't do it mam,' said Laila to her principle when she heard of the punishement for the other girl. And so the other girl's story ended with her parents weeping before the principal while Laila was free, freedom that soul begets . . . with happiness. Although, the inner sadness still persisted.

In a way, it was a sad conscious waste of life it was for this once upon a time soulful child for whom love was the only way of life. What harm did she do to others, to be living a life she didn't want to live this only Laila could answer by the reasoning of the life she would discover for herself.

To all this God, was watching over her just the way he had watched her innocent affection and care towards the needy. He knew that this girl's bitterness would ruin her further. He often heard her praying, 'Thank you God for I am living a happy life. Happy times full of fun. A time when Laila can be who she wants to . . . doing what she so wants to.' God, as kind as He always is to innocent souls like her's, decided to help His child for now she was a bigger needy than the one she showed her mercy to, in her mother's guidance, for years. God opened one of His old register's and asked the universe to cordially return her goodness, back to her.

It was a dull Sunday. Laila sat by her window with a plate of cold breakfast of Appam. She was nibbling it without looking at the food as it was low on variety and equally low on flavor.

'I hate this damn meal,' she grunted to herself. 'I have to study so much . . . what to do. I feel so sad all the time. What to do to me here, I am so lost. I wish lost was less ruining.'

She sat bored and wretched, cupping her cheeks with both her palms and looking away straight out of her window.

A Volvo bus passing by from Mysore to Bengaluru, pulled over, to drop a few passengers on it's way to the local bus stand. Laila's eye's widened as the bus moved on on wheels. She kept staring at what surprise the bus had on it.

Behind it was a hoarding which read 'Come, celebrate your life.'

It was an advertisement for a new dance school in town, which she ignored but what she noticed below was the punch line, that brightened her face and spirit, filling her with life to the brim with excitement.

Above it was the picture of the red hot Stiletto oozing with passion, with silver pointed heels exciting enough to invite her to step in it right in the moment she casted her eyes on it. Those were the pair of high heels, she always dreamt of wearing, when she saw it for the first time in the shop's window in a boutique of a five star hotel, in Chennai. She was only nine years old, but it's memory stayed in her heart, like a blue print of the constitution. The same colour, the same style, the same passion and the same madness to step in it, was felt by her on this mundane Sunday.

Unaware of the breakfast slipping off her plate, her neck straightened and she smiled away to glory soaked up in the lust of the high heels and the bus drove away from her sight leaving the red stilettos behind, on her mind.

'I want one. I want it.'

She whispered passionately to herself, determined to get herself one, as if she was stroked with a tender feather. She felt as if she had some divine water from some celestial spring from somewhere. She wanted one and now everything else seemed of less significance to her; so overwhelming was the power of passion, for high heels that the more she pictured it disappearing with the bus, the more she wanted it. Distance, pumped her passion, as it does to a lover. And then, an idea clicked in her mind. She rushed to the phone booth in her hostel and made an international call, immediately.

'Hello! Could you please connect me to my father. His name is . . . Anand.' She said courteously and apprehensively to the receptionist who took her call in a hotel in London, where her father was attending a meeting with new importers for his leather products. 'Anand Mallya,' she said nervously.

'Let me check. 'replied the woman. 'Sorry lady! He is not in his room.'

'Please I need to talk to him, It is an emergency,' replied Laila. Then she paused.

'His wife . . .' she hesitated, like a bad liar always does, 'is . . .'

'M sorry. I can't help you, his line is going unanswered.' said the woman keeping up the standard of the hotel she refused to help, though very politely.

'It's an emergency. His mother is . . . .' she hesitated and she cringed for lying and then she said, 'his mother. She is dead.' She was dead, much before Laila's birth. So it wasn't a lie as it appeared to her. It was a wise use of a truth as a lie.

'Her mother is dead. M alone at home. there is no elder and my father is there, in London.' She sobbed.

'Oh!' the receptionist gave in and her voice changed, into sympathy. 'Goodness gracious. M sorry to hear that.' Said the receptionist, from the other end of the line.

'That's ok. By . . . by the way . . .' m his daughter. 'M alone here. My mother . . . my mother . . . she has collapsed at the news of the death.'

Said Laila, crying for help. 'I can't handle it. M just . . .'

'Child, please hold the line.' She said nervously responding to her crisis. She dialed an extension and she said,' He is in the conference room, I will connect you to him immediately.' Laila was dancing moving her shoulders in a shimmy, then back and forth, up and down, smiling ear to ear quietly. And thus the next person she got on line was, her father. Her lady luck gave in to her this time as luck does happen to the one with resolute mind and determination to get what they want in life.

'Done', he said in a go, 'from now on I will pick two pairs instead of just one for your mother. You put your heart to your studies, my angel. Love you loads.' And he disconnected the line. He found his reason to make up for the lack of time he had for her as far as their interaction was concerned.

Life got a little better because though he was in a hurry to cut the call, he was none the less, the man of his words. She had more to look forward to than her thick boring books and she had more to handle than her exam pressures as her collection of shoes began to swell. In two months time, it outnumbered the entire collection of her hostel mates put together. Be it the satin stilettos or the one with high end Italian leather in it's heels, sequenced booties to her ankle or the one ending at her knees, peep toes reveling her toes and or the covered slip on, sporty peppy sneakers, to colorful pump shoes, if trend had it in Milan, Paris and London so did Laila. Multi coloured or unicoloured, neutral coloured or loud, there was one thing common to all her foot wears, all of it had high heels that could leave one in awe. Sky high heels the ones that resembled her spirit when she wore them. Wedge heels, to pencil heels, block heels to tapered one; she amassed a breath taking collection. It was like a walk in the paradise for the girls who got to see her collection in her room. Her glamorous glossy foot wears gave the girl her happiness back and no matter how momentary it made her ecstatic, it made her happy. Her soul was enjoying it and so was she. She was at peace with herself.

Each new pair of heels that entered her closet, restored and strengthened her faith in God for He was giving her what she wanted. She chose to overlook what she didn't get in life thus peaceful state of mind was inevitable. Her enthusiasm was now on crutches trying to regain balance and enjoy her time for as long as she could. Her life energy began to flow in ripples, through every new pair of heels that she received from her father. And despite the academic saddle on her tender back her laughter began to echo far in the hallway. It tore apart the grim silence of the dull studious heads with sleepy eyes. She slipped into being quite a prankster in the laboratory and had a way to cheer up people during the boring rounds of lectures because a happy soul and well nourished soul brings happiness to others without a second thought to it.

Her company was becoming a pleasure to those who loved her and a dream to those who envied her. Deep within themselves her college mates admired her zest for life, her shoes and her kindness that was slowly returning back to her being. Laila now had an intelligent mind and a kind heart, a blend that was a reason for her popularity and result of taking a stand for herself to fulfill her passion for high heels.

This Laila, was happy but her happiness now an escape too, which meant she still was running away from the voice of her soul instead of submitting to the challenges of that life, which her soul wanted her to live. For the unenlightened souls around her, she was like a miracle owing to her soulful kindness. It was unseen in the entire history of their campus because, there they were studying medicine for a respectable job, upward social mobility and position in society while this girl was studying for her father and then for merely curing the sick, giving them a new lease of life. To the rest, their degree spelt money, for Laila it meant a way to care for the sick and a full stop next it.

Five tearful years passed by and Laila graduated with flying colours to be known as Doctor Laila. Her parents, Anand and Andrea along with Catherine, attended her Graduation ceremony. They were probably the proudest parents to watch their child repeating the oath of Hippocrates, to serve people selflessly.

Her father gave a standing ovation to her achievements and to himself too, and deservingly so because he had successfully murdered his child's happiness by pushing her to do what he wanted her to do. Anand sure did deserve a pat on his own back.

Back at Chennai, all her domestic helps were elated and overjoyed to welcome her home. This memorable day was marked by an enormously lengthy Puja ceremony followed by scrumptious lunch, then a dance and an elaborate dinner, to wrap up the day, as the sun set behind them.

From a new born red cheeked chubby baby girl, to a tall and lean teenager and now a willowy high heeled stunning doctor, they had all the good reasons to celebrate the day. Laila shared a personal rapport with all of them and reciprocated their feelings even if it didn't mean a great deal to her, Andrea noticed her child and that she was becoming weary of the world. Andrea, who until then was elated at the completion of Laila's degree she nonetheless, wanted her daughter to know life at it's core which world weariness alone couldn't have generated.

Andrea felt an aloofness in Laila, and somewhere she felt that, a time would come when her daughter would realize that the real pleasures of life lies in going inward and not in the life, her father was compelling her to live.

And for Laila, it was a degree she worked very hard for and now she had to work even harder to pocket some more of it. But, kind as she was, she did smile at people to brightened their hearts.

But was medicine her passion? Or was her passion entirely away from her towering degrees? She had to stop thinking about it because this Laila was weak so just like what happens to the leaves in spring, her life flew with the wind due to the lack of an unwavering determination, from her end.

———◆◇◆———

CHAPTER 1

The haziness of human life ends with our journey inward.

There was someone, someone who went missing from the celebration; someone very friendly and loving. Someone, only the innocent or the spiritually awakened, befriends all. It refused to turn up on this day like a high class celebrity. It had withdrawn from giving her company because, It told her one thing, whereas she did another. It felt ignored and malnourished, ill treated and worn out. So even the day her achievement as a qualified doctor was being celebrated, it didn't turn up to participate. This 'it' was her soul, who went amiss.

And when soul goes missing, misery takes front row in our lives and sadness gives full attendance, never forgetting to turn up on the daily basis, as our inner happiness is the reflection of our proximity to the soul in us.

So every time Doctor Laila looked around, she found herself profoundly lonely and wretched. She couldn't connect with anybody. How could she and with whom would she connect, because a person with a missing soul never connects to anybody owing to the turmoil within them. So endlessly she searched for something undefined.

She was becoming highly self centered, thinking merely of her life, her sorrows, her miseries and of her tears, which bred despair. And, 'an unhappy person is a dangerous company, for they would try to give you the same suffering as they go through in the past or present,' so had she heard from her mother.

Thus the ceremony of her Graduation ended at her home's premise but not her void.

In the little life that she had lived, she was amassing troubles as though, she were living a curse. Her smile was fading away, and anger came up too soon and stayed for long.

Her high heels, were turning into an ineffective balm because now, her soul longed for a life she was running away from as soul changes its direction with our life's journey.

Another new trait of hers was to blame people. Easy way out. Her soul went on a holiday owing to this. She began to live in a fallacy—a fallacy of life based on lies and haziness. As it happened, the next bigger killer of her inner happiness, in the row, was marked present.

On the next day the twenty two year old Dr. Laila, sitting on a steel and leather reclining chair, was mumbling to herself with brightness filling her eyes. 'What if . . . God does a magic,' she imagined, 'and my father sets me free from his clutches. Oh my!

What a life that would be . . . aaah!!!!!' She exclaimed with a cascading surge of happiness rushing through her. 'Then my life would be full of all things good. Aaah . . . !' She imagined blissfully as that was the life she wanted to live.

'Laila,' she smiled to herself, 'then would wear a . . . Prada dress with a bright matching stilettos.' She gushed. 'I would then not be referred as . . .' she gushed again, 'and . . . be called a princess . . . why my life sucks? What would Laila appear then?'

'Psychiatrist.' Harshly said the person walking into her room putting a quick end to herself talks. Laila's face became somber as she diverted her attention to the man. 'That is who I want you to be. You shall pursue psychiatry for your M.D.'

She bit her lips in her aloneness and stood up, as a mark of respect for the man standing before her. Her head was bent low.

Looking half up, 'but father,' she resented tenderly, 'that's a bit too heavy a specialization considering . . . my capacity and my . . .'

'You don't have to carry subjects, on your head.' Replied her father. 'You just have to put more hours into study. My success as a business man is known to all, so you better follow my ways.'

'More hours?' contemplatively she replied as she was reminded of her dark circles around her eyes. 'More than twenty four hours? Is that what you are . . . asking for?'

'Fill this.' He said flinging several sheets of papers joyfully on her study table, 'and please, don't compel me to be rude. I am your father, show some gratefulness and be a good child to your parents. Make us proud

Laila.' Laila stood helplessly, blank in her mind, watching him tame her. 'Fill this,' he moved closer to her chair,' and then I will scrutinize the details and get it posted, on your behalf.

And if I may ask you, what is it that you want this time my dear angel,' he asked with authoritative love, 'what would my Laila say to it, as an answer? I am sweet as long as you allow me to . . .'

'What would I want?' she asked herself like a child. 'Umm . . . that . . . would be . . .'

'But that should go in the making of you, as a successful post graduate, my child?' said her father putting another clause.

To this, she wanted to laugh at the duality of his gesture, but since that would have meant disobedience to him, she remained poker faced and said,' a pen. All that I want is a pen. Besides if I am unhappy how would bring in happiness to someone else?' She didn't get any reply. She flipped the papers on her table and repeated, 'I need a pen to fill in these entrance forms, father.'

Holding out an exclusive gold tipped Swiss pen from his pocket he said. 'Here it is my child. And you can keep this with yourself. This is for you, my adorable daughter.'

'Prodigal,' she replied correcting him bitterly. 'And thank you very much, for this pen. I value it greatly.'

He stepped back on hearing her reply. 'I didn't expect such derision from you, 'he said turning his head away in disappointment. 'Did you know what specializations makeout a person . . .'

'Smarter and sharper. I know. I understand.' She replied with emotional detachment from him. 'M aware of it father.' She said waiting for him to look back at her in acceptance and that is what he did. She looked at him in his eyes, 'I may not be the best child around father, but I nonetheless would give all my time to appear smarter than I am . . . and also, to appear wiser than I can be in that environment, in this life time and doing what you expect me to do. But someday, I shall quit it all for my life. And that day doesn't seem very far from now.' Then she paused to think what always occurred to her,' I feel an unease everywhere I go and everything I do . . . except for one thing . . . that makes me forget the world.'

He opened his mouth in a bid to speak and then paused in anger. 'I don't get it my child what is breeding difference of opinion between you and me. Every time you say something . . . regarding your career, you tend to moan over it!' She kept mum, whereas he continued his conversation. 'Has your mother ever mentioned to you that I had a friend. His name was Aseem and he,' he paused in grief and continued, 'died.'

'He d-i-i-ed then his purpose must be complete for that's when death comes.' She spoke with not as much interest as he expected from the sympathetic child like her. 'M, dying too.' she mumbled.

'I didn't get you. Did you say something?' he asked cryptically. Not much pleased by her response he said, 'you must be a doctor but to me you remain just a child and please remember, you are taught to always respect your elders.'

'M sorry if, if I . . .' she spoke flipping through the papers on the desk. 'If I offended you. But I didn't quite know your friend in person, father. What more could he mean to me, than a stranger and how much tears you want me to shed over his death.' Anand was disgusted at her reply but remained cordial as he had a motive to achieve. He maintained his peace and wanted her to fill the entrance form with her signature on it.

'I am feeling a little dizzy in the head.' She said. 'In fact yesterday . . .'

'Hold on! Just hear what I have to tell you,' he said, 'and then you are free to lay on the bed for as long as it takes you to recover from that dizziness of yours.'

She was stunned. Fear gripped her and then sensing his temper and having nobody to rescue her, she replied by the guidance of her inner self. 'Fine. Please go ahead. I shall manage.'

'You see, you and I, do you hear me clearly, YOU and I, are working towards a dream. A dream, I envisioned the day I lost Aseem Khan,' he explained affirmatively.

'Who?' she asked tenderly.

'You are so forgetful. As I mentioned a moment ago, my friend A-a-s . . .' He replied.

'Oh! But then, he is dead . . . so why . . . devote our time to him? It will make you sad unnecessarily.' She interjected as all that she wanted on that tiring day was to fathom herself living her dream.

'Laila,' he said angrily losing his patience. 'Aseem, suffered from an illness of the mind without a cure, Schizophrenia, a psychotic disorder with an early onset. In his case, the onset of the illness was at nineteen years of age. And as it happens in psychosis, Aseem had developed symptoms of audio hallucinations. He heard voices that made him live in a different world, not that of the sane but that of insanity. At twenty he ran away from his home, following the voices that drove him to act just the way it wanted. Hell broke loose on me, when I heard of him going amiss, I ran around like a bereaved lover looking for his love in every house in the vicinity as I could remember Aseem visited and roamed in our colony.' Laila giggled quietly imagining her fat father running around.

'Enraged I dashed in homes in the neighborhood, peeping under their table and tossing their chairs in a jiffy to find Aseem, in case he was playing hide and seek with me like he did in his childhood. When I didn't get any precise leads, the scene got alarming and then I reported to the police.'

'So what did the police do?' she asked. 'I fear policeman . . .'

Troubled, he looked at her, 'You fear police . . . ? Outta everybody????'

'Yes,' she replied.

'There is no reason for you to fear them,' he answered breaking away from his conversation regarding Aseem.

'Amm . . . I fear . . . because I don't want to do anything wrong . . . you know as that would incite them to come up against me . . .' she replied tenderly.

'What . . . ?' said Anand. 'Don't be a fool . . . and most of all never fear, they are my pets. We keep them in our hand. Oh about Aseem, we were to head all over the city on a lookout for my loving pal. But before the results would have materialized, news came from the police that a young man's body matching the description of his friend, was found over run by a speeding lorry on the highway. The body was soaked in blood and bones broken into pieces scattered on the parched highway.'

'So this is how he died?' She enquired in a state of mild mental agony owing to her sensitivity.

'Yes. And the memory of that sight and the entire incident had left such a harrowing mark on my mind that from then on I set a mission in my life; to construct a mental hospital, in his name. And in doing so, we would save other families who, due to lack of adequate treatment, helplessly lose their loved ones.' She timidly filled the forms, the ones flug at her by her father.

But on this day, in a bid to pay a tribute to his dead Aseem, the one Anand forgot to save, was his own child. He killed her.

Laila fought her tears back and thus her application form to all the premier colleges of the nation were duly submitted.

In her essay to one of the institutes, her father made her write, 'dedicated to the cause of mental health in India and keen on improving the plight of people suffering from the lack of care and information regarding mental hygiene.' Blatantly stupid, she felt as though she was served vinegar, instead of the sweet lime soda in the restaurant called life.

Our life is quite like a restaurant wherein we have the liberty to choose what we desire and on failing to do that for ourselves, no steward(person), is to be blamed because what we get on the table is what we have chosen out of will or force.

Fate favored her father's choice and hers too because sometimes God sets us free to do enough wrongs till we get tired of our own decisions. He waits for us to grow weary of living by people's choices because then, an urge comes from within, with the velocity to chase our dream which then takes us on God's path. On the contrary, we tire ourselves of pleasing people, making our soul weep, then we choose to nurture the compulsion to follow our own path, our own life, our own choice and gain union with our soul.

She packed her bags, wore a pair of new blinkers and forced a smile at people, as she waved good bye to them, to march ahead with composure, as required for the cause, as noble as this one. As for her glamorous high heels, well they were left behind at home, to weep for her return.

'I came from London, this girl made me feel so loved that I never felt home sick and never missed my country's warmth. Now I feel so lonely, I want to commit suicide,' said a young orphaned silver high heels to another footwear in the tall cupboard.

'No. Don't you ever do that. You are a slick hottie.' Said the brown old thigh high boots from Italy. Like the Italians, this old man was a style icon in the world of her cupboard.

'Zitch. Stop flirting. M not in that mood,' said the silver hottie weeping like a running tap.

'Don't you remember what Laila told us before she left?' it replied in his husky voice.

'What?' she asked stamping her feet like a hot babe in distress.

'She gave us a flying kiss . . . . though I wanted a French one . . .' he spoke teasing her.

'Oh come on, just tell me what she did say,' she nudged him angrily.

'She said I love you all and 'll take you all away with me someday. Now you wipe your tears and pray for her return.' Replied the Italian wisely.

'Yes!' proclaimed a pair of strappy white heels from Singapore. 'We will fly, high and high, so says my soul.' She spoke with a smile that cheered up the entire closet of gloomy high heels. And so, the wise boots and the sexy strappy heels made them feel sheltered and hopeful. They no longer felt like orphans though they did miss the beautiful Laila who adored them dearly and wore them passionately, taking them around the town for outings. They loved her and so did she. They felt better to count days in hope of her return. We all feel better to live with hope in times we least expect and most require it.

At St. Allan's, a hospital cum residential institute built on the outskirts of Bangaluru and spread over a vast area of one hundred acres, arrived a pretty faced Laila wearing a navy blue sweat shirt and jeans; unlike rest of the students. Men turned to notice and rejoiced at her sight.

With her wrist watch ticking she changed into formals and as per the laid out schedule of the institute, she headed for the assembly hall for a formal introduction with the institute's faculty, staffs, layout and with the seniors doctors, who were salivating to be introduced to their freshers; some to bully them while some were hoping to find romantic love and the rest like her were merely following their set schedule.

Laila was the bird they all eyed to trap and they had good reasons to do so. But unfortunately the girl stared at the floor looking uninterested in either being introduced to them or to impress them for mutual benefit. She got up and followed the man who took them around the campus and gave out the details of hospital and how it functioned everyday.

St Allan's there were five major departments namely; Adult psychiatry, Child psychiatry, Drugs rehabilitation centre, Family therapy and Neuro-psychiatry. All the five centers were located in six different buildings. Each ward had its own set of staffs, nurses and doctors, including three senior consultants, three senior residents and three junior residents. Then there was another group of paramedics as well as psychologists and psychiatrist social workers. They worked as a team. The senior residents were doctors who were in the final year of the course and the junior residents, were the first year students of M.D. in psychiatry.

The fresher were referred to as the junior residents. And as a junior resident, Dr. Laila had to start from family therapy ward which dealt purely with family issues and severe tensions in marriage. She was posted there for the next three months. She was expected to read the old case files, attend classes to educate her self appropriately on the relevant topics and take up new cases for diagnosis, treatment and therapy. For this, she had to work in consultation with the senior psychiatrists, who guided and grilled them by the virtue of their knowledge and expertise. Time went by and then came a time for her to bid good bye to this ward and to move in to her next posting, that was the gruesome adult psychiatry ward.

Adult, as she was alike all of the first year students, she coped up well with the erratic work schedule, academic pressure, bad food in the hostel cafeteria. She did her laundry at mid night, sat through the unending hours in the library and tiring hours in the out patient department. Dragging herself from the bathroom to the classroom, she managed to survive this part of her struggle to stand by her father's dream. But there was something else, something within her that weighed really heavy on her.

It was emotional resilience, a prerequisite of being a successful psychiatrist which she lacked, enormously.

Emotional resilience, in a way was also an irony of the profession, which dealt entirely with the human mind, logical and not to forget amygdale (the emotional brain.) The part of our brain which bears strong resemblance with an almond. Strongest of doctors, were affected by the array of emotions they dealt with on the daily basis. It did disturb them, as what they dealt primarily was with negative energies of people and negativity of the body and mind. Energies that stood for everything negative and gave them live stories of ; how lively lives transformed into chronic and lonesome illness, how families fell apart due to somebody losing his mind to an extent of not recognizing even his beloved fiancée whose only dream was to marry him. How a care giver, a young mother killed her own child because she made him sit on a wooden plank in her kitchen and forgot all about him. The child fell down and died as her illness had relapsed unnoticed by her family, how a father locked all his family in a room while they were sleeping like a log and set it on fire because his voices guided him to do so. The real stories of how men, in the effect of mental illness, put an end to everything happy was being narrated here at the St. Allan's as a fixed routine.

Furthermore, the treating doctors and the team of specialists would get so thoroughly suffocated at times, that they exhibited secondary symptoms of the illness they treated. And why not, negativity at that level has rippling effects. It makes us see the world exactly the way it isn't.

It happens to all of us at times, when we live life with negative people around us. We begin to sound and think like them to the extent that we seize to be with the beautiful mind that we are born with and forgetting how good we thought life to be. We get so caught up by other's negativity that wrong begins to look the only right and our life looks soggy.

Post the diagnosis, along with medication, intense therapy was required for a short and long duration depending on the category of illness. This then made room for long list of areas that called for a rapport with the patients; some short termed and many long term ones because to bring the patient to a comfort level we need to interact with them thereby gradually winning over their trust and confidence which enables them to confide in their treating doctors, for their speedy recovery and good health.

Nobody knew, when the bond is formed just like we don't know when our enjoyment of coffee turned into an addiction for us. But then unlike a coffee shop, the pleasures at a mental hospital are very few and far because with the kind bonding comes issues of relapse of illness.

Then comes a sense of failure in treating the patient, who just sometimes back left all healthy and cheerful now returns as he was admitted. It was quite a compelling heart breaking issue for the doctors. Relapse, is like a land mines for the treating doctor, it blows up not only all their efforts but also their emotions, in a go.

To add to the agony, there were patients with mental illness that had no cure. Only treatment and/or life training was available for them. The family members of such patients regarded their treating doctors as God or just an equivalent to Him. So it was but natural that they expected them to work miracles to recover their loved one. On failing to accept the reality of the doctors' limitations as a human being they would cry bitterly, begging the treating doctors to help them or blow them into pieces just as the illness blew up the wellness of their loved one. Despite their heart wrenching plea, doctors knew within themselves that they had no way to help them because they were not God. But just justification was not enough either for their belief or for the patient's family.

The doctors felt dejected and fought an unending battle within their own self, not accepting the fact that it wasn't their own fault if there was no cure available and that relapse of illness is a way of life with some of the illness, so they should ignore it with utmost honesty. In other words, one felt the same sense of failure when a bank gets robbed in the broad daylight, despite high security. The guards were there, well qualified and well armed too, yet of no good. Who do we blame then, the efficiency of the robbers or that lack of it, with the guards. The harm is done, nonetheless.

Then, there were patients who could neither afford to pay for the medications for the illness that ran a chronic course nor could they lead a normal life without the pills. The reason could be as simple as, poverty. What does one do in the capacity of being a psychiatrist, it sure is such a high profile job, both at medical and social level. What should they do to such poor patients, leave them with a harassing life on the pavement where if not the illness, the rain or the cold would kill them or let go of the professional difference and quit their jobs as medical students and take them all to a camp and tend them like one does in Somalia with the famine ridden and starving people?

Helplessness ruled supreme and pain gave them its tearful company. Such was the life Laila was compelled to join in and live, not merely because it was such an emotionally demanding profession but because she was never cut for it. One of her passions was to help people and not to suffer with them by living away from her soul.

Further there were patients who were admitted for treatment in the hospital, and languished there as post the treatment, no family or relatives came forward, willing to shelter them. It seemed, they had had enough of their ill relative and also they had cared enough for them to have the audacity to betray them forever. For them hospital was the dumping ground and an easy way to wash their hands off their ill relative. Their bills lay pending for decades. So, even if they had recovered and by fluke there came forward some care giver for them, the bill were mountain high to be paid on their behalf. So the idea of taking them home was dropped like cherries in the pudding. For the hospital authority, letting them out on their own was not a safe idea because they are mostly unable to manage all their daily affairs entirely by themselves, because of their high sensitivity to stress. And stress also increases their chances of relapse. So the last resort for such patients was to perish in the confines of the hospital bed, the safest option in the eye of the hospital management too.

Sympathy was easy but help was far from available.

Pain of rejection was the primary predominant emotion needless to mention the torture of being in the same room with other ill patients who would yell and moan all night. Such an environment can give stress to healthy mind needless to say to the one's who risk a relapse.

'A person who first lost his mind, lost his family too, then again losing his mind was an easy escape from the life which they didn't choose all by themselves. Display of profound sufferings had no end in the hospital, for it is not a fault of anyone, it's just sufferings magnified,' often thought Laila, to herself.

There were some patients picked up lying in the streets. During their recovery, they had nobody to visit them or enquire about their well being. Doctors were their only visitors and confidante, briefly empathizing and escaping before the patiences' sufferings got them. Tears would well up in their eyes, as loneliness and sorrow engulfed their meek malnourished bodies. On special occasion like festivals, it was virtually impossible to look in their eyes and not be moved by the treachery eating up their lives as though their accounts of Karmic debts of past birth were far from over.

Despite witnessing and understanding such aspects of others' life, it was imperative for doctors to be emotionally detached from their patients. Their interaction had to begin and end with their case files. They were expected to forget, that it was one human being's interaction with another. So there remained two possibilities, one the practicing psychiatrists faked their detachment or the second, they did drugs and alcohol, to temporarily combat the stress stemming from the endless sufferings in all forms imaginable, in hospital.

One such experience after another left Laila disturbed for days on end. On one end life had taught her to love and care for all and on the other it expected her to remain detached and distant. A whirlpool had started to do rounds in her mind. Her conscience was shaken. She didn't know which way to go, as life began to close in on her. She was neither able to cope up with the demands of the profession nor was she determined yet, to simply to call it quits. And when all roads are seemingly closed life gets difficult and winding.

Laila desperately sought guidance from her soul with faith, as It was her only confidante who would lead her on the perfect path, a path of passion and of bliss, a path of success where happiness is satisfying and work is convincing especially her soul. And so she started to meditate as taught by her mother.

'If we get lost in life and depend on our soul with positivity towards our soul to God within us, God leads us on that path as life unfolds. He becomes the light that illuminates the darkest of tunnels of our life.' So Laila began to realize through meditation and reading Osho's writings.

Her fourth posting was in the famous ward of the hospital the Dead diction centre-a well known ward all across the nation for its high success rate of prognosis of the patients coming here for the meagre price they pay for their treatment. So like everything famous has something unique to it, low cost and effective treatment was the secret of the fame that this ward drew to itself.

It was her first day, when wearing her white coat Laila reached late for the medical rounds that were being held in the general ward of the department. She bumped her body into the gate in a hurry to enter the ward and save any further delay in reporting to her team. On reaching the inside of the building her rush lost pace, for the round had started exactly at 9 o'clock, bang on time.

'Oh my, m half an hour late.' she said to herself as she stood and peeped from the entrance door terrified to draw scorns from the senior consultants, whose life went exactly by their watch. One would wonder what was the exact time they served their spouses and how stressed their spouses must be if they got late winding up the kitchen at night. 'Horrifying and funny,' it was said, it must be for them in as much as it was for Liala, now.

Standing by the door, she was trying to decide the right moment to butt in. But because her mind was gripped by fear, she couldn't find her way into the general ward with twenty beds each of which could be seen clearly from the door. She fluttered her eyes thoughtfully and stood there biting the inner skin of her cheeks in a bid to find an excuse and\or an opportunity to move in without being noticed.

'I think the motion is loose in my stomach,' she pondered over her illness, an imaginary one,' Hmmm . . . shall I bunk this class and join the next one as I had fever in the morning!!!!! Good one, but just fever would not do, this is St. Allan's,' she said, 'High fever. She replied. Better. M proud of myself . . . situations,' she making a sad face, 'they force me to lie for cover.' And then she gave up and turned back to walk away from the ward.

'Ohhhh! Forgiv' . . .' she said in regret as brushed against a nurse who was walking past her. They both stared at each other as one was a nun and the other a student caught without a skirt in a convent.

The nurse looked at Laila's face, it was pale with fear. Her hair was dishevelled as she had run half a kilometer, from her hostel to reach this ward. The nurses suspicion grew.

'Ah! Hi! M a student.' Smiled Laila taking her in confidence before the nurse would have raised an alarm for a mentally challenged set loose. 'This coat is mine, it reads my name, here. See.' she said showing her name embroidered on her left.

'The attendance isn't over as yet,' whispered the old nurse in a bid to help.

'Shhh! Is it?' she replied hushing her in frenzy as that was the best way to escape the scorns and erase the delay. She could now escape from reporting late and from lying about her stomachache and high fever, too. She hated lying anyways. 'I owe you this.' She said playfully to the nurse, 'a chocolate. Tomorrow. Done. I will get it.'

'Here,' said the nurse showing the notebook 'the attendance register is with me. Move in,' she gestured and walked away from her in the opposite direction to fetch medication and a syringe for a patient on the bed number two.

Laila stepped ahead, 'God please you save me, this is the last time.' she prayed in whispers and peeped in the ward room. The team of doctors had moved far away from the door and were busy examining the patient on bed number nine. Thanking God, she stepped in the ward as quietly as does the sly cat stealing milk and placed herself behind Dr, Sandeep and next to Dr. Sneha, both of who were luckily her batch mates. She projected as though she was left out of the group, by sheer chance of positioning rather than an intentional mistake of joining them late. Gradually, they gave her way and she stepped a little further joining the group, smoothly. Smooth, yes it was though it didn't remain that way for long.

Securing a safe ground, Laila looked at the new team members as that according to her was more important than the client's case being discussed. She began to count the number of arms because looking up to do head count would have meant her lack of attention as a student. 'Twenty arms' she said, 'one including mine. It equals to ten people in the new team, two more than the other ward.' She looked at the patient; he looked as bored of the doctors as was Laila. She chuckled and pumping her courage, and fed her curiosity. She looked higher than their arms, to their stomach, then shoulders, their neck and she had to stop there, somebody elbowed her form left side. It was Dr. Sandeep.' Where were you yesterday night . . . I saw you in your . . .' he said playfully.

'Where did you see me, in your dreams? I will make a complaint,' said Laila mocking him. He elbowed her again hinting at the consultants looking in their direction. 'In your half naked . . . night dress . . . It barely covered you.

She regained her concentration and geared up to check out the new faces, very seriously. 'This girl's innocence had some guts.' Though Dr. Sandeep in his mind as he saw Laila's head was the only one looking away from the patient lying on the bed. 'I wonder if she can get away this time.'

'You should have told me I would have stood there for some more time to settle the virus of ogling in you,' she chuckled.

Across the bed, from left the first in the line stood Dr, Arvind the famous old cannibal as seen by her eyes. The senior most consultant who was known to dart toughest of questions on his students, especially when least expected. And that was not the end; he had the flair of cross questioning his students to rule out any guess work attempted by them. Though the new students feared being a part of his team, later they thanked him and their stars for having a teacher like him for the knack of working with a presence of mind was a compulsive art he taught them.

Next to him stood Dr. Shreeyesh the short and dusky young senior resident, who was mostly nodding his head in silence and in agreement. He had helped Laila several times in the library, when she was new to the institute, clarifying her doubts and satiating his hunger for female company. So he too was a familiar face for her.

'You saw me wearing a bikini version of my night dress????? Right!? Wonderful. And you have come here to study Psychiatry . . . God save you!!!!!!!' Then she giggled with him. 'Cobwebs . . . are not here.' She whispered as her eyes met Dr. Arvind. He gave her a nasty stare for giggling in the ward. 'Cobwebs Sir . . . hush . . . hush.' Both she and Dr. Sandeep felt silent.

After an hour thoroughly bored of her learning, she yawned and looked at the man standing next to Dr. Arvind. On his left was a stunning reality, a reality too real to be a psychiatrist whose sight evaporated her laziness turning it into a passion like a magician taking out a rabbit from his hat. Wearing a peach coloured shirt with its sleeves folded above his elbows and a rimless sparkling cleanglasses that sat handsomely on his flawless complexion. He was one hell of a man straight from a magazine's cover. Laila's eyes froze on him. He was over six feet tall with the cutest smile she had ever seen in her entire twenty three years of life. What a miracle he was, like a Greek God dressed in modern clothes and wearing a white coat.

To Laila, he looked unusual for the profession, as though he were a ramp model disguised as a doctor. 'My my!' she exclaimed, 'what a man, the man of the ward.'

Oblivious of his good looks he was down to his duty talking to another senior resident unfamiliar to her while the others looked at Dr. Arvind examining the patient. Though his lips were moving Laila could not hear a word and then she noticed her man smiled again while his conversation with the other man was still in progress. This time she noticed something new. 'Dimples. He can't be cuter.' She whispered to herself and life couldn't get better than this!

She was going dizzy with excitement and the freshness that a newly found love begets. She thought, God had just given her a reason to continue studying there. Her heart jumped with joy, as she stood staring at him.

'What is your understanding of the case?' Came a voice shaking her from the romantic paradise she was hibernating into. She stood speechless, pretending to be in a trance. Not a word regarding the case had been registered in her mind. So there was no way she could have given an understanding of it. For in so far, she had only understood and acknowledged her experience of falling in love, the rest didn't matter, atleast not until this moment, to her.

"Sir, I . . . . I . . . am . . ." She stammered with much difficulty. Forget about the case, she didn't realize as yet who among them had asked the question. She looked at the walls to find invisible clues and then she glanced at the special someone, who was smiling at her from across the patient's bed. Yet the mystery prevailed as to who had asked the question and before it was too late for an answer somebody across her spoke curtly.

'Yes, I know, you are Laila. That pretty much completes your,' sir sir . . . I m . . . 'My question is for him, not to you', came the stern reply. She got an electric shock realizing it was the cannibal who asked the question, Dr. Arvind.

She realized she had begun to perspire. 'O'! I am so sorry . . . to . . . have . . .'

The shark had spared her from its fatal bite. Phew! She rested in peace. And now it was Dr. Sandeep' s neighbor's turn to bear the bull by the horn.

"Sir, I think . . . ." responded the doctor next to her Dr. Sandeep with a steadily fading confidence in his voice. "Sir I firmly think . . ."

"Firmly-think. Huh?" responded Dr. Arvind with a heavy dose of sarcasm. "This isn't Bournvita quiz show. So," he spoke with disappointment, "no wild guesses with me. Either you know the answer or you don't. And you," he pointed a finger at Laila, "better stay awake during my classes." Her heart skipped a beat. She looked innocently at him not knowing how to respond to it.

"Yes, Sir." Came the faint reply form her, the lamb. She knew, she was caught red handed but she also knew that God had saved her from facing Dr. Arvind's fury, as he let her off with a mere reminder, which was unusual of him on a regular day during the morning rounds. Laila, straightened up her body taking an attentive stance. But straightening up her mind and taking her eyes off the handsome consultant, was any day more difficult than studying her entire course content of the year. She was waiting for Dr. Arvind to wrap up the case which would have given her some spare moments to sink into that romantic fantasy, over and over again. Suddenly her mother's wise words crossed her mind, "for every choice we make in life we pay a price, willingly or out of compulsion." and that rang a bell in her head. Being caught next time was too heavy a price to be paid for choosing to publicly admire her man, the man standing across the bed for who knew what Dr. Arvind's temper could do to her final result in the examination. So Laila promptly promised herself to be mentally present along with her physical appearance for attendance.

Her promise to herself came quick, unaware that love has a spell that draws one's mind like the thread draws the kite that flies high and high in the blue sky in an attempt to get away from the thread. The vast blue sky despite its infinity can not hide the kite or withhold it from being pulled back by its thread. Such is the compulsive pull of love, the love Laila had fallen in.

The more we run away, the more it chases us.

'Dr. George, could you please explain the case to the class,' said Dr. Arvind calling her prince charming with his name.

'Bingo!' she said to herself, 'I came to know his name. The George of the jungle . . . zitch . . . the

Tarzan of my heart.' She repeated, 'Dr. George! How sweeeeeeeet and God is S-W-E-E-E-TER for he gives me everything I desire from life. WOW! What could be a better start,' and she smiled to herself for now God gave her a reason to keep looking at him without the fear or guilt, which apparently was the only wish on her mind.

'Sir, the patient could give the correct answer to, a3+b3= (a+b) (a2-ab+b2) because his remote memory is intact. That is why,' and he paused, 'he remembers his past clearly.' And then he turned his head to look at the patient. 'He is a twenty two-years old mathematician, who had cleared the entrance exam of the Indian Institute of Technology in his first attempt, but his ranking was not enough for him to qualify for mechanical engineering, at IIT Kharagpur. It was a major setback for him and the next day he packed his books and sold it to the scrap dealer and began taking alcohol towards which he had very low tolerance previously. He was reported to get violent for no apparent reason and aggressively abused anybody at any given time. Gradually his behavior became unmanageable at home and by twenty, he turned into quite the opposite of his earlier sober personality. He remembers the formulas of mathematics clearly, till date.'

Laila was shaking her head attentively as if she were keenly listening to the client's case history delivered by Dr. George. Though in reality she was in another world altogether, unaware what would happen next for her innocent nodding with the data unregistered by her head.

'But there is a catch.' Interrupted Dr. Arvind with a grin like that of Monalisa in the famous Picasso painting, only if the painter would have given Monalisa a flat nose, a man's voice and a stethoscope around her neck.

'Yes sir there is, a catch.' Confirmed Dr. George with dimples which was more attractive than the client's unique case history, to Laila.

'Is there a catch to you too, my handsome?' she joked to herself as by now she was swimming in a pond of love with him.

'Nurse, please give the patient a piece of paper and a pen. And,' commanded Dr. Arvind 'and for God's sake, change his bed sheet immediately. It's unhygienically dirty.'

'He should come to men's hostel,' whispered Dr. Sandeep to Laila, 'his definition of unhygienic would change,' Both sniggered while the nurse shaken by his rage flew away to fetch a fresh bed sheet handing Laila a note book. 'We don't wash for years.' He informed.

'AW-WEEKH!' Laila felt an urge of puke, though she laughed at the disclosure of secret form the men's hostel.

'Sir!' Said Dr. Sneha finding it the right time to score some brownie points, 'I have a spare sheet. We can use this, if you don't mind.' and she passed on a sheet of paper with a special smile to him.

'Thank you.' And he sniggered and firmly looked at the patient, 'Eklavya, please write the answer to this equation, $(a+b)3$ and apply this formula on the numbers I shall give you.' He instructed the patient.

'Um . . . did you see that oldie smile at our . . . ?' said Dr. Sandeep sinking in the fun, 'like an old lion mating with a cub. We better watch out for Dr. Sneha, she steals the show smartly. We will become sidekicks.'

'What are you saying, Sandeep,' said Laila breaking into an embarrassing smile, 'focus, or else . . .'

'Come on, grow up Laila,' he snapped. 'That cannibal is burning for . . . ahem . . . ! You got it.'

Laila looked at him and said, 'Grow up and shut up for now.'

Ekalavya had snatched the paper from his hand and after a minute got up to stand on his feet onto his bed and began dancing wildly throwing his limbs all around and stamping hard on his bed. 'dhoom dhoom . . . move your body . . . . dhoom dhoom . . . . dhoom again and rock your body . . . . dhoom dhoom . . . .' He sang on the top of his voice and kept dancing. It was as humorous as wild as Laila couldn't have imagined.

'Eklavya . . . Eklavya . . .' shouted Dr. Arvind. 'Sit down. Sit down and solve the sum. I will get the guards to tie you down. You better sit down.'

'Dhoom Dhoom . . .' he shouted back looking at him and did gestures swinging fist and thrusting it at him and back. He moved his body like waves 'Dhoom . . . dhooom again and rock your body . . . dhoom dhoom . . . .' The three junior residents laughed and moved back for their safety.

'One kick of this mental on my mouth,' said Dr. Sandeep to himself, 'and I will lose whatever is left of me.'

And then Eklavya fainted. His thin body revealed his green veins while he lay passed out on the bed. Another nurse responded with a glass of water and dripped some of it on his lips while the team of doctors looked around at each other shaken by his sudden dance moves. Hiding her laughter Laila breathed deeply to calm herself and to regain her soberness.

Ekalavya opened his eyes and sat up on his own looking at Dr. Arvind. 'Yes Doctor.' He spoke in a way as if it wasn't the same him who had danced crazily a moment back. This was new to Laila and to her batch mates.

'Write the formula on this paper. $(a+b)3$ and apply it on the numbers 6 and 2.' Said Dr. Arvind casually, not giving any importance to how he behaved just a minute back. He was by far more used to such uncalled situations than any other doctor on the team and thus the only one to handle the patient gracefully. He looked at the team and checked their expressions. They all except for Laila had masked their laughter and stood with serious expressions. Her face was sober, it was her eyes that wore fun in them. He stared at her, more sternly than he sounded through his voice, to her.

'Done.' Said the boy. Dr. Arvind took the page away and turned it towards the team, 'this', he said 'is the catch.' The page was left completely blank with the equation on the top and a signature. 'Dr. George, could you please explain the team, what caused this behavior.'

'Sure sir,' said Dr. George and he looked at everybody in the team, old and the new. 'The boy suffers from the delusion of grandiosity, due to which he believes,' he paused, 'undeniably that he is the super star Hritik Roshan.' A ripple of giggle followed behind Dr. Arvind's smirk. A name of the popular heartthrob was and his talent broke the monotony of the room. 'Though his remote memory is intact, his immediate and recent memory is damaged. His analytical side is damaged due to which he is unable to solve the equation and neither does he remember the dance that he displayed in the previous moment. The patient . . . .' And Laila began to lose his words. Her mind turned into a children's fair, where anything and everything seemed possible and fun too. As it's a quality of innocent mind to convert the impossible into possibility, at a lightning speed and so did she. For her and for all such inexperienced lovers, just a glimpse of their first love is the end of all that they ever wanted.

Logic, they say is for the fools and only their love is real. It was the spring of her love life. Clenching her pen between her teeth, she swooned with emotions and images of a fancy marriage with the handsome consultant.

'Ahem! Ahem!!!!' came a loud cough from an ailing patient. It was loud enough to bring her mind back to the hospital. When she realized where she was, she remembered what she was meant to do there. Gently she looked around, her batch mates were writing notes. Hurriedly, she opened the notebook in her hand and began to scribble. After a moment, she looked up and looked around again and saw Dr, Arvind looking at her. She hated his speculative glances as it reminded her to keep her focus limited to the subject matter but focusing in anything other than in their love is hated the most by any lover. So did she. Yet out of her fear from him, she scribbled faster to save her skin from his verbal lashing. Fear, it does smartens us, in ways undesired but very much required out of us.

'What's going on there?' Came a female's voice. Everybody looked up. She gestured at Dr. George like a traffic police to stop. 'Is that the attendance register you are writing in?' asked the psychologist, Dr. Poorva, a respected senior member of the team, the lady with least words among the seniors and most flawless white coat. She was fuming with temper.

Laila's body trembled with fear as she flipped the note book she was scribbling her note in. 'I . . . . Ya. 'The room felt dangerously silent like a dungeon.' MAA-AM!! I am . . . sorry. I . . .'

'Excuse me Mam, don't worry. This one is of the previous month. I had discarded it a little while ago. We are yet to get the fresh one for this month.' said Dr. George saving the damsel in distress just in time.

'I see!' said Dr. Poorva, 'and then he casually resumed explaining the details of patient's diagnosis. Unlike his patient, Dr. Geroges' immediate memory was sharp enough to lie in her defense. As the class got back to normal, Laila gently lifted her eyes and looked at him with honor and gratitude, for she didn't know a stranger kinder and better looking than him and a life better than the one she was leading. She smiled to herself and like the other fellow students she got back to making her notes, thought not in the attendance register anymore, but in her own mauve coloured note book with the picture of yet another high heels on it. She had bought this notebook all the way from Japan through a good friend of hers.

The team of senior doctors heard all the details given by Dr. George and with an absolute confidence in him they approved of what he spoke. Their liking for the young consultant was unconcealed. As flawless as his image, Dr. George barely left out any information and spoke with absolute clarity giving way to the complete understanding of the case to all the residents. Besides Dr. Arvind's wrath had an unspoken compulsion on each one of them. They all felt no less than soldiers on the battle field, and their fingers moved on their note books, as if they were pressing the trigger of a machine gun, compulsively to save their lives and honour before the team. As the explanation of the case got over, the house was then open to queries.

'Is this alcohol induced psychosis?' asked Dr. Shreeyesh from Dr. George, as smartly as he could act before the team to prove is reasoning ability to the senior consultant too.

'What else do you wanna call it Doctor? A pizza induced psychosis?' replied the psychologist Dr. Poorva. She was furious at the way Dr. Shreeyesh was exhausting the latters, energy and her patience. It seemed she took a special liking of the handsome George.' Ofcourse it is alcohol induced psychosis. The genesis is very much alcohol in this case. Is it not Dr. Shreeyesh?' He didn't reply for he was embarrassed to speak anything smarter than he already did. Dr. George saved Laila and in turn God saved him through Dr. Poorva. Laila was content.

'Ok. We have the next patient waiting for us.' Announced Dr. Arvind calling the shots and signaled the team to move to the next patient's bed. 'Any other query would be taken after we complete the rounds. We are pressed for time, ladies.' He said looking at Dr. Sneha.

Dr. Sandeep, the entertainer pinched Laila, and said, 'we better warm up or the early bird will fly with the worm.' Laila giggled and said nothing in return. She couldn't play the match using both her hands, so she preferred to stick to her own love life.

As the round was about to end she got something special, a friendly smile from the ever so handsome George and as an icing on the cake, it came with his dimples. 'Aaah . . . !' she said as it cooled her heart like cold water on a hot frying pan. And yes, it made her day. Thoroughly impressed by his appeal she loved the idea of belonging to a man, intelligent and ruthlessly handsome. She looked like a bunch of cherries; blossoming and pretty.

During the entire round of the special ward, all the dangerous vigilance from the senior doctors couldn't stop her from feeling the joy that the new posting had brought to her. Examining patients from one bed to another, in three hours, they completed the entire round.

Post the rounds, they dispersed for a tea break and she blissfully enjoyed a cup of tea with Dr. Sneha, her colleague and Dr. Sandeep who had reasons to soak in the fun and the sun of the open tea stall. They discussed the new learning for the day and the related treatment of the illnesses and Laila nodded her head in agreement. In less than ten minutes flat, they headed towards their next class on 'the alcoholic genes '. Laila enjoyed that too for there was more to her life than the joy of learning. The day felt as beautiful as it could be.

That class was followed by lunch break and more classes in the evening. Gradually it became so demanding that, sparing time for a detailed trip of the wonderland was invariably difficult for Laila though she did spend a lot of time with Dr. Geroge in her mind, throughout the day. At night her tired body felt dead asleep unconsciously bidding goodbye to all the memories of meeting Dr. George and with the hope of meeting him in her dreams.

The night turned into the next day and she was back to the hospital for more. In this posting of her, for the first time she got many reasons to enjoy her time in the institute. Dr. Sanjeev, a senior consultant of her group had been a straight faced person with a rocking sense of humor. He would crack his spontaneous jokes that were really funny and made learning less burdensome. On the second day he said, 'Psychiatrists are sadists. They are thrilled to see people troubled, or they would sit by themselves without work and money.' Laila giggled and so did the others.

Laila was happier than she was during all the previous months as a resident student. Though her interaction with Dr. George was limited to mere exchange of smiles she felt blessed as happy moments like these added to the happiness that she searched for. Just a few days back, life that seemed on the wrong track and in a flick was giving her reasons to smile. 'In ways like this, God keeps surprising us, to keep our faith in him alive.' She thought. Days went by one after another and Laila began to enjoy life in the campus.

The fifth day in the ward had a different tune to it. The team of doctors including Laila, followed their usual schedule of morning rounds. Today it was the day to visit the patients in the 'special' ward. In this ward each patient had a room, bathroom, television set, fridge and a spare bed cum sofa for a visitor.

The team of doctors entered the first room of the floor and the nurse handed a green colored case file to Laila. It was her turn to brief the team members regarding the patient's case history and current illness. Everybody were alert, despite the noise of the drilling machine that was distant but profound while Dr. Arvind, and Psychiatrist social worker, Dr. Radha, the two senior consultants in the team attended the session along with the rest of the seniors. Laila was briefing successfully and then came the tough part, though also the most relieving one, the time to take questions from the entire team. Relieving, because post that she would breathe free, free from the mental tug of war.

For Laila anything other than love, didn't suit her interest at all. Love had become her energy, like a pack of glucose to the meek. She felt buffered and stronger, in life than before meeting the handsome Dr. George.

She managed to marshal the queries very well, as it came to her and took a breather. And while she was relaxing, happy to end the discussion over the case, Dr. Sanjeev who stood four feet away from Laila, asked for the file for review. He had developed a confusion which he wanted to clarify, through the pages of the patient's file. He said he himself wanted to read the case file and only then the team would move to the next patient's check up. Dr. George, who on that day was, standing closer to Laila and mid way between her and Dr. Sanjeev, forwarded his left hand towards her, to take the green file from her and pass it on to Dr, Sanjeev. As she was handing over the file to him, her eyes fell on his fingers and she went breathless in a state of shock. The world around her came to a grinding halt and she chocked with overwhelming emotions.

All the dreams she had woven each day with him, were ripped apart in a mere glance of reality of his life, that mercilessly shattered her. Tears well up in her eyes instantly and she felt dizzy being reminded of the wedding ring on Dr. George's heart finger that yelled loud and clear that; he, belonged to another woman.

'File please', said Dr. George unknowingly dragging her back to life. And, thus along with the case file, he took her happiness away, tearing her dreams into tatters.

Beyond that moment, she had no time to react on her emotional crisis nor was it the time to ask life, as to why it did target her, so heartlessly. But her grudge found its way out. 'I didn't want to be here in the first place, I was pushed to study.' She complained to God.' You had no mercy on me?'

But why to blame God or life, when all that it does is to teach us new lessons through new challenges that lead us to become stronger and wiser with each new experience.

'Why did you ask the patient for an M. R. I. scan, Laila? We know herdiagnosis was depression? It costed her extra money and exertion. Any answers to that?' asked Dr. Sanjeev. 'She is a farmer's wife and we, as doctors should keep the patient's financial background in mind. Shouldn't we?'

'To rule out any lesion in the brain.' She replied.' The clients history suggested a major fall from her staircase, wherein she had severe headaches for days unending. It was also a persistent symptom, which occurred in phases.' She continued lifelessly. 'Moreover, Doctor Sanjeev, 'she looked at him,' sometimes in life, we need to prevent future damages by ruling out current complexities, real or virtual, like this one."

'Good.' came the word of praise from the old cannibal, Dr. Arvind. He was content to hear her reply, so honest and practical. She cleared, Dr. Sanjeev's query with grace and knowledge.

Medical rounds were still going on, from one patient to another and so she had even lesser time to address her emotions. It kept stinging her and her heart was hit very hard. And then it was her turn to plug her stethoscope in her ears and begin with the general physical check up of the female patient, who lay on the bed before them. Stirred from within, she responded to the need of the hour and camouflaged her grief and wore a unaffected face. But on a part of her body, on which curtains could never be drawn were her big and beautiful eyes and sadness engulfed it brazenly. For a beautiful woman like her, inviting Dr. George for an extra marital affair was not difficult. But her conscience, her long lost pal, reappeared to stop her. Her soul, her old pal smiled at her from within and guided her. Her conscience said, 'we will get you better bachelors my dear. Don't worry. There are millions out there.' And this time she couldn't walk away from her soul's voice which compelled her to focus on her work and let go of the handsome, intelligent but a happily married man.

The questions that were left unanswered by life regarding the sufferings of her clients were also the initiator of her belief in Karma, both past and present. Laila, had begun to fear her deeds in as much as she loved God for she was wise.

So she began to wonder how sad it is to wipe him off from her head but sadder would be seeing his home wrecked alongside ruining happiness of somebody else's family. For this, the girl's love life was detonated but the integrity of the character remained absolute. And with her character remaining intact, God was to give her a life as beautiful as she sat and dreamt.

She remained unusually quite during the rounds. After the rounds, when the classes were over, desiring solitude, she rushed back to her hostel and wept in the confines of her room. Her only strength in the given moment was her faith in God and in her soul. She reminded herself of what her mother would tell her,

'Failures in life, comes to show us ways, unforeseen and unimagined in that moment. God has different ways of leading us on our life's paths. So never question God and wait patiently with faith until the big picture is revealed. That is the way of the wise. Be wise and act like one too.'

Laila was indeed wise for her age and acted alike.

Wiping her tears she went out with Dr. Sneha at the popular Coffee House on the M.G. road in Bangalore. She smiled at the sight of the chocolate brownies sizzling on the sizzler plate with thick hot chocolate sauce poured generously over it. They relished the dish and chatted freely. It was a breather good enough to cheer her up. She didn't disclose a word regarding her heartbreak to Dr. Sneha. Laila, though was known to be a friendly, warm, trustworthy and kind to all, she always took her own sweet time to reconsider before taking their friendship beyond general conversation. She would notice her gut feeling regarding everybody she met. And in Dr. Sneha's case, she understood her to be more of a competitive colleague rather than a cozy friend. So, she found it better to bury the ashes of her heartbreak rather than to scatter it through a discussion.

The girls cleared the bill and headed to window shop. As they walked past shop, Laila spotted a lilac shiny strappy high heels spreading its arms, longing to be adopted by her. She zoomed in the shop and bought it without a blink. She smiled happily and life felt better. On their way back both the lady doctors laughed reminiscing Dr. Arvind's temper tantrums and the new wild adult jokes they had heard the previous day in the canteen. She felt better and got on with life.

This was the wonder of leading a path guided by her soul. Her faith in God, pulled her out easily, from what could otherwise have been a disturbing experience nonetheless, a waste of time and her life for a life lived away from the soul is nothing but a waste.

From next day onwards, she began afresh. Gradually she realized that her focus in her studies had randomly improved. She asked more questions and understood the details of the case better. And fortunately for her, her exams were around the corner making it compulsory for her to study to score good grades. Life moved on as she chose it.

In her next and second last posting, she was put in the child psychiatry ward. She was scoring better in all her subjects. What still remained her weakness was not her love life or lack of it, but her conscience. Once again it was her emotional resilience with her patients that failed her more than before. She was finding it difficult to stand by the sufferings she saw around. She was turning into helpless spectator in the name of being a doctor. She had the dilemma of her life knocking at her again.

On a night, while she was waiting for her dinner to be served in the mess, she was playing with her spoon lifelessly. An announcement was made, for doctors to report to the emergency ward, every cell in her body froze. The mess buzzing with people came to a standstill and the food was left untouched for that night. Nobody believed, what they heard, yet reality remained unchanged.

The radiant, twenty eight year old Dr. George was brought in in a coma stage. He and his wife were on their way back from a weekend vacation from a hill station Chikmagalur, when a truck loaded with iron beams rammed into their vehicle, smashing their car and their own bodies into pieces. By the time neuro surgeons here at St. Allan's geared to act to the situation, he was declared dead by the local government hospital in Chikmagalur. It wasn't his face, but his driving license lying in the dash board of his car that declared his identity. His handsome features were ripped beyond recognition, scattered into pieces of flesh. She nonetheless rushed towards the emergency ward, and paid her last tribute to the man, she loved deeply once.

This night of his death, was a turning point in Laila's life. It lit a candle on the altar of her life. The big picture was revealed and clarity was magnified. She realized her fortune of not being with him, by chance and by her choice. She barely could have enjoyed the togetherness with him for his death was hovering over. Her mother's wise words and her faith in God, had saved her from entering a swamp that would have had given her nerve chilling end. God saved her, truly loved her and certainly had better plans for her considering which He saved her from the harrowing trauma that would have dented her for a life time.

Her mind was bombarded with introspective questions on the same night. 'What if my death is near, will I die happy? Will I have done what I wanted to do the most? Would I meet God with a smile on my face? Will people see fulfillment in my eyes when I talk of my life to them? Will I die with desires or contentment?'

And the dizzying reply was 'No'.

'When I die, what would I say? Thank u God?' or 'Life sucks?' The choice was upto her and her only. She felt through this episode of her life, God's had given her clear signal compelling her to live her life, her way, doing what she so desired to do and always dreamt of doing without being dependent on people of her happiness so that, when death comes, Laila would die with least of regrets. As depressed and miserable psychiatrist would be looked up for her professional status, was not the future she wanted to see come alive and neither did her soul. She made up her mind on that night itself, to pursue her career entirely on her terms keeping her happiness in mind. She realized that life was too short and precious to waste it doing what others wanted her to do because in the time when we go through the ordeal, nobody feels the heat of the situation like we do as an individual.

Life was burning her like the blazing heat from the furnace. Laila gave up, for once and for all, the idea of living her father's dream and decided to chase her own. She heard the knock of her soul, the knock that gave new wings to her.

———◆———

CHAPTER 2

Dreams are the aphrodisiacs of life and impossible; only an unsighted possibility for the dreamer.

It was farewell ball of her batch at St. Allan's institute of Mental Health and Neuro Sciences, Bangalore.

The banquet hall in the campus was decorated with bright streamers, colorful balloons, flowers, chandeliers and candles. The male doctors, psychologists and psychiatric social workers of her batch came dressed in formal tuxedo suits, neatly back combed hair, clean shoes with an evident sense of hygiene at display. The females, the more blessed being of the campus wore formal but modest evening gowns with their hair done elegantly. This was night they looked forward to from the day they entered the institute of St. Allan as students.

There prevailed a sense of achievement among the passing away batch tonight and also, a strong sense of loss and of bereavement, from the good, bad and the beautiful time they had spent in the hospital. That night, alike the nights of all farewell they found beauty in the most nightmarish experiences at the institute and they were to carry it as a somber memory, to cherish. 'It's the way of the world to enjoy what's gone by and sulk the beauty of today,' thought Laila as she entered the hall room.

The farewell opened with a formal prayer and words by the cannibal, Dr. Arvind, 'It has never been and nor will be,' said the Dr. through the micro phone, 'undemanding to get in and to, bid adieu to, our St. Allans institute of Mental Health and Neuro Sciences. It's a night of grief for me, in as much as it is to you my dear beloved students the respected future doctors of the world. But in this grief goes out my good wishes to you and to your future. The world outside is waiting for you whereas the world inside me in lament . . . It's heart wrenching for me to see you leave the campus . . .' and he continued with his farewell speech.

In a navy blue tuxedo suit with a scarlet tie seated in towards the back and end of the tiered semi circular seating arrangement, remarked Dr. Sandeep, 'The cannibal is seriously sad. He needs a hygienic bed sheet from our ward to wipe his tears.' He turned to look at the lady doctor, in a black backless evening gown with her hair tied in a glamorous lose French bun with a flower on the side, seated next to him, 'Ah! Who is this?' he said and rose a bit from his seat in disbelief. 'I suggest I lodge an F.I.R . . . there has been violation of the rule in the ball room.'

'Ahem!' said Laila, looking in his eyes unmoved by his attention. 'Defiance is my game.'

'Oh really! There is an emergency then,' He said with a grin that turned into a smile, 'can I take the size of your shoes, Cinderella? I have one made of glass with me. If it fits you, you will belong to me. I am Dr. Sandeep, the price on the lookout.'

Laila smiled unable to handle his attention, she said 'behave yourself Sandeep. We are in the public eye and I must say, you look handsome.'

'I have always been handsome, not my fault if you noticed it today,' he replied adjusting his blazer. 'Your loss.' Laila smirked. 'But what is different is . . . ahem' he coughed loud which distracted Dr. Arvind form his solemn speech, although he couldn't spot who coughed that loud. 'You know that man, that old cannibal . . .' he dived in her ears to whisper, 'He wouldn't need a Viagra . . .' he looked at her pristine beauty, 'just a glance at you . . . aah and he would . . . he would be in the clouds . . . floating.'

'Hush!' she said going red in the face, 'watch your words Dr. Sandeep.'

'Why only words,' he said regaining his posture, ''m watching everything . . . I can't afford not to and you see,' he said and paused. By now Dr, Arvind had concluded his speech requesting to head for the dinner followed by the ball dance. In excitement everybody rose up from their chair and began gathering around the dinner table. 'That three tiered cake over there, that as our wedding cake. So would you mind walking down this aisle with me Dr. Laila,' he said, 'don't be so heartless. Come on. I may begin to weep . . .'

'Enough. Let's get going.' She replied and walked down the tiered aisle with him on her side, turning heads in admiration. She could notice quietly, their heart's skipping beats looking at her. She looked down, watching her steps for her high heels needed her to walk carefully while Dr. Sandeep looked around, taking the crowd checking out his friend, as a personal adulation. He grinned and walked gallantly.

'Our examinations are due,' said Laila in between, 'so prince Sandeep, cut down on your pomp . . . and walk straight with me to the dinner table. Heaven forbid the professors notice you flirting with me . . . they may take it otherwise.'

'Marks!' he exclaimed walking along side, 'you don't have to worry about that, I will stand first this time round.'

'You look very confident tonight,' she answered, 'is it amm . . . because of you are walking with me . . . , or you are for a change, studying that hard?'

'I study very hard,' he replied staring at her from top to bottom, 'and will do so till my last breath sitting next to you, in our clinic, together.' Laila didn't reply and on reaching the dinner table he gave her, her dinner plate first, walking along side he served her the dishes before he serving on his plate. Which he took after her.

'Chivalry,' Said Laila, 'it makes you more handsome than you are prince Sandeep.' He laughed soberly,' I must say, you are sweet especially tonight.' She genteelly glanced at the three cuisines; Indian, Thai and Chinese. 'Give me some more of the cottage cheese dish.'

'Sure! Besides don't make presumptions,' he replied serving his own dinner, 'you are yet to taste me.' Laila blushed hard and looked away. Gradually her batch mates walked towards them grimly enjoying their last formal get together as student's of St. Allan's. Tonight they hankered to spend another year in the institute's campus or so it turn out of their conversation.

'The dinner is over my ladies and their mental men,' he said to his batchmates finishing the food on his plate in fifteen minutes and so did the others,' now grace the dance floor and you Dr. Ganpat no need to smile too much. I understand you are glad in the arousing company of the dazzling Laila but, excuse me, will you doctor, I am the one who's gonna dance with her, first. You may stand in the line, like others . . . there, as a waiting lister.' He spoke pointing at the men eagerly stairing at Laila from behind of Dr. Ganpath.

Dr. Ganpat stood shocked at the public disclosure of his happy smile on that night.

'Is it a sting operation,' he said shyly, 'I am happy to wait Dr. Sandeep.' and then he asked Dr. Radha, to be his dance date to which she was overjoyed.

'Happy to wait,' responed Dr. Sandeep, 'hope you are not left just waiting. By the way,' he said in style hinting at Dr. Radha, 'like feathers flock together. Men's talks,' he said looking at Laila.

'You didn't even ask me for a dance,' whispered Laila to Dr. Sandeep winding up her dinner while the students had started to fill the dance floor for their annual ball dance. 'That's too close a dance . . . I can't,' she said worriedly.

'If this is close, than,' said Dr. Sandeep, 'I wonder . . . how close is . . . ahem. Hey! Dr. Ganpat, is this the first time you are touching a woman?' He asked him as he was about to begin dancing with Dr. Radha. He glanced away and looked back at Dr. Sandeep gesturing him not to spoil the chemistry between him and his dance date. 'Good luck with that.' He waved at him.

'How many women have you danced with . . . ? You shouldn't have spoken like that . . .' said Laila giggling. 'He is shy of your humour.'

'Not many. Dance is about confidence and now may I ask you for our first dance?' he spoke nobly taking her hand and leading her to the dance floor. He moved her gracefully, swirled her around and pulled her close. 'You like it?' he asked looking down at her, holding her hand genteelly, in his hand.

'Aah . . . hmm,' she said and they danced more. 'Sandeep, I don't wanna practice psychiatry.'

He smirked. 'Are you scaring me or trying to do so?' he asked. 'Like a dose of my own drug of humour, Laila. Please not tonight, because tonight is as special, as are . . . you . . . to me.'

'No. It's a decision and you are the first one to know.' She said cutting his line of speech.

'Go ahead,' he said, 'if that is the quest of your soul,' He replied undergrounding his feelings, for her. 'I am not happy either, but I have no option, but to continue being a psychiatrist,' He genteelly pushed her back and turned her around holding her finger over her head. She smiled in her eyes. 'So, what is it that you wanna do?' he asked keeping a check on his soul's quest.

'I will tell you all about it, once I make up my mind entirely,' she replied.

He looked away and said, 'Your mind is made up, I know you Laila . . . it's something else that is holding you back.' She looked at him with a twinkle in her eyes and his eyes became numb. 'I will let you go, if that's what you want.' And their dance continued. 'But still reconsider it. I have been your friend for sometime and in that capacity I would want you to be happy and fulfilled. Don't leave Psychiatry altogether . . . for my sake,' he chuckled and felt a pinch inside.

'Why not let go?' she said resting her forehead on his chest, 'as for our friendship you are my good friend, and will remain so.'

'Lift your forehead Laila,' he said with a smile, 'my marks are at risk and so is my heart.'

'Let's change partners,' she said, 'or else you will have a hangover.' They giggled and changed partners and danced until midnight when the cake was cut for everybody to relish.

That week Laila went back to her home in Chennai for the weekends. Since there were just a few months left in the completion of her degree, she found it sensible to complete the course to be kept aside, may be, as a backup degree.

There were days it pained her enormously to be a part of St. Allan's, as she was losing her nerves. Her composure was out of her leach; she began to feel like simply walking away from the institute's campus on any given date. She had to calm her nerves recalling, her mother's word's, 'knowledge is like a dead snake. It has worth and use even if we think it doesn't.' which encouraged her to take up her exams and then move on but the biggest hurdle of her life, her father.

As for prince Sandeep, he set his love free and waited for it to come back. For him, his not started relationship was over and he moved on, or so it was in Laila's eyes. He continued to love her in his mind, everyday and in the hounding stillness of the nights too.

At her home, the villa spread in a vast area of six acres was on fire, as her father was enraged to hear of her decision, though thankfully her mother had had a word with him before she was to come down to Chennai to talk to him in person.

'You are prodigal indeed.' He said to Laila filled with scorn and annoyance. 'Seven years of your life, who but you can detonate it for an unheard profession? What pleasure does it bring to you to ruin my dream? Don't you see I am not keeping well these days.'

'My own dream,' she replied. 'A hundred years back who knew about psychiatry, father?' Her words that night had hidden faith that only wise could have understood.

'No but . . .' he responded. It was indeed very hard for him to step in her shoes and feel her pain of being in the profession, 'we had a word, we had a dream, didn't we Laila?'

'I am sorry to fail you but I am not cut for it. It's like trying to become a fish while one is a tortoise because it's shell will rot in the water if he lives in water only.' Was all that she spoke convincingly giving a clear message that she would not pursue his dream for life was hounding her to break away and follow the quest of her soul.

'Photography is erratic. It's a hobby. You can do it along side. I wouldn't be able to stand you roaming around with a camera in the jungles, or in people's marriage parties, or . . . or . . . in circus. Is this how you want to live your entire life Laila?' He spoke with antipathy as it's easier to find logic in matters we are convinced about and against matters we are not open too.

'Where' she said, 'in jungles? What?' and she chuckled though maintained the decorum. 'Yes, I will ie. if my work calls me to shoot with jungle as the back drop, I will go to the jungles father. That would be my work.'

'You will go to marriages in our city also calling it work, dedication and . . . . ?' He ran out of breath due to the disappointment. Laila went blank for his health was at risk but then so was her happiness, her dream and her life.

'That's not fashion photography, honey.' Announced her mother entering the scene just in time. Her father aborted their conversation asking Laila to go to her room.

'We will talk about it later.' Said her father.

'Wait.' Said her mother, 'this is about her life. We have to have a serious talk. Let her do her part and we will do ours. Please.'

'Andrea, what are you talking about,' he spoke with aversion. 'Photography has no future, no money, no certainty . . . no fixed salary, what is there to talk about it that too seriously. She will continue with what she is doing.'

Andrea looked at Anand, 'why didn't you study to become a doctor?'

'I couldn't. I didn't have the resources.' He said, 'and the opportunity to study medicine. There was no appropriate environment for it.'

'Or else you would have?' asked Laila with a smirk and disgust in her voice.

'Perhaps,' he replied.

'Or perhaps not because you are emotional,' she added. 'Easier said than done, father.'

'Yes, I am emotional, I am very emotional,' he answered with an objective of grating her dream off her mind.'

'In that case, you couldn't have become a psychiatrist. You couldn't have done it successfully,' said Laila, 'nor can I. It's has killed me. Spare what is left of me father. It ruined me to the extent that I will become a patient and not remain a doctor. Please don't be so unkind and pitiless towards your own child. For God's sake, father, let me be who I want to be, than die being who I am miserable being.'

For two months he used silence as a measure to force her to change her decision.

But Laila's thoughts were unwavering. She wanted to navigate her life by her choice though garnering his support was imperative for he was her father who somewhere in his heart loved her and every love does call for sacrifice, which he had to understand. She was resolute in her decision and was prepared from her end to give a polite but persistent explanation as much as she possibly could have, despite her lack of exposure to her new profession, the one, she wanted to explore.

And before she would have given up on giving logical explanations, and moved to emotional blackmailing, he became placid and changed his mind miraculously.

God's grace was apparent in Laila's life and her prayers were answered quicker than she believed. She kissed her mother for understanding her and being by her in the real sense of the word.

Parent's support are and will remain a blessing for their child because in doing so they make their child unconditionally loved and accepted, which is a performance enhancer.

As every human soul hankers for support from each other and form their loved one's, the elder's who guide them, from their understanding and life experience. Such children are lead a much happier life than the one who's struggle is enhanced by indifferent parents who withdraw support from their children to please themselves and people. Their love remains conditional and thus turns the child sour and cynical, snappy and bully instead of turning them into being, wise and caring.

'How do you feel?' asked her father over the phone form Chennai while she had returned to St. Allan's, Banglore.

'Better than I fathomed, thanku.' She replied.

'What are you thanking me for?' he asked not finding a worthy reason of being thanked by her.

'For your love. It's my guiding light father,' she replied, 'I know you are not happy, but I will not turn you down.'

'You didn't turn me down,' he replied, 'I need to understand the possibility a human mind withholds and I am going to do that through you.'

Laila couldn't respond for a moment, she was touched by his support. 'It's quite an encouragement. That's all that I could ask from you, father.'

'Yes, I infer I have not been as loving as your mother and neither as wise,' he answered, 'but I will try to, I know she is never wrong and also it takes courage to be who you are. But still you see Laila . . . psychiatry isn't that bad an option for your career.'

'No confusing talks honey . . . she will feel low and unaccepted. Besides it's not fair to levy our desires and dreams on somebody else's shoulder. It can be brutal for such children frustrate easily . . . you know what troubled and killed Aseem . . . will kill Liala too,' said Andrea as he was holding the line.

'Hellow . . . hellow! Laila are you there?' asked Anand.

As for Liala she began to realize as to why she felt distant from her father naturally despite he being so pampering. 'Yes, I am.'

'That's what . . . I will hang up . . . your mother is here . . . on my head,' said Anand.

She smiled and thanked God for his support and they hung up on each other lovingly. He then thought to himself, 'as an elder I should understand how delicate children are and how much our support matters to them. I have hurt my child, may she forgive me.' One dreamer giving up his dream for another was praiseworthy and called for respect because in doing so, he gave her the freedom to chose life and follow her soul, which is the seat of God within being. "Many in this world have a quest to follow their soul and the talent,' said his father to himself, 'may the good God lead them through their journey.' After this he began to rattle his head again as how to stop his child from treading the path of his dream.

Laila's exams got over and results were awaited, her foot wears were partying in her cupboard as her own dream took her from Chennai to the city of infinite possibilities, Mumbai.

A city that has invisible threads to weave dreams and visible resources to make it come alive. A city, in which people despite it's fast pace of life find time for a stroll on the beach, for daily prayers, for quick gossips, for elaborate festivals, for street food and time for falling in love. Mumbai, the city that embraces any migrant who can afford her pace of life, her high living cost and the palpitating rush to make ends meets. This city in specific, is said to feed desires enthusiastically. If new things happened, it is said, it hits this city, first.

New trends and style wears off rapidly in the volatile lifestyle. Laila, accepted the life Mumbai offered and then came the charm of the newness, in abundance. She saw ample of reasons why the city feels like a hot cup of frothy cappuccino kissing our lips in a winter morning. It has temptation and it's own charm to it.

Famous for the match box stacked one on top of another, in the concrete jungles of Mumbai, she hired a one bedroom flat on the sixth floor, with unheard ease. Not only that, her bedroom's window opened in a huge park surrounded by fresh green coconut trees on all it's four sides. A view that was as relieving and refreshing. Her building had twenty four hour water supply and white marble flooring, a rare combination in the old buildings of the suburbs. Moreover, the façade of the building though old, was far from being dingy and dilapidated. Freshly painted in lemon yellow with blue borders it was recently repaired as though God wanted to set it ready for her arrival, just the way she desired in her mind.

After all the wise knows that impossible in reality is actually the limitation set by our own mind.

On familiarizing herself with her locality and settling in with her new surroundings, he started to meet different photographers, old and new, to get firsthand experience of the real aspects of the profession. She used contacts from the directories and from a friend she had in Banglore whose younger sister was a fashion designer, there. It was Dr. Sandeep's elder sister, Ella, who helped her with the accommodation and directed her over the phone how to get to the place where she wanted to visit. Laila traveled to different parts of the city, from town to the suburbs, on the local trains, a mode of commutation with a live of it's own. It is as mean as it can be in it's speed, dumping people under it's wheels and leaving them standing on the platform if they are new to the pushing and pulling technique of boarding it. And then it is equally concerned in the way it connects one part of Mumbai with another. A mix of meanness with some kindness, it makes the passengers just like the way it is. Laila stood patiently in the long but very fast moving queue and bought her ticket. "Fifth platform" said the man at the counter while handing her the ticket. The train was on right time. She ran grabbing her ticket towards the platform which required her to cross the over bridge and get down the flight of staircases to board her train. While she was on the over bridge, the strap of her high heels came off and she was stranded there.

'Oh No!!! I cant miss this one,' she shrieked as the train came and she was rushing to make it to the platform. She ran again and she faltered to a fall.

A young boy stood before her as she gathered her nerves, 'is that the train you wanted to board?' he spoke handing her, her ticket which had fallen from her hand. He staired at her pink premium I-pod.

'Yes,' she replied rubbing the dust off her pants and taking her ticket back from his hands.

'Look there.' he said pointing towards the ladies compartment. 'Now tell me could you have managed to board that compartment?Good your heels came off. Everything happens for the good.' Laila wondered a this wisdom, though not quite sure of what he said, 'Look down,' he repeated and she did giving in to his confidence. She looked down from the over bridge to where he pointed. She could see women were at a tug of war pushing and elbowing hard at each other. They were yelling shrieking to make their way in the compartment. 'Nobody seemed to care for anybody but for them selves,' thought Laila. The worst sight for her was, an old women who wanted to get off at Andheri station was crushed in the stampede. Somebody tried helping her and the train started to shunt, so the women who was helping left and boarded the train. Laila's heart melted at the sight. Thankfully a gentleman on the platform helped her to stand on her feet and find her way out of the rush.

'You look new.' Said the boy as the train shunted.

'What makes you say that,' she asked tiredly, 'you look quite experienced.'

'Somebody with an high end i-pod, trying to make her way in the inhumane SECOND CLASS compartment is what only a new comer can do.' He said, Laila could see fatigue on his dusky skin.

'Thank you for briefing me. I didn't know it was this bad.' She remarked recovering from the shocking sight.

'It's Mumbai expect help anywhere though not trust anybody. Always wait and watch. And this,' he said in a relaxed tone of voice, 'is not that bad. It's seems bad because it's new to you. You have to know the technique of pushing and of being pushed and now look there,' said the boy and ran away as fast as he could form Laila.

'But hey!' she yelled trying to stop him, 'I couldn't . . .' The way he was rippling across the crowd, it gave her a fright, but he didn't stop. And there he was on the platform, making his way in the second class general compartment with ease, despite the same rush.

Then he stood at the entrance, possibly to get off at the next entrance. The entrance was without gates, looking up he waved a thumbs up sign at her with a sunny smile and the train began to shunt and whistle taking him to his desired destination. She waved back at him with a smile.

He left behind a sweet memory and a wise lesson. Nothing in life in as difficult as it seems the first time, we just have to find the right technique to be able to conquer our fears.

'I couldn't thank him,' she gibbered and picked up her broken footwear and headed homeward walking as carefully as she could. 'It must have been God,' she thought to herself, 'he wanted to guide me. Thank you.' She said resting her hand on her chest in gratitude and then she went home and changed her shoes and came back to the railway station, bought a first class ticket to board the next train with ease. 'I don't have the strength today to board second class compartment.' She said to herself though the next day she wore a flat shoes and learned the technique of pushing and being pushed and avoided the office rush hours. 'why call for trouble to prove my strength, I rather avoid the maddening rush whenever I can and use my energy for my work.' A wise decision indeed.

As she met different photographer and saw the shoots in progress, she got visually acquainted with the erratic work schedule, the stipends given to the assistants, the kind of work expected out of beginners, constant updating camera skills and the long arduous road to success. While she was still in the last leg of getting her degree in psychiatry, she had started with her ground work on the subject of fashion photography.

She squeezed out time to read up books on successful photographers and their entire professional journey. She found there were some common links running in all stories, and silent sufferings were one among it. And now when she came face to face with reality, she saw how much hard work went in the clicking of one right picture.

It was quite demanding then to march to the tunes of two entirely differently professions but she did put in that extra hard work which helped her gain an insight. Passion is one thing and sensibility is another. To be successful, the wise mixes the two of it together, instead of shirking away as just dreaming about making big in life is unwise because the path of living a dream requires endurance and exposure. A dreamer has to begin with faith in God because soul's have a distinct voice, which comes from God. God gives us that quest knowing we will succeed if we follow that path. That apart, a dreamer has to be tensile mentally taking obstacles in their stride and pursuing their goal. And as we do that, God walks along side, protecting, sheltering and loving us while helping us increase our endurance and strength provided we are open to learning and progressing with a resolute mind. When we make persistent efforts, we do reap the rewards, sooner or later and sometimes, unexpectedly.

It was on one humid bright morning that Laila was coming down the elevator, and she met Mrs. Matondakar, the secretary of her building. A short and thin woman in her late fifties, she looked towards Laila and asked, 'You are a doctor right?'

'Yes! Aahh . . . Yaah.' She was unable to find exact words to begin explaining her career change keeping in mind the newness of their interaction. Laila presumed that being the buildings secretary; she must have read the N.O.C, no objection certificate that mentions her profession as a doctor. That was a truth in as much it was a lie.

'So is my daughter.' she replied shaking her head as she spoke.

'What?' said Laila lost in confusion.

'A doctor. She lives in the U.S. She just bought her own house with a swimming pool and jacuzzi, just the previous month. Anyhow, what is your specialization?" Came the pompous reply and the query from the lady. She didn't even bother to introduce herself, such was her curiosity to scan Laila inside out, as a new member of the society.

'I see! Nice to know that, I am Psychiatrist too.' Said Laila unmoved by the woman's showcasing, for Laila was not new to wealth and neither was she the type to envy people for what they earn.

And in a flick of a second, jealousy gripped her hard and tight. The woman's voice changed from sweet to being competitive. 'Oh! Same as my daughter.' she replied. Interpreting Laila's calmness as a cold response to her words she added gleefully, 'She is planning to buy a another car, this time a Mercedes. in the coming month.'

To this, Laila raised her eyebrows, looked in the lady's eyes and smiled with a message that said, 'Ok, All right. You win.'

Wisely, she looked away and asked, 'how old is she, if I may ask?'

'She is, just 38 years old.' Replied the lady confused by the abstract query.

'Well, her assets well suits her age. I am twenty four. But anyways, wish me luck for I desire to live my dreams just like her."

The lady was embarrassed by her guts. She was left with no choice but to display humility as her age demanded instead of downplaying a person half her age.

'Oh! That's wonderful. Why don't you move abroad? It 's by far more paying to do the same work there.' suggested the woman in a week tone of voice, blended unevenly with arrogance stemming from her ego. Though momentarily, concern for Laila was also apparent on her wrinkled face. Laila to her, certainly didn't seem like drawing a hefty salary for one she lived in a hired flat and managed her chores all by herself. Moreover, her annual rent agreement had no mention of allotment of parking space for her car. She had no car and neither could her income afford it, as it seemed to her.

Laila, choose to withdraw and change the line of conversation, for grace was her second nature. Understanding the woman's insecurity without a blink and considered it absolutely useless to prick her any further. Besides, she was also sure the woman wasn't familiar with what it takes to be a psychiatrist, or else she would have spoken a word of appreciation with equal pride for the efforts put in by her wealthy daughter in her work rather than making a cheeky display of her assets.

"No. In fact I am giving up psychiatry to pursue fashion photography. I am looking for a right photographer to assist. I haven't found one as yet" replied Laila confidently unmoved by the woman's suggestion.

'Oh! Really? 'said the astounded woman, relieved that her daughter has just lost a competitor.

'Yes.' Laila smiled in confirmation.

'My nephew is in the same line of work, why don't you speak to him. He may be of some help to in this regard. He is good at his work. His name is Varun,' she said politely for a change.

'Oh! Varun. Is that what you just said?' she confirmed with amazement, 'I have heard of Varun Chawla. He is a well known photographer.'

'Yes. That is him, my nephew.' She said nonchalantly.

'It would be very kind of you to refer my name to him. He is senior person in this field, it would certainly be of help to have a word with him." said Laila humbled by the help offered to her.

'Sure. No problems. Come by to my flat in the evening, I will give you his contact number. M in a hurry now. See you!' spoke the woman disembarking from the elevator.

'Thanku! See you!' said Laila and they parted ways heading in different directions for their respective work places.

Her faith in God gave her good returns. Varun, a tall and lean forty five year old fashion photographer with a long list of credentials, including four awards as the best photographer of the year by the Photographer's Guild of India and another one by the International Association of Photography award to the first Indian, met her at his home and hired her as one of his assistant photographer thereby successfully inaugurating her journey into the sensational world of fashion photography.

CHAPTER 3

*Mind, the most complex organ of human body
is also it's, the most productive slave.*

The day was lovely in the sunny autumn. Everything seemed easier and slower, relaxed and warm. She stretched her arms and got up from the bed, changed into red and black track suit and headed for a jog on the rocky and muddy Versova beach. On her return, the sweaty Laila dried herself under the fan and dashed to her bathroom. Relentlessly, her sculpted body took pleasure in every drop of water gushing from the shower onto her, until her stomach called for attention.

Patting herself dry, she wore pink sleeveless shirt, tucked in neatly in black corduroy pants that ended an inch above her black heels and a thin black belt with snake skin impression on it, around her narrow waistline. Spraying a generous amount of floral French fragrance onto her clothes, she served herself a hearty breakfast of frosted cornflakes with some dry fruits, that set her pace for the day. This was unsual for her but that is what transition are all about. Somebody so used to being served was serving herself.

This was her first day to work and to her amazement, there was not an ounce of nervousness in her. Her mind in the early morning did throb with excitement, but now as she was all set for the day she felt deeply calm, from within.

The type of healing calmness we get when we arrive at the right destination, the destination one's soul travels for long. The next moment she felt a deep sense of relief, though her journey was about to take off today. It was indeed something very unusual as if she were being blessed by an invisible and super natural healing force. There was no dichotomy in it because in Laila's understanding, this was not a destination but the commencement of her new journey.

It could be a place, relationship, activity, object or profession. The uniqueness of this energy is directly related to the purpose we are meant to achieve in this life time. Everybody who is close to their soul does feel it one time or another in their entire life journey. It's an unspoken signal, that what lies before us is what our spirit seeks and loves to the core. And also that It was meant for it.

Laila kept breathing in the energy with a soulful smile. She felt an invisible aura which, far from being scary embraced her body. It was not scary in that, when He Himself is with us, to help us live our dreams, what is there to fear His embrace?

It was an unfelt experience for her and what made more special is the fact that we, no matter how capable, can never create it.

It comes to confirm to us that God is watching over us and that He cares to be by us even in our aloneness. In aloneness which has the capacity to make us complete.

> 'This world is wild and I am just a child,
> Please be with me, even in the darkness I can't see.
> You give me light and hug me tight.
> So that in my trials I do succeed and
> In my victory pure remain my deeds.'

These lines from the girl's daily prayers were heard by the Almighty, as a result today was the day, the once upon a time stunning but sad doctor was to begin living her dream as a happy fashion photographer. The universe had to pass on her good wishes to her and applaud her, in a special way. And it did so through this beautiful energy.

She looked at herself one last time in the mirror and saying a bye to her flat, she locked the door behind her and headed to the bus stop.

On her way to catch the bus, the only person to shade herself under the umbrella was the sultry photographer, Laila. Though she loved her Sun God, she cherished his company only while spreading her clothes to dry everyday and in winter, to keep her body warm and happy. She noticed that city dwellers were so used to burning under the sun that it felt weird to carry an umbrella in that crowd. The famous Mumbai tan was obvious on their skin. 'May be . . . .', she thought to herself, 'they are too busy worrying about worries, that guarding their skin is not even a secondary concern for them. But who wants a damaged skin. Naah! Not Laila,' said the girl to herself. Right, she was in her analysis and wise to protect her skin because as goes the famous Buddhist thought, our body is a temple and thus should be worshipped and preserved as here resides the soul;the seat of God. And also Laila had learnt the rule of the universe that if we don't care for ourselves, nobody else will.

Unfortunately, the crowd around wasn't wise like her and neither as careful as she was in small ways. Not a surprise, people out there constantly stared at her and envied the peace and the glow emanating from her skin while they ignored the casual secret behind it. Be it our life or just our skin, if we care, so does the universe. And when we care we get in grove of loving our body and soul, together and who but the unwise does not want to feel the experience.

Squeezing her eyes to shield it from dust of the narrow Mumbai roads she prayed for the arrival of her bus. The bus came by and on the next stop she realized she had boarded the wrong bus, which instead of going left from the signal was to take a right to turn towards the road that would lead to Bandra. Of this, the kind ticket conductor of the moving bus informed her, when she gave the name of her destined bus stop. 'What stop comes next?' she asked him panicked.

Then he asked, 'Where do you want to go to?'

'Oshiwara,' she replied holding the bar above her head to support her body.

'Get off on the next stop and take bus number 118 and go backward to the stop which we just crossed and from there catch another bus 222, it will take you to your destination—' guided the conductor.

'What? What numbers did you say?' She asked, as she swayed with the bus's moving wheels. Being bad at mathematics in school, numbers were far from her understanding when given in quick speed.

'Madam, your bus stop.' Said the conductor directing her to move ahead, towards the front door, which in BEST [Brihanmumbai Electricity Supply and Transport] bus, is the exit door.

'Oh no! It's too early. M not ready for this.' Said the girl helplessly looking at the man as she spoke. 'Oh!' Her palm began to sweat. She didn't know how to manage it all by herself in a new and a fast paced city like Mumbai.

'Get down,' he said, 'and ask somebody. Go!' The wise conductors message to her was that when we get lost on out path, we should pause and look around for leads.

She got off the bus in confusion and she prayed. She stood at the bus stop and watched the cars pass by and the signal that regulated the traffic. In her mind she was planning and plans weren't turning effective because she was worried. It was getting difficult for her to take the pressure that was induced by her urge to reach the studio on time, while she couldn't find her way to it. Her confusion mixed with lack of knowledge, compelled her to stand by and think overwhat the conductor said.

'His words implied to look for the lead that would clear my confusion,' she said to herself, still standing at the unknown bus stop.

Everything seeming so confusing and then she noticed somebody, a man around her age, looked at his watch and appeared amused by something she saw. Then he crossed the road. 'He got down with me,' she murmured, 'didn't he? He did. He was lost too.

He got down here and didn't know where to go. Then he made a call and now he is doing the needful.' And then she made up her mind and the next moment, she stirred clear her mind of all the dilemmas and chucked the helplessness crap. By now Laila was honing the skill of being a decision maker of her life. She was fast becoming the master of using her mind to weigh the options for herself, on her own.

The traffic light went red and she crossed the road successfully, to her revelation. She turned her head to right and there she spotted the man. She followed him. He spoke to the auto rickshaw's driver, giving him the name of a place in the way that sounded like an enquiry and then he sat in it zooming away in no time. Laila did the same. She waved at the autorickshaw, spoke with the driver and jumped in it as coolly as the ice cube dropped in a glass of chilled Martini. She was a quick learner. Giving herself comfort, lots of love and right direction was now her way of life.

As a new comer, in the zooming life of Mumbai, she was saving herself from turning bitter, lonely and lovelorn, in every moment of her life.

Sweaty and happy, she reached on time. Her choice, for the moment was wise and thus different, for Laila was a wise Indian with soulful German blood. She gained immediate inspiration, thanks to the man for inspiring her and to her, for following him wisely.

On reaching the studio located in Oshiwara, she pressed the door bell and stood waiting for a response. Her first bell went unanswered and so did the second and the third one. Laila stood there puzzled, as there wasn't there any response to the bell. Reminiscing, that supernatural energy that had embraced her confirming her move to be right, she was still awaiting the response. She was about to ring the bell for the fourth and the last time and just then the door creaked open.

A young fellow around her height wearing extra baggy blue jeans and green round neck t-shirt with the handsome Italian footballer Totti's face embossed on it, came forth. He had big eyes, a small goatee on his chin and messed up wavy hair and a band holding his hair back just like the footballer on his t-shirt. He stood before her with the lower half of his body behind the door and the other half facing her, hiding as if he wore nothing below. Little did one know that it was just his style of opening the door as was it to look carelessly cool.

'Ahhhh . . . Aaah . . . I', he paused to wipe his face with both his palms, 'I . . . . I . . . . was sleeping. You are?' said the fellow, in a muzzy voice.

'Hellow!I am Laila.' Came the reply from her in a soft voice.

'Laila? Umm . . .' and he stared at her to recall if there was a model with her name required for the day's shoot. 'Luscious lips' came the voice in his head. 'Okheay. Allright. Umm . . . . I am Joy. Joydeep Sarkar. Ummm . . . . Come . . . come on in.' And he stepped back to let her in. 'Aaah . . . sorry I forgot your name.' 'Haven't you heard you duffer, 'what's in the name', anyways', remarked the voice in his head, 'life is about opportunities, the ones like this one.'

'No problem.' Replied Laila and stepped ahead to enter. Before stepping in the studio she bent to touch the wooden threshold with her right hand and put the same on her head asking God to bless her with a good day at work and a pleasant career ahead.

As she stepped in, the first room was a small reception area, with photographs of Varun's recent shoots and some newspaper clippings neatly pinned on a long rectangular board. She was walking behind Joy who led her into another huge room, the actual studio.

She got the shock of her life as it was worst than the general ward of a hospital. To her, it appeared less like a studio and more like a store room unattended from ages. Opened books of nude women posing were strewn on the floor. There were innumerable lights kept as if one was pushed against another in frenzy, drapes falling from the couch, used thermocal glasses and leftover food spilling from the packets. Garments, lying haywire and newspapers scattered on the studio floor. Added to the picturesque effect to the dinginess were the yellow dim lights, like that of the night bulbs. She kept standing dumbfounded.

A tic-tac sound came from behind, to which she turnedaround half heartedly. It was Joy crazily switching of the high voltage lights like a novice on the piano, to improve the visibility of the room and to feed his desire which was to see her curves, with an absolute clarity.

'Is that good?' he asked.

'It's much better.' She replied to him innocently. She felt a relief and dutifully thanked God and then to Joy, which was a mistake on her part. Mistake, because Joy had a mindset that interpreted gestures his way. And if innocence was always rightly taken, as was not in her case, the world would have been a sweeter place.

'Okhaey! She's friendly,' called the voice in his head again.

'Do you . . . live here?' she enquired. She felt concerned as to how he managed to live in that mess with bad order of the leftover food and no bed to sleep. This enquiry was a mistake.

"Ammm . . . . Aaaaahhhh . . . ." he gazed at her figure. The lack of sleep, to the lack of words and now from lack of words, he lacked sensibility. 'Bloody you put so much effort in winning women; chocolates, flowers, gifts, soft toys and long phone and hotel bills and here she is wanting to be in bed with you.' Said the voice. 'Take the hints quietly.' 'What did you say?' he asked in confusion rubbing his lips with the back of his finger, he was thinking. 'This is your call. Sweep her off her feet. She is game . . . already.' suggested the voice.

'You live here? It's such a . . .' she spoke softly narrowing her eyesbrows.

'Who me?' he cut her before she would talk any further. 'No. I . . . ieeeee . . .' And he scratched his eyesbrow and smiled more in a way of a controlled laughter unable to believe his luck today. 'Well, I don't. I don't . . . . ahhhh . . . . live here. Aaaah . . . I just sleep here sometimes. You know what I mean. Amm . . . somethings can be done, anywhere. 'Nervously he wiped his entire face to cross check as if he were still asleep. 'Man! Tall and toned, she is all yours.' Said the voices inflating his ego. 'But then . . . . models are very dumb!!!!!!!!!!!!' warned the voices. So what, may be someday dumbness will be in vogue! You sound more interested in her and keep pacing ahead.' 'Luckeeeeeeey boy!' He said to himself.

'Hey! M sorry what did you say was your name? 'and he offered her a chair to sit saying 'Sorry again . . . . ammmm I kept you standing for so long. Take this, this is more comfortable. More cushioned,' he rubbed his lips, 'and . . . . you know . . . what I mean . . . .'

'Laila.' She replied, 'thanku for this, chair.' As she sat on it mulling over his line, 'you know what I mean.' Because she failed to understand what he means when he says so. To her, his mind seemed scattered and as loose as his baggy jeans whereas her own mind was hovering around meeting Varun and initiating work. In the absence of both the aspects she felt low.

'Laila,' he repeated in a poetic mood, 'WOW! That's such a sweet sounding name. You live alone? I mean . . . . What I meant is you live near by?' He spoke unleashing his interest in her, unaware of who she was and why she was there.

'With men there is always a chance with women,' she spoke as she began to get his point very slowly. 'Is it not?'

Sometimes, we have nothing to learn for a long time and then there are days when we are left open to learn so much.

'Hell, no. I didn't mean like that . . .' he replied. 'M not flirting or anything like that.'

'Hmm . . .' she said and giggled on his intentional mistake but saved herself from making her third mistake. She didn't utter about where she stayed and with whom. Her soul had signaled her 'to be careful', as the guy looked confused as well as one with wandering mind'. On the contrary she was trustworthy and had no experience of what could come next from him. He was a stranger, the one with designs on her.

'Anyway. Near or far it doesn't matter. What matters to me is what is in the heart.' Came the superb next line from the poet.

'WHAT?' she said perplexed. She was right in following her soul's guidance to her but where she was not so right was in cutting his conversation then and there. She didn't know that saying a calm shut up was the easiest way out. Unaware she giggled and giggled evenlouder, 'what was that you said?'

To her it was utter nonsense. But to him, it made sense because if all would go well, he would have been overjoyed by what his luck offered to him. 'Party time Joy' called the voice.

'What? Oh that!' He acted as if he didn't know of what he spoke. He giggled along not because he found his own words funny but because he wanted to impress her by coordinating with her mood. He rephrased it and said ". . . forget it. Ammmm . . . I was just kind of curious as to . . . . you know . . . . where you live. I mean if I could be of any help . . . . you know what I mean?"

'Oh that's sweet of you. Thanks,' she replied, believing that he genuinely wanted to help as she was unaware of fast pace flirting in which, lot can happen in disguise. The girl was yet to learn her lessons like all the innocent women do.

'Oh you know what . . . . last night it was me who managed the entire shoot all by . . . . myself you know. Varun let me call the shot. I asked him to chill and I did aaa . . . fabulous job. He complimented me and said I would make, big in life.' Laila was listening. She was kind of impressed too.

'I will shoot you today, It was crazy yesterday night, you know what I mean . . .' he said shaking his limbs, while he spoke.

'Shoot me?' she said cringing and grimacing at him.

And the phone rang harshly scattering his absolute fiction, into unseen pieces.

'Yeah! M good . . . believe you me . . .' he attempted to continue with his story, but the phone rang harsher and harsher.

'Zitch! Uffffhhhh,' he said scratching his chin furiously, ' . . . excuse me lady. May I say my princess. These people have no other work . . . you know what I mean . . . man, it's sickening!' Laila was confused like an owl in the daytime who makes faces as it can't see clearly *what is going on around him.*

Joy got up and leapt like a leopard to its prey, wanting the call to be ended as soon as possible. Furiously, he clawed at the receiver and said. 'Hellouuh! Yeah!' 'Wow the girl is dumb and alone. One free with one. Yahooo!' celebrated the voices on the eve of Joy's victory.

'Who? No.' He responded like a chilled out dudemoving his jaws, chewing nothing in his mouth.

'Who??????' and now his voice changed like a clear blue sky suddenly hit by thunderstorm. 'Oh! . . . Ohhhhoh! OHmy???? Ya . . .' Panicked he turned around to look at her "Ohhhhh . . . . oh my God! Ya, sure . . . . yayaaya . . . . I would. Ya . . . . Ohya, yes. Byeh. No I didn't . . . Ya sure . . . sure. Bye." By the time he hung up he was breathless and began rubbing his face really hard shirking away from accepting nothing but the truth.

'I am sorry.' Said the stud losing his vigour like a tyre, deflated suddenly. Puzzled, She glanced at his face. It was white with fear. 'Lack of blood to the brain' she recalled her lessons from her degree in Psychiatry,' what went so wrong with him?' She asked to herself.

'I was . . . I was . . . very sleepy.' He said in distress. 'Damn you! You messed with her . . .' came the damning voice in his head. And he further begged in apology rubbing his palms with each other in regret. 'M so sorry! Aaahhh . . . . aaam . . . . I didn't ask . . .'

'Sorry for what? Besides, you weren't that sleepy, Joy. You were just ignorant.' replied Lailawith smartly delivered wisdom.

Her word's left him horrified and gasping for more breath. Ignorant, yes he was because he presumed her identity and also the purpose of her visit as per his suitability and never bothered to enquire as to who she was and what she was looking for at the studio.

Now as he came to know that Laila was neither lacking education nor wisdom and she certainly wasn't a dumb model, though she looked as stunning as one. She was Doctor Laila, the newly appointed assistant to Tarun and in that capacity Joy's colleague. He was still sinking in the reality post answering the call. 'Varun would be here in an hour.' And he got her a glass of water to drink. Fully awake into his newly anointed role as her colleague he said, 'I will arrange the studio. You can wait in the reception.'

"Thanku! I shall wait there." And she got up and headed towards the reception. Her soul saved her again.

Now images flooded Joy's mind of Varun holding him by his long hair and banging his head against the wall, yelling curses at him. He was then kicking him with all his strength, between his legs. 'Oh!' he began feeling the pain. Turning him over he was kicked hard on his back, to which he went flying out of the studio like the free shotshot by David Beckham in the world cup.

He was out of his mind thinking about the embarrassment he would have to face if his behavior gets reported to Varun, he stared at the wall as dumbly as he never before. 'Oh! I will be like an emperor whose elephant goes mad amidst the battle.' He was dismayed. 'You will be damned in front of such a hot doctor . . . and you deserve it . . . . you dull head. Your image is ruined. You will be turned into acrippled superman, crippled to the bone. Now wear your red brief over your blue pants and prepare to move around in a wheelchair.' Came the voice from his conscience. Better late than never.

When he regained some nerves, haphazardly he jumped around the room to collect the trash strewn all around, as that was the only way left to save his skin, and to decrease the punishment that he could foresee for himself. 'It will leave a good impression on Varun and score some brownie points.'

'Crippled superman, on a mad elephant. Ou dada!' he said fearing Varun's wrath. Buzy as he was for a change, he did find time to think of Varun cancelling his arrival due to a bout of diarrhea . . . or may be he breaks his leg . . . or slips from the staircase . . . . just any of the above and remains at his home. God, but then . . . . this man will limp his way here.' Butted in the voices. 'May be I'll wear a cloak and break both his legs. That will be good . . . . Ufffhhhh!' he replied to himself. 'But what if you fail or get caught in the act', checked him his conscience. 'But what if you don't?' said his mind leaving him in confusion. 'ZinadineZidane, among the biggest name in football was not spared for his behavior and neither would be you for yours, dear asshole', confirmed his conscience with absolute perfection and confidence. His mind now had no answers.

This life of ours is a battle between our mind and our conscience, the spokes person of our soul. The mind tricks and wavers but the soul speaks only one language, the language of love and that of peace. And that is why those of us who wake up to the call of our soul are peaceful and unconditionally loving, as well as always fair in their ways. Whereas the rest live in chaos. Listening to their mind, same mind that pulls them in a black hole of tragedies and lovelessness.

Joy was no different. He was in a habit of listening to his mind and his misconduct with Laila was an obvious result. His forehead was profusely sweating as his wicked mind went endlessly ticking from one thought to another.

Laila, on the other hand, sat like a nervous new bride not knowing left from right in a new home yet she was clam. She did feel lost in the new environment, unfamiliar guy and unseen objects around. It also felt weird to sit at work place and remain without any work, for Laila's body and her mind was used to movement, eyeing work like one has to in a clinical set up. Though she thanked God that she was spared from the berserk pace of the Mumbai's life style, still sitting idle was not a desired option for her.

Patience. She had to learn and teach others as her life would unwind.

Time lapsed and doubts began to do rounds, empty mind became the house of devils. She thought to herself 'has he actually hired me or was it in the passing? Or . . .' she blinked her eyes, 'I think it was just to please that aunty . . . . he said a yes to me in her face? Oh God, what am I to do now?'

Just in that very moment, the swinging doors of the studio flapped open and Varun, wearing a rugged jeans and an Ed Hardy t-shirt rushed in, like a dart, with speed and aim. He was lean, tall above six feet with long face and aquline nose. He was polite with a distinguished demeanor. Laila was thrilled to catch a sight of him, just like a child lights up on catching the sight of pink cotton candy. 'Yeepee!' she said to herself. 'He is here.' And on this day, she realized two aspect of her work, one she was dressed up too formal for the profession and secondly, for Varun, the definition of one hour meant half an hour, flat.

Joy's luck on her didn't work but she did save him from bearing Varun's wrath on that day. But, then it was Samantha, a model who complained Varun about Joy asking her out on a date. Apparently, he called her at midnight 'just to say hi!' and from a hi he went high on her. Ridiculous as he was, so was his fate. Varun instantly took action against him thereby making him apologize to Samantha in his own presence. And as the girl left the studio and Joy, he on the spot got verbal lashing from Varun.

'This is my studio not a brothel, maintain the sanity of my temple or find yourself another place to work.' Yelled Varun outraged at Joy's behavior. It had taken him all his life's efforts to make and maintain his reputation in the profession and such misdemeanors, though miniscule in appearance could damage his repute in a go. 'And you work just anywhere on earth, if you don't maintain the dignity of your profession, God will never forsake you and neither will your profession.'

Laila, the wise one had intentionally ignored the matter on day one. For one the gravity was not intense enough to bring it to Varun's notice, so confirmed her soul and also because she had the faith, that it wasn't for very long that Varun would come to know of it. 'Our wrong does get checked in this life or another,' was what her wise mother had told her when she had checked Laila putting salt in Catherine's tea instead of sugar. For four days, Laila's misconduct went unnoticed but on the fifth, she got caught with the spoon and the jar of salt. Naughty as she was, she was equally blessed to be born to her wise mother who checked her with rights words.

Back in Mumbai for months on end, Laila's work revolved around the camera and Varun's assignments but never actually with handling the camera. "One should know the tree from the base to be successful in scaling its height. Otherwise the trees with weak roots may fall while we are still sitting atop,' was Varun's mantra for her. He was right indeed, because if we climb without knowing the tree from its base, we may be caught unaware of the tree's dangerously weak roots, is uprooted which may result in our fall, despite our pleading innocent of it. Because it wasn't the tree's fault if we weren't wise enough to decipher its state before we climbed atop. She worked with the best in the business, the one with perfect fingers, to the one with the best pout, the one with sunny smile and the one with the most voluptuous bust line. It awakened her senses to watch them strut around and catwalk in the sky high heels like a mystified fantasyland where everything is so fine-looking and gorgeous. As a child she would wonder to herself, about the flare displayed by these models in wearing revealing clothes. She would watch them on the television and ask herself, 'how come these India born and bred, women carry themselves with grace and élan in attires that barely covers their bodies. They never falter in those heels and how come they never feel cold, they mustn't be human beings. They must be angels.'

Blasphemy, blended evenly with fabrics draped them, in the name of pret and haut couture. Honest to herself as usual, Laila as a little girl, deep in her heart desired to wear it all, but it was the social barriers that limited her scope then. Now that God had got her to live in a trendy metro, she tried fine-looking garments she always stared at in awe. She developed a passion for clothes and preserved the one for heels. As for high end glamour, she as of now left it as the realm of the models.

The cat named curiosity still did rounds and with regular observation and interaction with models she realized that, for some of them, it is an inborn talent to carry glamour as their second skin just like one is good at mathematics or in singing, from birth. While there were others, who were born with a beautiful face and took to modeling as a profession, there by being compelled to experiment with different fabrics, cuts and style. Comfort in these outfits came to them with practice and so did their flair for glamour.

Propelling their talent was the attention they received from people at events; the more they got the more they wanted or rather commanded, that too with elegance and poise, that was far beyond the capacity of an average person. These professionals are blessed by Goddess Venus, the deity supreme of beauty, making them attractive for reasons defined as well as ambiguous.

It is difficult to pinpoint why exactly a model is stunning, we just know that's how they are. It's as simple as honing our skill in just any other profession, then of course fate is in play when it comes to success and fame.

Enhancing their comfort was yet another, subtle fact that Laila discovered through her observation. Everybody in the team including the light boys are so engrossed in their work and are so used to shoots and models posing in bare minimums that they gradually get desensitized to it. And if by chance, when a new worker joins the team and acts as a discomfort to the models during the shoot, the models cope up retaining their focus as a professional demand, or else, the photographer is informed to take action against the worker.

Laila respected the muses and appreciated their sense of style, for she always had something to add to herself as a learning from others. She would chat up with the gals sometimes to build a rapport and at times to understand why it was that they preferred floral fragrance by Kenzo in summer and a spicy note by Versace in winter.

It was a new world for her and to gain the most out of it, she would ask questions when she couldn't find an answer to it, on her own. She read extensively from fashion to locations, to cameras, to people to keep herself abreast of new developments around. She would sleep with books and wake up with them. And yes, far from the painful world of medicine, fashion and camera came to her rescue when her life energy was fading at a lightning speed.

Our desires indeed are a reflection of our future and as a direct correlation she had stepped in a profession wherein lay her soul and to which supported her mind and body with enthusiasm. She had the courage to say a 'yes' to what the world would ordinarily say a 'no' and in keeping the reins of her life in her hands entirely, she was living a fulfilling life and with unending happiness.

She would silently watch him at work throughout the shoot, finding answers to her queries, until the techniques of handling the camera and light's positions went way past her logical mind. And if everything could be understood by our eyes, this world would have been devoid of the significance of human interaction, for which words came into existence. The master does help the good disciple provided he sees in them a deep passion and devotion.

Everyday, she would make sure the floor of the studio was clean; the background papers all rolled neatly and all the props, like balls, variety of chairs, fur stoles, sports equipments, rugs, plants . . . . werein their respective places. The green room was kept neat for convenience and decorum. Laila, would check every aspect of the studio, a tendency she had developed at the hospital, during the morning rounds of different wards. Old habits, as it is said, truly die hard and fortunately so as in her case.

As a routine before Varun's arrival, she would ensure the flashlights were in perfect working condition. And for this, she wouldn't call for Joy's help or assistance ever.

On one day she pulled the stool and stood atop it. Then she realized that she neither had a new bulb with her nor the skill to replace the old one. But she was not the one to give up, this she had settled with.

So with lots of efforts and some nervous laughter she did managed to near about change the fused bulb and clapped in joy because for her it was big deal, a success story to be narrated to her parents, even though for them it was the work of the electrician. And in her excitement she forgot that the stool on which she stood had a broken leg and thus she had the fall of her life.

The miracle of the day was, Joy. The real superman for, who caught her just in time like an actor in a

Bollywood flick, so perfectly that he saved her from crashing on the floor from the skyhigh stool. And the bigger surprise was that he neither took advantage of her nor did he speak a word in the entire episode. He got her a bandage and sat next to her comforting her for a while until she was ready to get up and get back to work.

'Let me do it for you.' He said offering help.

'I wouldn't learn if you help me all the time . . . you know what I mean,' she giggled.

'Hmm . . . I know well what you mean.' He said calmly. She got up, took another stool, checked it's legs and she learnt to fix the bulb.

'Thank you God, I learnt a lesson without causality,' she said to God in whispers. Her rescue was a miracle to which she thanked God and laughed her heads off every time she narrated it to people. The light she fixed did 'fire' (in the lingua franca of photographers) and so did her list of achievements, big and small.

After checking all the lights of different flashes, she religiously cleaned the lenses of Varun's Nikon D-300 SLR, which was treated no less than a new born baby, with extra care and tender yet firm grip. Laila's fingers had the feel of a novice lover full of passion for each other, even though her muse was inanimate. It's a quality of unprecedented passion that it chooses to forget the loud difference between a living being and the clinically dead. Her love remained unabashed and flowed freely; nature had to respond to it, without fail but with right efforts and patience.

She promptly made notes and took no holidays. The girl never felt sick for her life energy was flowing in her with optimum perfection. A life she wanted and worked for was the life she was leading, what then would hamper her good health.

Progressively, Varun made her to be a part of the planning and execution, of all his shoots. Whether it was a product shoot, a portfolio shoot or that of an ad campaign, Laila would do it with effective skills and drive, always. She would call up the required professionals; models, makeup artists, hair stylists, and outfitstylist to check up on their availability. She would get them together, to decide and arrange for the entire outlook of the model including the props required. Once the shoot date was fixed shewould a day in advance, call them up to confirm, cancel or just to remind them about the shoot's date, time and location.

Slowly but surely, Laila developed the conviction that Varun was the person with whom, putting right efforts was in favor of increasing her familiarity and expertise with the profession.

We all need immediate role models in our life, to inspire us and to leads us, because then their specific energy comes to us by the universe. Therefore she chose Varun very carefully. He, as she found out, was very well educated on his subject, was experienced for over two decades in the profession, thoroughly dedicated, humble and had the flair of training a fresher with unseen patience and grace. He put words to untold wisdom and had a fair degree of detachment with the people he worked with. He would teach and check his students' learning regularly so as to ensure they were well groomed, to fly away to their own nests, one day.

Another despicable task that Varun was teaching her out of compulsion was collecting payments on his behalf. 'Money,' he had explained to her, 'is a magnet which attracts powerful when it is with us and can be a suffering, when we have to collect it as our payment from others because it's is a companion with whom even the wealthy don't want to part ways with grand erffortlesness, in lieu of services they take from us.'

To him, as to others Laila's clear big eyes were a testimony of her trustworthiness. As her experience progressed, it dawned upon her that, 'when we have to shell out our payments, our needs teach us to master this skill, without choice mostly. We all have to pay pending bills, buy groceries, give maintenance for the apartment, refuel our vehicles and save deposit money for travel and any emergency just in case and our list is endless. So one is compelled to chase or request their clients to pay the their dues either with or without constant reminders together with denial for further work. He also taught the girl never bow before money. 'It's a sure killer of passion that we have towards our profession.' He told her many a time.

Step by step, she became meticulous and professionally wise. Varun had inspired her to work with pure passion and had ingrained in her all the abilities of being a good photographer. There was yet another lesson learnt from him which came as a bolt from the blue.

On a regular day of shoot, the makeup artist was awaited and Varun had a visitor without a prior appointment. Caught up neck deep in work, Joy informed him about the visitor. Varun could barely recall the name given to him by Joy and he marched towards the reception area, which was an adjoining room separated by a door with a knob.

As Varun saw the person, his mood lit up freeing his face of all its worries. He was Anirudh Randhawa. Handsome by his own perception, this sturdy looking business man with droopy eyes, was passing by the studio and had dropped in to revive his old friendship. Anirudh, was his school friend and lived inWorli, which was quite a distance from Tarun's residence and studio, both. So over the years the distance in geography had also distanced their acquaintance with each other.

Varun in high spirits hugged his friend, who hugged him even tighter and invited him in and sat him on the sofa in his studio room. Going by his friend's preference, he ordered some coffee and chatted throwing glances here and there, in a fit to recall the days gone by. Since they had met after a long-long time there was a lot to catch up on each other. Anirudh, who smelled of musk on his body and an Omega on his wrist, spoke entertainingly displaying humility and alacrity pleasing to behold.

'I saw a stunning customized calendar at my friend's place and you know what?' He spoke with a child's wonder, 'I knew you shot it. I picked it and I did read your name on it. It was spectacular.'

'Thanks,' came a polite reply from Varun.

An apparent element in Anirudh's mode of conversation was his faith in God. He sounded like a sweet child who swears and lives by the holy book. Word's like, 'by God's grace only . . . .', 'God saves me always . . .', 'I go to the temple every Tuesday . . . .' etc. came out like water from the spring, in abundance and naturally. But there was more to him than met the eyes.

Anirudh expressed a strong but courteous desire to have lunch together, to which Varun hesitated. He instantly making work as an excuse he said 'Oh having lunch together would have been a pleasure but my shoot is already delayed. Everybody is waiting.'

'No problem.' Said Anirudh, 'I can wait for your lunch break? May be we should take these people with us. We'll have a blast together.'

'Oh! That would be nice . . . but you know Anirudh, it will take me atleast3-4 hours to break for lunch. We are short of time today and it's already 12.30pm by my watch,' replied Varun diplomatically, desperately expecting a non compliance from the other end.

Otherwise patient, Varun didn't seem to be in a mood of obliging him beyond that hour. Laila was wondering, why on earth Varun did behave so unusually because underneath his diplomacy was disappointment, like he has with his clients who don't pay up on time leaving him in a lurch.

'Fortunately . . .' said Anirudh 'I have time. I will wait.'

Any more excuses would have sounded blatantly rude and wastage of time. So without wasting time any further, for which he was already pressed Varun composedly agreed to the offer. But being focused, he excused himself to carry forth with his work. And thus Anirudh drove him to give in to his demand, a specific trait of his since his school days.

Humble as Anirudh was, he waited relaxing his back on the sofa with his folded arms resting on his abdomen. His body absolutely still, but what moved around the room were his eyes following Laila, everywhere she went.

With thoughts of gratifying his twin interest, food and friend he had more to look forward to and yes, he wanted nothing more, at least not for that day. Without waiting for Varun's help, he attempted several times to introduce himself and strike a conversation using Varun as buffer to secure his authenticity. He was smart enough to think of using Varun's noble image, to get closer to her, as one usually tends to go by the image of the person one knows relatively better. In this case it was Varun she trusted and respected. Ideas of holding her attention darted one after another through his mind. Though, twenty years older than her, his passion was unstoppable and wild, and that made him restless from within, with a calm fake exterior, that he had developed with years of practice.

As the shoot began, Laila stood before the laptop watching the photographs as was being clicked by Varun. Instinctively, she shot a glance at Anirudh, as she felt he was staring incessantly at her. He in turn maintained his stare in her eyes, narrowing his own eyes as he smiled at her.

She smiled back in courtesy and looked back at the laptop screen. The images of his smile flashed in her head over and over again. She recalled the way he smiled, with his eyes squeezed, she recalled the colour of his eyes, it was malicious.

He had his mission on the loose, she on the reverse had turned scarlet in the face and lost her focus. She found reasons to rush to the green room and check in the mirror if, in anyways she was provocative in her appearance. Uneasy and twitchy, she wanted to find faults in herself. 'It is easier to check oneself rather than confront the stranger.' She thought nervously. She rushed back to work thinking she didn't register it right, whether the way she noticed and felt about the matter.

It was a mere self creation or was it actually the way it was. To her dismay, the latter stood as the blistering reality. His stares were still as persistent as she didn't want it to be. Not from any man, especially not the one in his age.

Panicked as she was, she went back to the green room. Standing in front of the mirror she pulled her t-shirt further down, even though it wasn't, by anyways, showing any skin from her belly. She peeped in her neck line and made sure it sat intact on her neck. Even though it didn't show a fraction of an inch of her cleavage, still she adjusted it for her satisfaction. Her hair was neat and nice but not good enough to her contentment. The upheaval, raked by Anirudh's eyes led her to cross check in her mind, if one in a million chances, she had sexual overtones in her own behavior. And after a through intense scanning of her ownself, Laila found no answers because there were none.

But what was there was, her faith in God and Varun.

As she returned to monitor the photographs on the laptop screen, and wiped her porcelain skin and bit her lips nervously. Just then, Varun shot a glance at her and that was a miracle. His fears for her, from Anirudh came alive. He knew well enough that, in a city which eyes the innocent, it is an eccentricity to have high respect for men for reasons like age. He was watching over her despite his workfull in progress, for he knew Laila was new to direct sexual advances like this one and she wouldn't believe easily that a man was eyeing her, for one night stand over and above her imagination and experience.

Laila's cell phone vibrated in the front pocket of her jeans and she went numb reading the words. 'Leave right now.' The message was from Varun, who went to the rest room to send it to her. Laila was sure he had his reasons to say so, but she wasn't sure if it was the studio she was asked to leave or her job.

A sense of fear engulfed her, more profoundly because at his studio she was living her dream. He came back to the camera and work proceeded. She was too scared to look at his face, to interpret his state of mind. She stood there blank in her head and then eventually, her soul gave her the courage to look in Varun's eyes, for once before she left. And when Laila did manage to look at him, Varun intentionally looked away, from her.

'Add just a few years more to Anirudh and he could easily pass as her father but . . .', thought Varun to himself, ' . . . this by no means meant that, he was not swaying like a wild beast ogling at his prey to tear her into pieces.'

He was but a man, and such are the instinct of men who live away from their soul. Flesh remains the centre of their world and God merely in their words. But as long as there would be demons, there will be God. And as long as there would be God there would be protection from the beast.

He was giving instructions to the hair stylist 'iron her hair. Make it straight. It will highlight her jaw line.' Laila was watching.

Another glance from her went to Anirudh. She wanted to rip him apart. And in that she made her first move, though just in her mind.

Then again her mind went to Varun. Casting her eyes down, drowned in guilt, she regretted doing innumerable rounds of the greenroom, right in the middle of the shoot, that too without Varun's permission. Guilt and more of it, as well as sadness inundated her mind. She was embarrassed to the hilt and deeply pained by the fact that it was too abrupt and severely disturbing end to a journey she was enjoying so extensively.

Quietly, she picked up her bag and headed out of the studio with her mind dipped in unbearable pain and agony, to hold a sensible conversation with anybody there.

'Hey Laila!' came the firm voice. It was Varun calling her name, 'I forgot you have an appointment with the doctor. Carry on. We will manage it here.'

'Who?' came the dwindling voice of the dazed bird, with broken neck, 'what?'

'Doctor.' and he looked her in her eyes and gently moved his own eyes to his right, in a way that hinted at Anirudh. 'You forgot.' His being more obvious than that would have costed him his friendship. 'You have to go.' Thankfully and by God's grace too, she got the message. She smiled at him in relief and in pain and as Varun smiled back at her, her eyes went moist. She looked at him for yet another moment and stood speechless.

In a city, where she had nobody to call her own, this man's protective gestures had touched her deeply. He was straight faced to avoid giving any leads to his honorable friend with dishonorable intentions for he could have chased her outside the studio, may be followed her to her home. Laila pounced at her hand bag and disappeared like a mouse who manages to free itself from a trap.

Varun was the first to notice how his friend's eyes glowed when he first saw Laila, as he entered the studio room. He knew, he was immediately provoked by nothing but her innocent good looks. Further, he was fairly familiar with Anirudh's way of life, his chivalry was his mask to please women, who were either lonely or innocent. He also knew that his sole intention for pressing him, to dine with him, was to buy time and opportunity to ask Laila out. And his asking her out would have had serious repercussions on the girl as she was innocent and inexperienced about such thrills.

Women for men like Anirudh are like wine, different flavors to be enjoyed with different food and mood.

'This was the reason his voice had disappointment while refusing to accept lunch with Anirudh' realized Laila, when she received Varun's call that evening. Her heart pumped more blood than usual, and throbbed harder than ever for it was her first close brush to the wild side of the celebrated life in Mumbai. But, when there is faith, there has to be a saviour. She gradually sprang back to life, when Varun taught her the easy way out of situations, alike.

It's a special quality that women are born with, to be able to know a persistent stare coming from a person near or far, in her direction. But where we fail mostly is, in counteract.

'Stay alert from men despite their age and when they stare, then you, as a rule of thumb, stare back in their eyes until they lower their own gaze. For all of us, have the inbuilt capacity to realize their wrongdoing and keep a check on their instincts. They have to and they should, be reminded of their limits. And now you will stare back hard and settle their lust on them instead of being its victim.' This was a kind gesture and encouraging too because it came from a man who she admired and respected. And this respect, has love and effortless submission to somebody who led her on her soul's path. 'Be strong, if you want to be successful,' he told her.

So this day on, there was no messing with the girl. Her eyes did just what she had learnt from this harrowing experience and though it took her time to practice and master the skill, she nonetheless tried to stand for her defense, once and for all.

And when we try honestly, we improve with time because every effort receives its reward.

Laila was no doubt, wise for her age and time, but then we are all vulnerable and weak in different ways, all our lives. If we were safe always, we probably wouldn't think of God ever and neither would we fear our deeds. God knew this even before, he created us. Thus, inevitably he made us both, vulnerable and strong, in ways obvious and latent, like some of us score high and low physically, some mentally, some financially, some emotionally, some spiritually, some sexually, some academically, some in creativity, because at the end of the deal He wants us to feel equal before him always. That's his sense of equality. And at times, when we feel vulnerable, we should call for Him to help and protect us.

With so many directions to tread, she had no time to think of anything but work and more of it. God had laid the table in an impeccable manner;one dish of opportunity was served after another. So, to live our dream, it's required of us to be clear about our desires and work towards it with patience. We should be on our marks to grab a dishout of the platter, casually known as, opportunity. As for her, as she was wise in giving her one hundred percent, with faith, devotion, hard word and zeal to absorb, all that she could learn, as an intern.

Laila was also wise enough to realize that her impressive degree in medicine was her past and that it should never come in her way to learn the skills of her current profession. She kept a check on her ego. For ego, is a shrewd weapon, upon which we need to keep a constant watch. Every time it raises its ugly head, we should stamp it down because, ego wickedly reminds us of our achievements, in a way that becomes an impediment for us. It tells us how much ahead we are of everybody, instead of telling us that learning and learned are always waiting ahead of us on the roads of life. What it doesn't tell us is that we will be superseded with ease, if we don't work on ourselves constantly. And in doing this, we should always remain humble from within and keep ourselves reminded that if we stop to learn, no matter how old or young we are, we will stagnate and stagnation is regression.

For the wise Laila, the day she would die would be the last day of her learning by the grace of the master within us. This she was wise enough to know and accept needless to say, she made right efforts to evolve as a person as well as in her profession.

With this approach towards life, her passion to learn new skills and her humility became her stepping stone to popularity. It was common to hear, 'Oh! You are Laila. Varun refers to your name often . . . .' to, 'Hey Laila! Good job huh . . . . we quite often hear of you . . . .' to, 'Finally, we get to see you . . . . Varun mentions of you frequently, seems you do quite a good job at work.' In all this Varun's pride in having her as his assistance was unmistakably loud as was her unprecedented efforts to learn and learn more. She took a fancy to the world of fashion photography or rather Laila chose to give her best as genuine efforts always stand out in a crowd of millions. Because God too is watching us at work and then he brings to us what we well deserve. Passion indeed spills onto others with ease, given it comes from a woman daring and genuinely devoted to her work.

CHAPTER 4

If silence is golden, its defiance is platinum.

Spring, the lovely season and the local florists had done their bit to mark this occasion with unsurpassed happiness. Flowers tied in bunches, twisted as wreaths and passed through threads, holding it together as garlands, embraced the walls and pillars of the villa, like a toddler's arms around our neck; tender and unadulterated. The garden smiled too, with deep purple orchids, bougainvilleas, cosmos and pretty red roses, blooming neatly from the rows and lanes. Ducks dived in and out of the fish pond cheerfully, and her pets rejoiced.

Friends, family, relatives and neighbors', all rushed towards the Chennai airport like the water gushing out from a barrage, excited and impatient. Some among them clutched garland in their hands, some came with bouquets while the others with mere emotions stood at the airport as if in the airport was to land President Barak Obama disembarking from the plane.

Their bubbling enthusiasm was unstoppable. Obama's disembarking was important, but not as important as was Laila's disembarking for them for one their own lovely girl meant the world to them and secondly, their bond with her was not political. Their connect was strongly emotional. No doubts that in current times politics is indeed very important, but despite its powers, its love that survives even after one loses all elections of life, because the frenzy of the latter never fades, like the loud promises of politics.

People couldn't contain their hearts from meeting the girl and tell her how precious she was for them. Every time they heard the deafening sound of an aircraft making a landing on the runway, their eyes would glance eagerly at the huge boardwith black base and with the flight's information in white. And every time it didn't read the word 'arrived' next to Laila's flight's schedule, their mind dipped in momentary disappointment, though never in disheartenment.

Such was the obsession to receive the girl who today was returning home after completing, a long one full year and eight unthinkable months. After an hour's wait, the airlines staff made an announcement that it was bad weather that had caused the delay in her flight, for another good three hours. Their heart beats raced to hear the announcement over and over again, as their girl was traveling alone; the first young girl in family and the only child too, to travel that far without her parents escorting her.

Countdowns began and also the yelling at the airline staffs, two of whom were overheard talking amongst themselves, that it was not bad weather but, the late boarding of a foreign dignitary from Algeria that had caused the delay of the flight. The Algerian heat was now on, full on at the Chennai airport, at the staffs who kept their calm and had their young manager handle the issue with heavy refreshments and a hundred black t-shirts that read the airlines's name below the long beaked bird on the top left, next to the collar. It placated their suffering stemming from the separation from their loved ones on board.

Who knew then that, image's sustainability matters so much not only on earth but also to the ones, flying in the air.

Exactly a good half an hour before the delayed scheduled hour the wheels of majestic flight finally touched the Chennai airport, and then there she was making an exit from the enormous glass doors of the arrival terminal leaving to the awe of everybody. Eyes widened to take a larger visual sweep of her magnificence.

Wearing a white and black Capri pants folded at the brim, a white body fit top, a small black cropped jacket matching her pants with sparkling patent white high heels and huge white hand bag, she clearly stood out from among the crowd of innumerable classy passengers who got off that flight.

Stunning was the least to describe her appearance and enhancing her beauty were her long silky smooth hair that flew gently across her face which she kept tossing back frequently. And needless to say she was doing what she was good at, leaving people gasping for more and more.

Pulling her hugered suitcase on wheels Laila headed towards the anxious crowd of familiar faces, with the appeal no less than that of a celebrity. As she walked closer, and with every stride of her's she walked them to another world, a world of appalling disbelief and a world of grief, for all those who loved her deeply or faintly. The mystery to this beauty was ever so shocking, shocking enough to surpass all their previous lifetime experiences.

Her expected embrace went missing. Her hug was no longer a genuine act of bliss she would display to greet people who counted days on their fingers in her wait. It was very unjust to the souls gathered at the airport who in their wait were like the parched barren lands looking up towards the clouds in agony and anticipation, of the rain. No doubt, catching a glimpse of their angelic girl, who always cared for them even through her physical absence, was an immediate relief to their overwhelmed hearts. She did put an end to their unabated wait but what didn't end there was, their sense of disbelief. Just in nick of time their night of the moony emotions turned into a haunted nightmare. She looked weaned from nourishment and her behavior, weaned completely from the most important element that bonds one human with another, an element that separates us from animals, birds and cockroaches, an element that changes the hormones in our blood and body, an element which we have all known by different names yet treated it all the same, the element popularly known as love.

Far from good, in her newness was a glimpse of unhappiness and corruption to them.

Corruption was an easy possibility, for she was a humble young girl living alone in a city of crime and drugs, pursuing a profession in fashion, easily trusting and trendy in an effortlessly attractive way. Needless to repeat, she had a willingness to help the needy and who knows which needy person could have approached her with disguised intentions. Moreover, Mumbai, the city that never sleeps is also famous as a city that snatches the happiness of the innocent compelling them to sleep forever and leaving their families sleepless for a life time. The mystery was getting deeper in her silence.

Physcialy, Laila's eyes were flapping together lazily, demanding sleep and solace rather than responding to the love all around her. She looked cold and disoriented to every eyes that awaited her home coming ever since they first heard of it.

Unfortunately, the gossip mills had began to churn faster than expected despite, the spotless image Laila had, so far.

'She wasn't even introduced to him . . . . why did she smile at him?' Said, her own father.

'Is she sick at head?' murmured her popcorn eyed cousin from behind her thick glasses with her eyes blinking at the speed of Act II corns turning into popcorn, in a hot pressure pan.

Words buzzed across her friends, relative and staffs, who were a part of the entourage present to welcome her there. The evidence catapulting the buzz was her smile to her new driver, Irruvar to whom she wasn't introduced to.

'What the hell?' yelled her infuriated fat aunt to her husband, 'did she come from a hard day's work at the coal mines . . . or was sheploughing fields in Mumbai?'

Her doubts regarding Laila darkened her already swarthy complexion as she blazed at the injustice meted out to her by the girl's attitude.

'The side effect of her glamorous life style,' came the curt reply from her slim husband who sat crossed legged with a ultra slim figure matching that of a long legged girl. Their car, placed fifth in the line of the convoy of six cars was being driven back to Laila's home for a well rehearsed warm get together. Far from warm, this one was to be a heated get together and this soothed this man internally. In his line of thoughts, today he did find a match for his own out law son, Laila's cousin who was jailed in Bangkok for over nineteen months. He was spotted selling contraband goods, and was dragged back to India after doing time. Here his father and her uncle, sat tall with confidence like a cricketer bowling out an ace batsman, in the first ball itself.

'You mean . . . .' she looked at him sternly, 'glamour is a forbidden fruit and those who take a bite, are doomed?' Her voice had ample of cunning innocence, as if at fifty two years of her age her mind didn't know nothing about the subject she was delving into.

'Certainly. I had told her parents a thousand times, GET THE GIRL MARRIED. You know, I was a hundred percent sure she would stray. I was DEAD SURE.' Replied the heroic cricketer all set to become a domestic scientist.

'Marriage isn't an end to every issue, so you keep quiet,' added her aunt.

'No longer would it have become his headache as per what you see today, that's why,' said her husband.

'What if I say the same to you? In anyways we have to teach her a thing or two and in doing so she will open up and tell me all about what's happening in life in Mumbai,' she retorted biting the nail of her first thumb.

'Yes, yes . . . we will sit close by her,' said her husband merrily.

'Anyway we haven't had anyone to chat about for long . . . may be that's why my lord Shiva has sent her.' Replied her aunt cheekily.

Was it fair on their part or was just a human tendency to stab the dying bull to celebrate their strength no matter how faint, one could be left to wonder. But as the way of the unwise always is, their tongues was as fast as the fans of a helicopter though far from rising above, their soul dives and falls face first.

In the car behind them Laila's neighbor the Subramaniam family's youngest daughter Illa, younger to Laila by five years spoke adjusting her skirt that were too short to cover even her entire thigh. 'It's cocaine! It's very in thing in that society.' Came the Californian accented voice from the Indian her, courtesy her playful career as an call centre executive in a mobile company.

Turning his face sideways from the front seat, asked her brother Manii, 'in which society? Come again.' His tone mocked Illa's own way of life, which comprised of drinks and regular late night parties. Manii had so much love for Laila that he didn't care a damn for anybody's talks.

Twitching her face in defense she replied, 'Don't you act unaware! Where else . . . in creative societies. They work better when they are high.' She furnished the information with maddening anger looking left and right at her parents sitting on her either sides to gain sympathy as well as for confirmation, as she knew Manii would lend a deaf ear to all her replies.

'Hmmm . . . It could be so,' butted in his father, a chief engineer, filling in the dead response from his son. And the conversation continued from cocaine to Konkani curry, Laila's favorite dish, at their residence.

'This girl was always too fancy, she could never cook. I gave my recipes many a time, but all in vain,' sulked Illa's mother just in time to do her bit to fuel the fire. 'I never found her a home maker types. You know . . .'

Blaming it to his lack of appropriate information or his one sided love affair with Laila, Manni chose to stay loyal to her through his silence. She was a cherished dream for him and unfortunately he never found an equal match to her which kept him single in her wait and in wait for a twist of fate, that never came by in so far because of his silence. Yet, whether she did drugs or was a terrorist in her own soil, what remained unchanged between him and Laila was his love for her. Something in life like love becomes stronger even in silence, just as silently as coal changes into a diamond and turns into the strongest and most cherished gem on earth.

'Homemaker? When on earth did she get time to be a home maker?' Replied Manni after he finally gathered courage to speak, in her defense and thus indefense of his silent love. His parents and his younger sister remained unaffected, but atleast he made an attempt, better late than never.

'Shut up!' said his sister. 'Though an accomplished surgeon, you are very foolish. And look at you,' she laughed pointing a finger at him, 'your bouquet is in your own hands. Did you get it for your ownself?'

Poor, Manni, bend low to look at the bouquet and held back his tears, seeing the flowers like his heart wilting right there in his arms. It was the first time, he so lovingly got this bouquet of beautifully fresh yellow roses for her, from the best florist in town, located a good twenty kilometers away from his house. He gripped the bouquet close to his heart for holding Laila that close, was a bleak possibility given his level of courage to express his feelings. 'Allegations are like wild grasses, they come up anywhere in any form,' explained Manni to his own head. His heart didn't need any further explanations, it was welling up with emotions and the excitement to meet her at the get together. He remained a victim of silence again while their conversation continued on her.

In the third car, Catherine proclaimed, 'baby doesn't look all that healthy . . .'

'We shouldn't have let her live by herself in Mumbai. It has eaten your girl . . .' pitched in Anna, a friend of Laila's mother.

'We will have to keep a close watch.' worriedly replied Laila's mother in a fading voice. Then confiding in her best friend God, she repeated her prayers in her mother tongue, German. 'God you love her more than me. Take good care of your child like you always do.'

Surprisingly, her love for her child was intact, like the way of the wise and conviction of the experienced. Clouded by their conversation, her heart did sink and swam in disappointment, as she stared out of the car's window. But, her conscience told her 'it's never too late to fix any issues. At least Laila is alive.'

Deep in herself, she kept her faith alive, for that is enough to lead us right.

A lack of interest, even in her parents was blatantly obvious as was her sloppy posture, and her eyes, were casted downward. Her mannerisms were indeed a way to avoid people for reasons like deceit and addiction. Her collar bones were jutting out in an unpleasant way, a way of the sick from Somalia. There own little girl was giving all evidences of fueling the fire of her doing drugs.

Was life unfair to her? Wasn't she happy with her career move? Wasn't she living her dreams? Were people targeting her for her achievements, that too at her very own home? Were their allegation a naked truth? What could be the probable reason for the onset of her addiction? What drugs was she doing—cocaine, heroin, smack. The plethora of questions hounded the entire household day in and out, for two days at a stretch.

It could have been the effect of taking drugs but not when she lived so close to her soul. Thankfully truth stood for itself. The 'druggie' bounced back to her usual pepped up self on the third day, smiling like sunshine from the foggy clouds: a sight we all cherish and want to stare endlessly at. That sun doesn't hurt because it is not meant to. It also has a unique beauty in it and in the same vein beauties like Laila are not designed to hurt the one's they so loved. And if they hurt, they do it in defense never in the form of mere attack.

'Stress, the lovechild of modernization,' spoke the girl on the third night of her stay in Chennai, 'is like fungus on our smelly feet; the more we close our eyes to, more it grows. In the bygone century, one thought stress happens to those we didn't know or to those on the television only. Today, it is all-pervading, all pervasive, omnipresent, sticking its neck out like a bottle of aerated beverage in our refrigerator. It is happening to those who work hard and to those who lay idle, to those who are battling marriage or are single, to those who are learning to walk and to those who have won an Olympic gold medal, to the skinny and to the fat . . . . not a name or an identity is forsaken.' This was her response to her mother, who moved her hands over her hair and had asked. 'Are you all right my dear? You seem very worn out.' when the girl opened her eyes wider than the previous days.

For two unending days back to back, she would wake up, walk herself unsteadily to the dining table, force her mealdown her throat into her raging stomach with depleted energy level, as though any extra time spent on the dining table could result in her collapse then and there. Barely managing to wipe her face with the napkin, she would get up and get going. Then, flashing a smile here and there seemingly even to the walls at times, she would dart straight to her bed room. And before one would take time to settle in their bed, Laila engulfed by her sleep hormones would be dead asleep.

With their emotions unattended or not reciprocated at all, suspicion and hurt was an inevitable consequence at home. Her father ripped open a suitcase which had a pair of men's underwear and a shaving kit. So it is a man . . . no wonder she left psychiatry; to have fun in Mumbai. Only to realize that instead of her suitcase he had opened his own suitcase in a frenzy.

Mocking himself he managed to lay his hand on her red suit case and what came out in large numbers was even more deluding but nonetheless very touching. Wrapped in shinny gift papers of all size and shape, stacked neatly in her suitcase she had bought presents for everybody. And the biggest of it all, a rectangular box wrapped in a yellow and silver paper, read his name 'PAPA' on it. Tears welled up in his brown eyes. Laila didn't take a penny from home in such an expensive city yet she managed to save enough to buy presents beautifully wrapped, with love. Touching, it indeed was, but the doubts didn't diminish from his mind. Not many are Manni who had the potential to keep the flames of his love burning alive, despite his right too, to be loved was grossly violated by the girl, if so, he claimed from her. And neither did he have Andrea's wisdom and faith. Some elegant and some chivalrous, but nonetheless they lived away from their soul and thus ended up making a big fool of themselves when, Laila awoke from her fatigued sleep.

Words could only describe and never really could explain her exhaustion to people. It is because when we suffer, it's only our body that feels the pains, the aches and the miseries. Not to forget that when we achieve what we had set forth for, we alone are applauded most for the commendable task.

'She did have in exhaustible courage, determination and most of all faith, but in person she was all by herself,' thought her mother leaning on one of the pole of Laila's bed when she woke up. 'After all, we always pay a price for all the choices we make in life,' she recalled her own words, 'so stress was the price Laila was paying. It is as simple as this.' And she smiled to herself mocking all the efforts people around her had put in to build the edifice of allegations against the innocent girl.

To blame her for living her dreams would have been an instinctual mistake and the way of the unwise. 'The usual fleet of servants was amiss, making her days difficult to manage,' explained her mother to Catherine, who then passed on the message to entire team of staff and jealous relatives who were burning the mid night oil, investigating Laila's addiction. Nosy relatives, eager to hear a piece of news as evil as themselves and stress, are part of our mysterious journey of life. And life is mysterious for all, as are the intensions of evil minded people. But when the wise set to live their dreams with faith and right deeds, God brings to us rescue just like oil in the midst of barren desert where once upon a time living was as difficult as it could be in hell. Yet in those deserts, like Laila people lived with complete faith in God and patience. And then came a time when oil was discovered in such abundance that today those very countries have the honor of being among the richest nation of the world, having unsurpassed wealth and luxury. Telling the world how hope pays when we mix it with faith and patience.

Reflecting the pace of her time she further added, 'if stress was not a dinosaur eating us all, exotic spas around the globe wouldn't be doing such a good business, mother.' She smiled through her eyes though her creamy complexion inherited from her mother had been partly eaten by the dinosaur.

"All that is fine. But I didn't quite like that 'fat' bit of your conversation," exclaimed her mother glumly, pressing her lips tight that appeared as if she were smiling to herself.

Drawing herself to sit uprightly on her bed Laila broke into a fit of laughter.

'OhGod! Mother, I said it in passing. Now for God's sake get over it.' Said the girl giggling, though her exhaustion was still evident in her body, after three days of uninterrupted sleep.

'In the passing?'—repeated her mother, looking at her direct in the eyes finding conformation as well as comfort to be comfortable with her size. Laila's girly laughter was compelling for her to break away from her serious face. 'You arent the type to talk without meaning it. Anyhow, I feel girls don't eat these days, they nibble.' she murmured to herself in consolation.

Gaining control of the mockery she finally responded. 'Girls are thin also because of stress, mother.' Battling defense from a strong woman was undoubtedly taxing but it sounded hilarious too given as came from a seasoned wise woman like her mother. 'Besides you are not fat by any given standard, you are . . . . ammm . . . . just a little, or shall I say just very little overweight, that too by a merely twenty kilograms, mother.' She replied sarcastically and then the room rang with loud laughter. The daughter's laughter targeted her mother's attempt to defend her body weight and the mother laughed in self mockery. The latter was wise to accept the loud truth which was not her obesity but her defence of it.

The wise know that truth cannot be hidden ever, no matter how tight one's defense is.

No more in a mood of giving any further discourse on the subject, either anorexia or obesity Laila inquired about the dinner.

The dinner was ready for the night and so was her father to display his love for his daughter. He drove himself in the heart of the city to get home a chocolate soufflé, Laila's most favourite dessert of all times. His daughter spoke little and ate like a death camp victim, finishing every drop of food on her plate in a hurry that only a deprived stomach displays. Her hunger was sharpened by her unending hours of sleep. The slave alike in Mumbai thus began to enjoy her time as a princess, at home.

'Here my dear girl' exclaimed her father lovingly handing over a sheet of paper to her at the dinner table, 'this is for you.'

'Oh! What it is dad?' she remarked in surprise and took the paper to read it.' Hope not another exam!!!!!!!' She smiled.

'I can't believe my eyes.' She yelled excitedly after reading the first page. 'Mother look . . . . look what I have with me. It's . . . It's . . . . you know that . . . .' She waved the paper at her mother.

'What is it? You look so alive!' she said smiling in surprise.

'One wild rose salt glow facial-forty five minutes, One aromatherapy massage with detoxifying oil of your choice—eighty fiveeeeeh minutes . . . can you believe this? 'and she smiled wider . . .' One Hot and Cold stone therapy . . . One personalized yoga and meditation instructors, followed by royal facial . . . . Oh my God, I cant ask for more . . . .' But there was much more, 'their Signature massage especially for the back-forty five minutes . . . . WOW! My back needs all that special attention mom, it's screwed. 'And she looked up smiling with joy, 'and,' she said with a pause, 'this is to last for five days and six nights, non stop!!!!!! I can't believe my eyes' and she danced a step or two beside the dinner table. In her hand was the print out of the reservations made for her at India's best ShriAnanda Spa, located in the foothills of the healing Himalayas.

'It's fantastic! Who told you about spas father, how did you discover it.? Unbelievable! Thank you so much.' And she hugged her father, who was as happy as her to see her thrilled at the surprise which in his opinion wouldn't have mattered much to her. She got up from her dining chair and sat on his lap.

Welcome to Formula One generation, an era in which people wear out as fast as the tyres of the formula one car on the race day. No doubt, there is a growing need of frequent change and refueling, relaxation and spas. Blame it on their pace of life and the thrill of it, fatigue is the order of their day.

'But,' he said hugging the girl, 'you will go only next week. We have spent sleepless nights in your wait my child. Spend some time with us too.' And he clapsed her hands with emotions welling up in his eyes while he heard Andrea brief with what Laila had just told her about stress.

'Hey! Sure papa, I sure am here for you and,' then she looked around the room and said pointing her fingers at her mother and the staffs standing around, 'and for you, and you and you . . . . And you too and all the rest of you.' They all smiled back in appreciation and she took her arms away from her father and said, 'Ohhhh! Wait.' She got up from his lap and ran to her bed room. In no time she returned back, dragging her huge red suitcase behind her and opened it with exhilaration.

'Oh my God.' said her mother looking in her suitcase, 'what a splendid surprise my dear!' and then she looked at her husband, in his eyes with contempt. And he looked away in guilt. He couldn't have felt more guilty all his life for giving in to his impulse and thus checking her luggage, hoping to find the worst of all things, drugs. It also suggested lack of trust in his parenting.

By this time the girl had sorted out what she got for whom. 'Sorry! It's . . . . ammm . . . it got terribly messed up in the flight. Phew!' Her father now wanted to become invisible, like the popular Mr. India, Laila so enjoyed to watch on the t.v. as a child and return when his consciences allows him to be back, which could be never, as well. He managed to look away from his wife and Laila and then said to his daughter. 'Hey! Look what I got for you mother,' and gave her a pouch like present wrapped in a silver paper with a pink decoration on it. It read 'My Mother, the best.' Her mother was touched and proudly opened her present while Laila handed over the rectangular box to her father.

Humbled by her efforts, he opened his present with a child like wonder forgetting his age as his mind forgot everything worldly, all the bull crap he had amassed from years in his head. The present had Carlton London shoes in it. This was different from all his previous footwear because, it was trendy off white suede which he didn't own previously, a perfect match for his off white linen pants and the first time ever he loved to wear something bought from SALE, a complete no for him previously. It gave unsurpassed pleasure to his feet and to his heart, for it had his daughter's pure love in it.

'Thanku,' said her father kissing her as he stood up wearing the shoes then and there in appreciation he hugged her. 'It means a lot to me, my child! Thanku so much.'

'Oh! Thanku you so much too.' said her mother happily holding the small light brown pouch like hand bag which haddark brown embroidery on it. 'I love it. It's so stylish! And so Mumbai.'

'You like it?' she asked with a big smile looking at them both of them. 'Yes. Very much,' came the unanimous reply from them and from everybody in the room who got presents from her. Some got simple t-shirt, some got fancy hair clips, some got school bags for their child, some got a pencil box, some got a small set of towels and Catherine got a pretty apron with colorful fruits on it's front. And everybody got one similar thing, the girl's love.

Laila was the only change her house had witnessed ever since she left for Mumbai. And of course, the other change was the death of her dog, Grace. He was a Dalmatian with less of black and more of white on his natural coat. Flown from England, he was a new addition to the family and a fast deletion from it, too.

We all die several deaths in our life time only most of us are not aware of it, as there are no visible remembrance, obsequies, wreaths and elaborate funerals. Laila had died, too, a several times. Her body weaned from energy whereas her mind was fraught with work and more of it. The difference separating her deaths from that of Grace's death was that, her spirit never left her body unlike her dog whose button like eyes never opened for his soul had parted ways with it's body to leave for heavenly abode. But in all this, God was with him then, in as much as He was with the Laila in her race of survival while she was on her right to living her dreams. 'He is with us all, dead or alive,' had once remarked the devout Catherine.

Thankfully now, by the grace of same God her love for Laila was restored and her enthusiasm refilled, up toto the brim. Her heart glowed just like it did twenty six years back, while she stood on the doorway to welcome baby Laila, on her first home coming after her discharge from the hospital. She felt the same joy of taking her from the nurse's hand as she wept for the first time at her home.

From next day on she lazed around, caught up with old friends, knitted with her mother, baked her favourite vanilla cup cakes, and visited all her relatives and the Surramaniam family with a box of chocolate chip cookies. And in doing so she successfully sweetened their bitter mouth and silenced their wagging tongues. Fun became the buzz word of her holiday. The weather, balmy and slightly cold, was the right type of fall in love. In love, yes, she was falling in love, in love with her life.

'You know in business the key word is . . . .' said her father picking up his cup of freshly brewed filter coffee in his garden, all in a mood of handing over the girl, not his will but the key, to being a successful businesswoman. 'Are you listening . . . . my dear?' and he got no response. 'Laila? Are you with me?'

'Oh! Oh yes . . . yes I am. What . . . what were you saying, father? Sorry, I was . . . .' She replied reacting to his words.

'Lost right?' he pitched in.

'Yeeeah!' she smiled.

'What were so lost thinking about. I thought you were staring at the birds just like you used to while solving mathematics . . .' he said with a sneer.

'Opportunities.' She answered bluntly while acting to be still lost. 'I was thinking about opportunities, father.' And she looked at him with hope in her eyes.

'Oh! That is weird. That is just what I was trying to tell you about.' He wondered at the coincidence.

'Like father, unlike child,' replied the girl smartly and winked at him. 'Right papa?'

'Yes, absolutely my dear child.' He said enthusiastically. 'Wait a minute. What did you say.' He chuckled. 'You, have become really smart. The magic of Mumbai is it?' he remarked.

She giggled and raised one of her eyesbrows proudly looking at him. 'No, it's genetic in that it is from mother.'

And he chuckled 'Now that . . . again Is, a smart reply.' Then he felt a fear. He thought to himself 'my child indeed has grown up mentally acquiring worldly wisdom but then, there is a very thin line between being worldly wise and being corrupt.' He pondered. Indeed, it's the excessively worldly wise who we call corrupt, because they play not only with words but with lives too. In a way he was right, talking out of experience but on the other, he was unwise because he wasn't aware of the power of positive thoughts and that of being led by our soul. Liala giggled and got lost in her maze of thoughts while her father relished the evening snacks fired in olive oil. He was part of the mantra, eat light and eat right though he still weighed ninety kilograms.

Opportunities are not only relevant for business but they also matters a great deal in our personal lives. And to avail herself of one such rejuvenating opportunity, sat the girl comfortably, cozy and excited on her way to Delhi. She took out the glossy brochure from her bag and began to read the details of the spa.

'Your seat belt madam.' Reminded the pretty airhostess.

'Ahhh . . .' said Laila distracted by the voice, 'Thanks.' Replied the smarty and clasped the belt down to her size and got back to reading her brochure, deeply engrossed in the little details. Lunch was served in no time and she relished the heavy north Indian food and then when she couldn't eat any more she reclined her seat to relax.

'Any doctor on board please contact the aircraft crew immediately, we have an emergency. I repeat, if there is any doctor on board, please . . . .' Repeated the voice again.

'Is there really no doctor on board?' thought Laila to herself, still lost in the charms of the spa.

'It's an emergency, any doctor on board . . . ,' announced the voice again.

'So sad, may God help the patient.' She said to herself. 'Aaah . . . . WHAT did she say . . . . EMMERGENCY,' she repeated. 'Hell . . . . I am . . . .' 'Emmergency', the word hit the girl like a lightening. She wildly hit her hands on the seat belt, unclasped it and in a frenzy to help, she got up from her seat like hurricane Katrina and WHAM!!!! came the sound. And she lost the world and the voice, both in a go.

'Hola! Como estas chicka?' asked the woman on whose lap Laila was blinking her eyes, partially open. It was the cabochon emerald on her fingers' ring that matched the deepest of deep green eyes of the woman who was looking at Laila from above, like a camera lens shooting a model lying down.

'Am I on Mars?' she asked herself, 'and what is this woman asking.' She breathed slowly, 'Did I board a U.F.O.' and she tried lifting her head looking for signs of familiar human life around. She was very much on earth, yet she panicked loud 'Ohmy God!'.

'No no.' called the woman pulling her back to her lap. 'Tengo no problemas.'

'You-hit-your-head-at-the-hand-luggage-cabin and collapsed.' Informed the air hostess as if she were reading news on the national t.v., with pregnant pauses to sound clear.

'Oh really.' And Laila held her head with both her hands and giggled. 'Ohhh! There was . . . ,' And she sat up to ask the air hostess, 'there was an emergency on board? What happened to that? I am so sorry . . . . I couldn't . . .'

'Relaaax!' said the women with a heavy Spanish accent. 'Me doctoorh. Estamuebian.'

'U mean . . . the person is dead?' and she covered her face with her palm in grief and guilt. "OH my God . . . what did I do" and finally she drew herself up from the woman's lap. Her head was kind of swinging the way it happens after a ride on the gigantic wheel in Disney land, Florida, while she was a little girl. She rubbed her face in despair and in vain like being caught in heavy down pour under an umbrella with innumerable holes. 'Here I am a doctor on board and yet the patient died'.

'Madam. This is for you.' Said another air hostess wearing a red lipstick and handed her a thanku note. And she smile perfectly at her, 'it's from the gentleman you intended to help. He is fine.'

'Oh! O . . . okheey,' she replied hiding her mouth in her palm, this time with lesser despair than before and then as the airhostess said, 'This lady doctor, our guest form Spain helped the gentleman and you too.'

Laila was cheered and happily turned her head to her left to address her Godmother like lady and said, 'Gracias is the only Spanish word I know in your language. So gracias madam.'

'De nada!' said her treating doctor, in Spanish. 'Water,' she said giving her a cup full of water which Laila drank slowly.

'Now, does she want something?' though Laila to herself in confusion, where as the woman simply meant, 'mention not' and she left for her own seat as the flight was to make a landing on the New Delhi airport.

Laila happy to be helped boarded another flight to Deheradun airport, where she had cab in waiting to ride her to the spiritualistic Rishikesh, ShriAnanda's location in the foot of the great Himalayas.

'Great.' Said Laila to the polite woman on the reception desk when the latter gave her the cards to swipe and enter her room, informing her that hers was 'the palace view room.'

Marvelous and calming were the two easiest words to describe the feel of this renovated palace, now a spa, formerly owned by the maharaja of the area. Laila looked around quietly as she walked to her room led by the bell boy carrying her luggage. She dumped herself on the bed and, worn out from the journey, she fished out her cell phone from her hand bag and made a call to her parents telling them one, that she reached the place safely and secondly that she was enjoying her welcome drink in a tall glass with some mint and lots of herbs in it to cleanse the toxic in her system. The daddy's princess was happy to have a palace now.

❦

CHAPTER 5

Self love, is the finest present
from one to one's self.

Shri Ananda, the spa was turning out to be a bliss.

'It felt like a heaven on earth and if not on earth where else could heaven be because it's the polarity of hell, so if we tend to feel hell on earth heaven has to be here as everything exists in polarity. Where there is bad, there has to be good. That's a universal truth,' thought Laila to herself admiring the place.

The landscape outside her exclusive room was transparently exclusive in its magnificence. The countryside charm was like an enchantingly breathtaking painting of a landscape coming alive from a frame. Her window was surrounded by cluster of clouds floating in and around and peeping from behind were the grooving tall pine trees playing hide and seek with the clouds. Wrapped in a warm pashmina shawl

Laila was enticed by their play wishing if she could join them too. She gazed at the high and humble mountains, the lazy green pastures on it, the willowy plants and the river so full of life and so free to be what it wants to.

She looked around soaking her eyes in nature's allure. 'Nature is beautiful because it is open to embrace and accept anybody, with same love and same warmth.' She pondered mildly stroking her face with the back of her first finger.

And like nature, people who accept us with warmth and equality remain close to our heart all our lives. Laila admired this aspect of her surrounding and prayed to be one such human being with the qualities similar to that of nature she was sopping in.

Her stream of thoughts was interrupted by a soft knock on her room's door, twice. 'Come in' she said and a slender man courteously pushed the door inward without using the knob. Seeing him gain entry she realized that the previous night, she went off to sleep leaving the door unlocked.

Purity can have carelessness to it and so did this girl like the mountains she was admiring, it remains unlocked and yet safe. God takes its care and ensures its safety. And equally safe and cozily she slept in her room far away from the noisy city rush despite her door remaining unlocked. Her sleep was almost like being dead; blame it on the peace there, the synonym of high end luxury in today's world.

'Namaste!' said the man. He wore a cotton long Indian Kurta over pants of the same fabric, neatly ironed and simple. 'Good Morning mam! Sorry if I disturbed you mam, I am the appointed dietician for you.' And he introduced himself as Gyan Singh. His posture was straight and limbs were long.

'I see! Step in, I am awake.' She replied wrapping herself closer in her shawl.

'It's a beautiful morning. Hope you had a comfortable sleep?' He remarked looking out of the window and stood with his left hand grasping his right wrist firmly, which manifested dignity.

'Yes I did. It is an extraordinary morning for me and beautifully so.' she supported his view. This opinion of hers stemmed from the serenading experience that she was having since she woke up that morning. Peace can leave some lonely while the wise enjoys it extensively, using it as the time to get closer to their soul.

'And you are fortunate to have this room.' Informed Gyan. 'It gives a view of the historic palace and the hills together.'

'Oh Yes.' She glanced at the palace building. 'It is a splendid combination, like two charming beauties standing together. One can't say who is prettier.' She remarked and both chuckled together. Her vibrant persona made Gayn's morning more enjoyable.

'Mam, it's time to make your diet chart.' He suggested.

'That sounds like being organized. I have been eating just everything off my plate, lately. Let's get started' she said. 'We can sit here,' said Laila pointing at the couch.

'Mam,' replied the man politely standing next to the door. 'Respecting the sanctity of the room, I will request you to please let me lead you to our special glass room. It faces a Himalayan peak and is flooded with natural light giving us a holy dip in nature. It is good for you, your body and your mind-" replied the man respectfully.

Laila heard every word attentively and agreed to follow the man to the room suggested by him. 'Sounds good.' She said giving her approval.

She was aware that every room has its specific importance because of specific energy present there. But in today's time our activities are mixed up, eating on the bed is in and so is sleeping on the couch in the drawing room. And a parallel trend is sleepless night and painful aches as our body reflects the same order as we follow in our day to day lives.

She picked up her heavy keys to lock her room and moved out in the corridor. As she turned to lock the room Gyan Singh said 'please, let me do it for you mam.' And he did the honor of locking the door, on her behalf.

'What a splendidly careless life I am enjoying,' she thought to herself in a state of bliss. But it was not her renunciation of the world and material pleasures that had got her to the five star luxury of ShriAnanda, it was her the simplicity of her life and pure thoughts. Thus this time too it was God refilling her with love by giving the girl what she so desired and required, as an expression of self love because, it's not always that we have to work our back's off to get what we want. Many a time the simplicity of our desires and the purity of our karma get us what we silently cherish and wish.

Gyan Singh walked Laila to the other room. The room with natural sunlight diving in from glass doors facing the Himalayan hills, was special for the purpose it was meant to fulfill. There were two comfortable chairs on both sides of a glass table in the centre of the room. On top of the centre table was a plain glass flower vase with a bunch of white exotic Himalays flowers dangling all over. Laila bent over the delicate glass table to get a feel of the flower and as she was to smell it's fragrance, 'mam' said the man and she gasped out of fear and immediately withdrew her fingers and turned to face him.

'Please have a seat.' said Gyan and forwarded a flower from the vase towards her. "This is a local flower.' He informed her politely and poured the green tea from the floral tea pot. Pampering, who minds it, not Laila for sure. 'Thanku! It smells divine.' she replied with her warm eyes shining with happiness.

'It has medicinal properties too.' And he gave her the cup he poured for her. 'Are you comfortable mam?' he asked expecting her confirmation.

'It's beauty with a purpose. Yes, I am comfortable.' She answered sipping the tea with jasmine flavour which relaxed her mind, awakening her senses, while he gazed at her looking for signs of comfort in her body. He appeared more like a holy father than a mere dietician, gentle and compassionate. For a change she felt safe in his company.

'So we shall begin with our work?' asked Gyan, as the part of hospitality from the countries' best chain of hotels and spa. 'Money' thought Laila, 'can get us to Nirvana provided we know how to bring it to use for us or else it leaves us being heady and egoist.'

'Yes we can.' She replied looking up at him from the cup.

'Your body,' He looked at her from one shoulder to another.

'What?' said Laila and jumped from her chair, spilling some tea on her shawl thinking that her fatigue had got the best of her and may be it had damaged her with visible scars. 'What about my body?'

The man smiled instead of breaking into a bout of laughter, at the sight and at her response. 'Please have a seat mam. Your body is a mix of pitta and kapha, the two among the three distinct forms of body.'

'Oouh . . . . Alright!She relaxed and sat back in her couch. 'I am sorry!' And she thought she didn't get the pretext of his conversation, she was sure he didn't diagnose a fatal illness of sorts in her. 'Who dies in a spa anyways,' she thought to herself.

'Pitta, imparts aggression,' said gyan to her. He paused to make sure she understands his point clearly, 'Pitta, is a body form which is known to impart aggression and also the lean build as in your case. Whereas it is kappha imparts soft appeal to you. Therefore you are lean and yet soft in appearance. It is because you are a mix of the two body types which is a blessing.' He looked at her in a way that congratulated her for the perfect combination that she was. 'Fortunately, your body doesn't require heavy exercises. Just a few right asaanas (work out postures) would help to keep you fit and would help combat stress very well. But,' he made a pregnant pause, 'you will have to watch your diet to avoid complain of acidity and cold. There are clauses attached to all body forms as far as imbalance is concerned, no matter how seemingly perfect we appear to be. That's because . . .'

'Because God believes in equality while making each one of us.' Said Laila supporting his last line. 'So true. I don't work out rigorously to keep my weight intact. I just pray to keep my body in perfect shape. And yes, the heat gets to my system sometimes resulting in acidity and allergies.' Amazingly right he was though not to her surprise for long.

'So I will suggest, you drink green tea instead of the regular tea as it's more acidic in for. And avoid high intake of vegetables like cauliflower, ladyfinger and heavy pulses especially at night time. Stick to eating medium spices. Remember, your body had internal heat naturally. And, please avoid curd after sunset.' He informed her calmly and jotted down the recommendations to her on a neat ruled paper. 'Sip water though out the day, it will balance the heat that pitta bodies generates.'

'Hmm.' She was taking a mental note of his words too.

'Ten minutes after having your meal, I would recommend you . . .'

'To drink luke warm water,' she interjected raising her eyesbrows in a question mark expression.

'I am amazed.' Said Gyan perplexed at how much more the girl knew. 'You do that already. No wonder your body is in perfect shape, mam.' Said the man, appreciating her intimacy with the writings of the thousand years old, Ayurveda.

'No my father does that.' Replied Laila. Gyan was mystified at her response. 'But still . . . . he is over weight. 'Her eyes looked sad to him and she kept looking in his eyes for answers that would help her find the way out for her father. Minds like her are ever so curious and concerned, and it' s in the latter that innocence resides.

'I see. But . . .' replied the man.

'But why is it so . . . ?' she asked candidly.

'Is it his weight you want to deal with?' He clarified politely as he was supposed to deal with just her diet and body construct.

'Yes.' She replied squeezing her big eyes to a smaller size like a dectective, 'And you are right' she opened her eyes brightly, "I, too, do the same after meals. My father taught me to do so."

'I believe, he is a pure kapha form of body. They can be bulky. Their bodies are entirely soft and rounded. Esomorph in English is what we refer as kapha body form, in Sanskrit, mam. He needs to be extremely careful with their diet and keep a close watch on the weighing machine as it can easily tick towards right.' He filled her with adequate information because for him it was a matter of kindness towards an innocent and curious child like girl.

'You are a genius.' She praised the man delightfully clapping softly for him in appreciation. Praising people genuinely was her way of life and so was in understanding things that were new for her. She had a zest for living life to the hilt and her enthusiasm was replenished everytime she had a new opportunity to learn, to grow and to keep evolving.

Gyan was humbled by her appreciation. 'No. It's simple. We need to understand our body, its assets and drawbacks. No one thing is suitable for every body type.'

'Except for God. He suits everybody, who lives with faith.' She replied confidently for the first time since she woke up on that cozy morning.

'Very right. That is a very wise reply. I believe in it too,' said the man sure of her wisdom and equally unsure of her origin because at the time of appointing him as her nutritionist, the spa's manager had briefed him that Laila was an Indian by nationality. But her creamy fair skin, coloured eyes and her construct were not matching her nationality and nor was her body language very Indian, in many a way.

It was perplexing and Gyan with his simplicity spoke his mind. "You are an Indian, mam?"

'Yes, I am and also half German. The German side is lean and adventurous and the Indian side is soft. Everything in vision has an origin you see. My body is a mix and so am I.' She replied in a flash, looking proud of her nationality and of her twin origin that had imparted her an ideal physical combination. The man laughed softly at her wit. She was wisely right. He checked his watch and informed her, 'It's time for your Yoga session, mam. May I lead you to the adjacent room, your instructor must be waiting for you there.'

'Sure.' And she got up leaving her keys on the table and walked with Gyan to the Yoga room.

'This,' he gestured towards the man, "is Daya." Both the names were complementing the ambiance and in real life too, when there exist Daya, which means kindness, Gyan, which means wisdom and knowledge has to be lurking around.

'Namaste!' said the man joining his palms and bowing to greet her. She smiled in a distant yet friendly way and gave her name, 'MLaila.'

'Very well,' said Daya and gave her a set of off white track pants and a similar t-shirt. He informed her that she along with a woman from Italy, would be joining him for Yoga in five minutes. 'She would be coming in anytime. You may change into your Yoga clothes, mam.'

"Ellow!" said the woman he was expecting to join them.

'Namaste.' Replied Daya.

'O' what a co incidence, we meet again.' said the woman this time speaking toLaila.

Laila turned over her shoulder, to check if the blonde was talking to somebody behind her, she saw white walls which indirectly confirmed that woman wanted was directing her conversation at her. Holding her yoga clothes in her hands, she stood there dazed.

'Ow are you?' said the woman and almost hugged Laila who was stiff with embarrassment.

'First men and now a woman . . . wasn't this supposed to be, beahhh . . . . serenading, rejuvenating experience nestled between the mountains and the massage?' Laila whispered to herself in discomfort. She looked at Gyan, who was her confidante waiting to lead her to the changing room.

'She is . . .' gestured Daya to relax the complicated reunion of two look alikes, one with a skin shade lighter than the other, 'the lady we were waiting for. Let me introduce you to each other."

'I know her.' Chirped the woman.

'Oh ya . . . You do.' Laila smirked covering her mouth with her palm. 'Ohya, yes you do. You do know me. We must be like the long lost sisters . . . although I don't rembember going to that big a fair people talk about young children getting lost and all that. But still . . . may be, you and I . . .'

'Remember, we met in the . . . aircraft on our way to this . . . ?' said the woman giving her leads to help her recall their previous meet, 'To here. This place.'

'Flight? I didn't take a flight to this place,' replied Laila dumbstruck. 'I took a cab . . . . U know the local taxi.'

'Yaah! It was taxing with that . . . .' And she was attempting to console her with her kind eyes. 'I was in the seat next to you.'

Laila pretended to recall, 'yaa. Right. U mean you were next to me instead of my hand bag. Right. Ok. That was good.' And she giggled. 'I don't believe in co incidence but anyway, what I believe in is that, we are due for an hour of Yoga. Her clothes . . .' and she looked at Daya to hand the woman, her set of track pants. She noticed Daya's hands were empty. 'Good Lord!' and before the co incidence would take a murky turn she prepared for her escape. 'She will do it without her clothes . . . I mean the tracks.'

Gayn and Daya stood witnessing the bizarre reunion of the two ladies. One connived and the other denied.

'Ieeeh . . . I will change and join you in a moment,' said Laila andignored the woman blatantly and marched towards the exit excusing herself, from establishing a link that would force her to acknowledge the stranger, who she had never met before as claimed by the woman. The one she met on board was from Spain and not an Italian, though both the foreigners had emerald green eyes. Moreover there was no blonde next to her. To top it all, she reached Shri Ananda in a cab from Deheradun and not in a chartered flight like the woman mentioned.

'I am already wearin' my tracks,' said the woman to her. Laila turned her head and looked at the woman's legs. She was indeed wearing her track pants. Now Laila

159

was tongue tied so she stepped ahead to get away from her traps. 'I am familiar with the schedule here. I am used to . . . coming here.' Spoke the blonde who had turned her head backwards to face Laila, 'I come here frequently. I love it.' Her elegance had a scheme to it.

Laila's pace of walk dropped. She took note of the mystery lurking from the woman's voice in the way she said her last three words, 'I love it.' What kind of love was she hinting at, wondered Laila to herself. She paused tostare at the blonde in her eyes. 'Ya, once we get used to doing something,' she remarked wisely,' we do it with ease the next time on.'

The blonde woman pondered and said, 'may be . . .' and she looked away. Laila turned her head back to her original position with that blondes voice ringing in her head. Her voice, this time had a lack of sense of belongingness to somebody, somebody she loved deeply, somebody who made her feel undesirable. Who would do that to her thought Laila. Is it a man or a woman, was the question. She was irrefutably very wealthy but lacked the fulfillment that emanates by possessing that enormous wealth. A common element, of the west creeping in the sleepy east. Moved by the woman's voice, Laila didn't walk ahead.

'I am Laura. Laura Chabbra.' Suddenly introduced one beauty to her younger and happier version.

Laila turned back hearing the woman talk, which stopped her from walking towards the changing room. This time again, she was talking to Laila. 'Wonderful. I will catch you guys in a moment.' And she disappeared in an anxiety to do away with acknowledging her deliberately, without actually knowing her. She escaped to the changing room and recollected the conversation. Such is the mind of innocent.

Due to Laura's Italian accent her last name Chabbra resonated with the word cobra to Laila. 'What was that . . . a cobra?' she chuckled. 'God only knows? May be, what she couldn't do successfully in her country she is trying it here with us, the innocent Indians. Who will suspect her anyways. Oh God . . . rescue me.' And she hung her clothes on the metal bar on the back side of the door. She was about to take her clothes off and she recalled, 'Or was that Chabbra? Well, that's an Indian surname?' she blinked a few times. 'Whatever. I gotta change and then would get back to the turf. One shouldn't run away ever.' said Laila to herself affirmatively. She took a deep breath, wore her new set of clothes that smelled of lavender. 'Awesome!!!' she exclaimed enjoying the fresh fragrance. 'Thanku you God for this. It smells of peace . . . and of you by me."

The changing room didn't have any mirror to let her catch a glance of herself. 'There must be some spiritual reason to it. May be . . . they want us to focus to be beautiful from inside rather than just skin deep.' Saying this, she unlocked the knob of the changing room's door. 'Aaah!' came the voice from her mouth spellbound by what she saw. The opposite wall had a large mirror that reflected the beautiful her, she was full of joy to see herself crisp like a new packet of cookies. Happily she adjusted the band on her hair that held it together in a pony tail. 'Time for yoga.' She said to the mirror, 'bye,' and ran towards the Yoga room.

Laura, the cobra was lying down on her mat, with her feet joint together and arms resting close to her body, as if she were dead. 'This is shavasan, the one I do the best.' She spoke, winking at her.

'Oh! I see. And this?' asked Laila as she saw the woman sit upright.

'Nothing. I am just sitting.' She replied. 'Waiting for Daya to commence the session.'

Laila bit her nails, at the awkwardness of the situation. Daya smiled looking at both of them and gestured Laila to sit on her lavender coloured yoga mat that well complemented the fragrance on her fresh clothes. The mat itself was very soothing and so was to be Laila's life ahead.

'We shall now begin with the breathing exercise. Please fold your first two fingers, rest them on your palms and keep your thumb above it, so that it touches your finger like this,' and he turned his palms to show them the exact mudra(hand posture). 'Do it very slowly mam.' He added. The women did just as he instructed them.

From one aasan to another he taught them to relax their body and mind that was giving way to silence and helping them to connect to their soul. 'The only sound we should hear is that of our own deep breath.' Said Daya. Laila was doing just as directed, just as a child heeds his elder believing that the elder will lead him right. Though elders are not always right, which she knew by experience, here she was being led right because, he, was taking her closer to her soul. It is this meditative silence that establishes and strengthens our bonding with God.

Though she had made her life a meditation, doing what she believed in and enjoyed doing from her soul but this was an extra topping which taught her to batter stress and keep calm. Laila's life was her choice, shaking hands with luck, for fate always awaits the seeker.

We should always choose our own direction for us and await destiny to join hands with luck, to help us to live our dream.

'Next, I shall teach you Taarasaan,' said their instructor, 'or the tree posture. Please stand up and keep a small distance between both your feet, lock the fingers of both your palms and stretch upwards. Stand on your heels and breathe . . .' he said stressing on the last word.

'Gosh! I can't do this one ever.' spoke Laura, standing without stretching herself upward.

'When we start with a negative approach, we ruin the positive chances of doing it,' said Laila softly. 'Please say it to yourself that you will do it and, then, you will do it. Think right and the consequence will change.' Daya and Laura stood with their jaws dropped staring at Laila. 'Did I say . . . something . . . unusual?' she asked Daya, considering his amazement at her words.

'One can't be more right, mam. This is how I started practicing yoga with guests but somehow . . . . I couldn't convey this message to them.' He replied honestly.

'That is because you consider your disciples, a guest. And you are right in way, because and not many, who come here as your guest, have the audacity to swallow the bitter truth if it comes from you. We are more comfortable hearing fabricated eulogies and praises, than being used to honesty. No wonder, there is a chaos in and around us all the time. We pay to hear lies, be it in a wellness spa or elsewhere. You are paid to make us feel good with an approach that suits us, nothing beyond that.'

The man stood speechless and so did Laura. They were in such an awe of her that their own mind felt numb, like a glass of cold water thrown at our face, opening our eyes compulsively. 'Lets gets back to yoga,' said Laila and they smoothly followed her words. The session was wrapped up with Laura mastering more than the shav asana (the dead body posture).

A steward, served them a tall slick glass of bottle gourd juice. 'How is your head?' asked Laura.

'Peaceful.' Replied Laila. Meditation was her central part of her existence; here she was learning new ways to reach the same goal, which was being close to the God within us, in our soul. The more closer we are with Him, the easier our life becomes and the wise like her know this universal truth.

'Hope . . . it does not hurt anymore?' she askedwith sympathy.

'Why? Why would it . . . . hurt?' Laila was left astounded. She was also mildly irritated by the woman's probing, as after yoga she was wanting to enjoy the silence within. Such small talk were not here prerogative, unless she felt a need for it, professionally.

'You had banged your head. It was . . . baaad. We got the doctor for you-' explained Laura, lovingly looking at Laila who was, in a situation she didn't want to be. 'Then you mumbled that you were a doctor who wanted to help the man on board. Then you fainted.' Scenes from her previous flight journey were coming alive.

She blinked her eyes, 'what happened to me next . . .' she asked her for complete narration, not sure if the woman was talking all truth of helping her or was cooking up some story which by fluke, matched her real life experience.

'Not much. You fainted and the lady doctor came and . . . next . . . . I saw you when, I was changing my flight, from Delhi to Deheradun.' She narrated correctly.

'Oh ya, there was somebody . . . . ,' Laila couldn't foresee an escape now because Laura was right, 'on the third seat. It must have been . . . . you. I am so sorry . . . I didn't . . . . notice . . . I was . . .'

'Into reading brochure of this Spa.' Smiled Laura, finishing her glass of juice in a gulp. 'I hate this bitter juice.'

"Ya, yes, I was reading the brochure." She replied frankly. "um . . . but this does good to our body, I gotta finish my glass of it. And I am sorry again, I didn't . . . aah . . . recognize you. Nice to meet you, again and umm . . . Thank you for getting me, the doctor. You are my savior and . . . ahhh . . . thanks a billion for your help.'

Just then Laila recalled something. An energy that states that there is more to the moment, which only time could speak of that she felt right in the beginning of their meeting. There was something within her telling, that this meet had more to it. What could it be?

A sad blonde in an expensive spa, there has to be a reason why God put them together here and in the flight too. The wise like Laila knows that co-incidences are merely disfigured puzzle that falls into the right place with time. 'It's . . . so stupid of me. I couldn't . . . recognize you here. M bad at remembering people when I meet them at random.' The honesty in her voice was apparent to the other women.

'It's perfectly alright. You were in a hurry. This place taught me slow down by the practice of yoga. I understand,' said Laura, 'we all go through times, we don't want to be reminded of.'

Laila looked at her and found the crown of unhappiness on her head. She wasn't expecting this dolorous, a reply. 'Ammm . . . yaa . . . yes, we do.' And she forced a grin bringing the glass closer to her mouth unable to sort out the mystery that baffled het. 'Who on earth must have made this woman so deeply unhappy and why?'

'M hungry.' Said Laura. 'Now that you are through with your juice, lets grab a bite. Come along.'

'Oh! How nice, you are thoroughly familiar with the place. It's a pleasure to have you around. I will catch you in a moment. I have left my keys in the other room-' said Laila keeping the empty glass, atop a table.

'What . . . you left your keys!Get it. I'll wait for yoou here,' said Laura some what shocked yet charmed by Laila's child like openness and warmth. Laila got up and strutted towards the room where she had her left her keys.

A man her age, another guest at the spa was sipping his green tea there. Without disturbing him, Laila marched in and was about to lay her hands on her keys laying on the table next to his chair, where she sat an hour ago with Gyan.

'That's mine,' said the man and she jumped out of her skin. She kept looking at the keys instead of looking at the man. 'You want it?' he asked playfully.

'That's mine.' She replied.

'Then you take it. Let us see which room it opens. Mine or . . . ,' he said seriously, in a mood to have fun.

'Mine.' She replied forwarding her hand once again to pick it it up.

'Your keys,' whispered the man, 'are with the receptionist. Gyan Singh took it from here. 'This,' he said, giving her a flower from the vase, 'is for you.' Laila still didn't look at him, tough she did look at the white flower he held in his hand for her.

'This belongs to the hotel.' She replied, unable to say something smatter though she answered in a flash.

'And you?' he asked playfully. Laila didn't respond and in the next moment she was gone from the room. 'Who do you belong to?' Thenhe yelled. 'Who do you belong to?'

She was nowhere in the sight. She stopped by the rest room to wash her face, embarrassed by the episode though undoubtedly the man's voice rang in her head over and over again. She stood there in silence, wiped her face with a tissue and walked out prim and proper.

'You got your keys?' said Laura meeting her in the corridor of the hotel.

'No, Yes. I mean . . . aah . . . it's with . . . at the reception. I want some water, my throat is . . . sore . . . no not sore . . . ahhh . . . It' parched. Let's have our breakfast.' She showed an exigency to have their first meal wondering if she delayed, that man could follow suit. So she and Laura sat by each other during the breakfast and decided to meet post the aromatherapy massage, for lunch.

In a moment as she collected her breath she thought, 'how clumsy of me, I should have atleast looked at him. Anyways, thank God for I ran to my safety.'

And then she was on with, the massage. It awakened her senses and rejuvenated her body. She felt as though she were floating, weightless like a feather. The stress was receding unbelievably from her body. From her head to her toe, she felt reincarnated. Her first dip in the ocean of Ayurveda and its ancient secrets of rejuvenating our body, mind and soul, was effectively relieving her of her stress. Thousands of years back, the east knew how to live healthy better than we do today. They emphasized on curing the cause of the illness and preached abstinence whereas the modern medicine, targets treating the symptoms and not the cause. It thus teaches us impatience and supports rash lifestyle.

Both the ladies at the spa got together for lunch, post the massage, as decided. Women on such matters, matters of beauty, are not particular in keeping their promise to each other as that could lead to their secrets for beauty go public. But both being evolved met on set place and time.

'I didn't mention, I am a fashion photographer, assisting a renowned photographer,' said Laila at the salad bar.

'Interesting,' said Laura chewing the lettuce leaf. 'My husband, is a great deal into photography. But I don't know anything about it, though I once posed for his magazines cover.'

'Oh! Goodness gracious, your picture must have come out . . . gorgeous, in the least. M sure people must have stared at it, for days unending?" and she gulped in a spoon full of carrot soup, which to her palate was, light and tasty. A good appetizer.

Laura rested her fork on her plate and biting her lips at the corner, she said 'ammm . . . I don't know . . . ?'

'So, you don't know how stunning you looked? How humble?' Laila chuckled.

'He didn't like my facing the camera. And so . . . I gave up on it,' replied Laura.

'He. Who's he?' retorted Laila surprised at her reply and disappointed at the photographer who didn't like her picture. It was close to impossible.

'My husband.' Replied Laura.

'O' said Laila, burning her tongue eating the hot tofu smoked in white pepper sauce with vegetables, on her plate, placed next to the soup bowl. She could't believe she was living in the twenty first century. 'You . . . with due respect to your decision, you . . . gave up on what he,' and she paused in disbelief, 'didn't like you, to do? Ouuch . . . !'. She sipped some water to soothe her tongue. 'I wonder how many sacrificial fire he has made you jump in, all along your marriage. And I am surprised, as to why he reacted so selfishly. He must'nt be a good looking man himself, is he Laura?'

Laura laughed cleaning her teeth off the food with her tongue. She was a very slow eater. "I don't know . . . You figure out when you meet'im," she retorted cryptically.

'This is insane. You don't look submissive, not to my eyes nor to anybody else's.' Replied Laila for she knew the danger of not living the life, one wants to. Once we begin to give in to other's desire without our own happiness in it, it is but obvious that we will be expected to submit, all the time. That's how the world works. "Do you realize, the oppressor oppress the oppressed?" Said Laila compelling Laura to look within her and figure out the reasons, why sadness gives her company instead of happiness, why she was not happy with her life and why she was lonely in her marriage. 'Life is not to blame always. We should see our mistakes and attitude which goes in it's making Laura.'

'Hmm . . .' Replied Laura, for there were way too many issues staring at her, from her life's windows. Some could be called, 'easy way out,' some was, 'giving in.' There was also, 'suffering in silence and preference to it,' and then of course was, 'getting used to the way life was.' Then, there were more windows which she didn't want to look at because when we learn to lose courage, it seems impossible to gather it on one fine day when we realize how miserable we have made our own self. On the contrary, those among us who live with courage, stand erect to face life head on and also live in a way that supports happy living.

'You decide for yourself.' Said Laila, 'I will help, when you require. We get helped when we are open to make efforts to better our life.'

'Ahhh . . . yes. Right.' Said Laura. She appeared to be in a pensive mood and they both had their meals in silence. One thinking about past and the other enjoying her present, the latter was Laila. She finished her meal before Laura, and said, 'you must be a foodie? Are you Laura?'

'Aamm . . . yes,' replied Laura, 'but I can't cook very well.'

'Let us stick to what you can do. Okhai?' said Laila with a smile. Making her best efforts to cheer the woman up and see freedom in her eyes and positivity in her mind and body. Life feels different when we change our approach towards it like she did during her yoga class. That unknowingly was a beginning of a transformation she must have awaited for it in her silence.

'So you enjoy food? Tell me in a simple yes or no.' and Laila saw a man doing some stretching exercise in the lawn, facing the dining room. She tried to steal a look. 'Oh!' she said getting back to Laura. 'M so sorry, I . . . . that man looked like an old friend of mine.' And just then the man turned, giving her a clear view of himself, as clear as she wanted it to be . . . He was well maintained and fit for his age, which was in late sixties.

'That man,' asked Laura surprised. 'He is your friend?'

Laila chuckled, 'Ahhh . . . . no! I . . .' and she broke into a spell of laughter. And she laughed almost falling off from the chair. Laura sat intact whereas, she was finding it hard to contain her laughter recalling the gaping lack of similarities between the two men, and how with abated breath she waited to catch a glimpse of his face assuming him to be the man she had met fleetingly in that morning. 'Curiosity, you see, can leave us breathless . . .' She said gasping for the fresh Himalayan air, Laura still didn't join her, she just passed a smile. 'Anyhow. You enjoy eating probably a lot?' She managed to speak with her laughter fading away.

'Yeah! Yes, I do. But how did you figure this out,' replied cheered up by the entire incidence and happy to think about food, as that was something she enjoyed extensively only when cooked by others.

'You eat very slow. And mostly slow eaters relish food. They eat enjoying the flavor and the taste of each bite.' Said Laila making a ball of tissue she was tossing it while she gave company to Laura. 'And having said that, I would go on to believe,' and she smiled looking at Laura, 'that you are a good cook. One has to have a love for the art that cooking is.'

'Hey! No . . . it's not an art. It's simple activity. I loved to cook, but . . . Indian food . . . I can't.' Replied Laura.

'You what?' said Laila hinting the woman to correct her attitude. 'Indian food requires long hours to cook it well. But then it teaches us patience in turn.'

'Yes, perhaps you are right. One has to stand longer until the food severs and the aromas finds it way out form the vessel to our nose and . . . . everywhere. Ummm . . . . I can and I promise I will try my hands again at it.' And she raised a toast to that achievement of hers. 'Cheers to that.'

'Cheers.' Said Laila holding up her glass. And both took a couple of sips.

'You will come to my place? I live in Mumbai . . . pleeez come by, sometime.' She requested like a child.

Laila was watching calmly. 'O . . . h! What a . . .' and she checked herself before uttering the word, 'co incidence,' to her. 'Yes I will. I owe it to you. Your wish, my command. And by the way, I live in the same city as you.' Laura was incredibly happy and seeing her joy, Laila felt a supernatural calming energy surrounding her.

It's an unseen trophy that God sends to us when we are kind to people selflessly. Here she made genuine efforts to cheer up a stranger, unrelated and unfamiliar. She helped her and felt for her cause without expecting any returns. And when we don't expect any return, God rewards us in extra ordinary way, beyond the dominion of the natural realm.

This spa was an indulgence in the scenic beauty of nature with the healing massages and detoxifying food. Laila was sinking her teeth in every bit of what they had to offer, for she loved indulgence this time round. And indulgence is also a way of self love, in such a fatigued state. And the wise know that, no life is life good enough, if there is no indulgence in it because our body and mind tire, which calls for our attention and love, to repair and rejuvenate our self and have the glow of relaxation on us, peeling off our worries and fatigue. Thoroughly, enjoying her package at the spa, Laila was happy and felt healthy as the shiny Arabian horses and flew back to Chennai to reunite with her doting father and her loving mother. Her holidays came to an end, in the next week, as was the call of her work, the work she loved dearly.

CHAPTER 6

Our talent is the God in us, who gets us;
bread and fame.

Holding a box of sweets in her hand along with a pack of white vanilla fragrance candles, Laila entered her boss's chamber, to greet him for the festivals of light, of eatable sugar animals, cards and fire crackers-Diwali. As she pushed the door that was left ajar, far from the illumination of the festival, the lights of Alexander's room were turned to the colour blue with the aid of the light emanating dicode(L.E.D.) apparatus and alike a fat old boxer, he sat with his head in his hands with his elbow resting on his table, on his enormous leather chair, that contained him, to his comfort.

'Alexander, can I come in?' Laila asked in a low pitch voice to match his mood.

'Who?' he said like a sad hero of an old Hindi film with his vision retarded by the dimmed lights. 'Is that not Laila?'

'Yes. It's me. Laila.' She said still trying to figure out the cause of his sadness.

'Come in my dear. Come in.' His energy was visibly low and his limbs were lifeless like that of antired ape.

Unsure of his state of mind and careful of it too, she said, 'Shall I come a little later . . . if it suits you?'

'No.' he paused, brightening the light, to white form blue. 'Walk in and have a seat. Over here.' He said gesturing at the chair he wanted her to sit on.

'This is for you.' She spoke forwarding it, 'Happy Diwali.' She greeted him gently to which he looked away for a fraction of a second.

'Heay! That's . . . . very kind of you . . . but,' and he gestured to her to sit, 'it's not . . . . required.' Laila kept looking at him to which he changed his response for he was sensitive to her feelings which were genuine. 'Thanku. I appreciate.' And he gave half a smile, a rare commodity which like the festival, came once in a year to light up his employees.

'My pleasure.' She said, wondering as to what caused him the exhaustion or the sadness. 'Most of the employees had taken an off in advance for the festival so there wasn't much work he had on hand. Then what caused the . . . ,' she thought to herself.

'All prepared for festival? Hope, you have a good time.' He said not quite in the mood to talk.

'Amm . . . yes, I . . .' She replied. Though apart from buying him the box of sweets and another one for herself, there was nothing she did in preparation for the festival. And yes she did buy the candles from the blind children's association, where every month she gave a donation of Rupees five hundred, from her salary. Women like Laila, know how to use their life keeping their sadness away and share her happiness from others like an oyster does to its pearls.

'Hey Alexander! Look what I got with me,' she said taking out a C.D. from her bright orange hand bag. My first out door shoot for our magazine." Happiness poured out from her. "Happening, it was for us and I hope . . . you like it, rather I pray you like it.' Then she paused to look at him as her tone of voice didn't cheer him up. 'Is everything ok with you? You don't look your usual self. It's . . . ." She searched for right words to convey her thoughts desirably, after all, he was her boss no matter how unofficial her concern was. She had to speak the right words. 'I am worried for you.' He didn't respond considering her to be way too young to understand him. On getting no response she spoke, 'ok! Here's the C.D. and it is ready for your approval.' Her face lighted up. She sensed his mood and then she hushed, thinking what if he didn't like it. He would let loose a terror on her like the Nazis on the jews. 'No problem. Fear isn't the way out anyway. So I may as well take the shouting and rework on it.' She thought to herself. He took the C.D. form her and Laila smiled at him again making efforts to cheer him for he was a nice boss. Somebody who was ruthless to his employees, only if, they failed to match his expectations, which was very often for others, but not for Laila for she kept her priority clear and landed her work always on time. On the brighter side, he as a boss was relatively less political and had a defined taste for favoring honest employees.

Both sat in silence, not knowing who would restart the conversation. Her apprehensions were gaining ground and then he raised his head to speak, keeping the C. D. aside on his glass covered teak wood table.

'How do you live without . . . . sssaey . . . ?' he stopped to look at her innocent face, 'It leaves me wondering? How do you . . . ?'

'How do I what?' she said with an intensity of having fire on her backside. He didn't fill the line. 'What's it . . . . ?' She was dazed as to why someone his stature and experience would take an awe of her meager life.

'You know,' he said with frustration apparent in his voice, 'my wife has threatened to leave me?' Both went silent once again, one out of his suffering and Laila, out of his sudden burst of emotions a side of him, he kept under wraps. His face twitched, 'Infact, she has already left me.'

The puzzle regarding his life was still ringing in her head. 'I understand.' She spoke, 'but, did you . . . by any chance . . . 'her face showed some discomfort. She bent forward, 'did you mean sex, previously?' She spoke relating his frustration with his query to her. She had had experience of how his talks were related underneath the surface. His asking, 'aren't you keeping well?' to an employee could mean, he is disgusted with the work.

'Yes,' he said swinging his head in amazement, though he couldn't clearly notice her embarrassment on his question, to avoid which, he smartly turned to his laptop and clicked the button for the gadget to start up.

'Just the way you can't do without it.' She replied flat. Alexander was shocked at her confidence and at her clarity in her voice.

'What was that?' he smirked in response given it came from her.

'Habit.' She said, 'I am not in a habit of it, sir.' She blushed red while her body showed a remarkable confidence in line with her witty reply. Staring in his eyes she said, 'And I am perfectly normal.' Looking away from his laptop, he looked at her to get her point clearly. 'And Alexander!Sir, I am straight.'

'Wait.' He objected. 'Don't defend yourself for the heck of it. It wasn't an allegation. My point is, you,' he said pointing a finger at her, 'are always working. Which is good. Trust me, it really is good.'

'Thanku,' said Laila. Her eyes glowed.

'But . . . it's ridiculous as well. Be it day or night, you are available to Brazentine. No . . . no . . . nooh, that's not a problem. The issue is . . .' he paused and looked deep in her eyes interrogatively, 'how come you are . . . still so happy . . . that too, all the time?'

She faced the challenge of his question and kept her empathy alive. 'Is this why you are sad, because I am happy . . . . all the time?' and to this he laughed out loud. Laila continued to explain. 'This is my work Alexander. I should give my best to it. Moreover, I didn't come here to . . . .' She paused, 'I came here to . . .' Life had sharpened her mind for her own sake. 'I am here to give you good work. I want to give my best to Brazentine, which is demanding. I would be glad to . . . . to fulfill my objective, as your employee.' She answered sensibly.

'That's good. But I am jealous. I am very very jealous of you,' he said seizing his laughter and throwing a protective glance at her for he loved her, for her innocence and freshly acquired tact in handling work pressure;most of all, his tantrums.

Today, to her surprise, he was like melting snow of a mountain; drifting away and away.

'I don't know much of you and your life, but, as a human being, I would tell you, what Gautam Buddha told his disciples hundreds of years ago. By the practice of loving kindness, we attain liberation of heart . . . and is one of the noble truths of the universe. Please abide by it and you will feel the difference.'

'Please give me a moment,' he said and picked up the receiver of his intercom and pressed the numbers to connect to the security. 'By the practice of loving kindness we attain the liberation of heart . . . ,' he repeated her words and looked inward. 'Ya, I believed in it as a child and then life didn't give me a second chance.' He clenched his teeth which was noticeable.

'Disappointment, when mixed with pain, comes back as anger. And this anger, when mixed with meditation, gives back love—' said the wise Laila.

'Love?' replied Alexander, 'relationships are about money . . .'

'Money? No, it's about love and love.' Said Laila.

'What love?' he snapped at her.

'Love that comes from the soul and stays by us, as love,' she smiled. Alexander smiled back with hesitation. 'The Katha Upnishad says, 'in the secret cave of life two are seated by life's fountain. The seprate ego. Drink of the sweet and bitter a stuff. Liking the sweet and disliking the bitter part of it. While the supreme Self drinks the sweet and the bitter. Neither liking this, nor disliking that. Our ego gropes in darkness, while the Self lives in light.'

'Yaaah . . . hmmm . . . . what do you know of life. Don't judge me?' he said.

'What I know of life is; it's eternity. The eternity of the soul(self) and the love, that heals . . . like the morning sun on a chilling winter.' said the wise Laila. 'This is all that I know of life. This is all that I have understood form my daily meditation.' There was a serene silence between them. She sat like a Virgin Mary with kind and loving eyes.

'Alexander you are always at work too . . . your mind is always at work . . . where as Laila's work is merely physical and . . . I am where my head is.'

'Limited to her soul,' he replied.

'Yes,' she replied.

'That is why . . . you are you and I am . . .' he said.

'You are me . . .' she replied, 'for being at peace doesn't mean we have to stop being at war. It just means that we have to stop fighting within ourselves. That is why, in this moment, you are me.' She said tenderly. 'How do you feel?'

He looked dazed and said, 'I feel calm.' He rested his hand on the table.

She said. 'That is my energy.' They shared the same silence. 'That is the energy of your soul, Alexander. Now it is upto you, to practice this meditative silence. And then you shall be the partially awakened one who will learn from his suffering by finding the cause of your sufferings and your faults in it and would share his joy as God's blessings, who will thus accept both the good and the bad, thereby becoming a seeker of God.'

'Aah . . . yes. Excuse me.' He said to her and he read the message.

His mind is always ticking to contemplate his next move, like my father.

Her eyes then fell on his laptop's screen which was kept midway facing her more and less towards Alexander. Her eyes widened in disbelief, as if it were not just a screen but a live skeleton that came to life. The caption read, 'MyHorny Alphabets.' Below it, it read; 'A—arousal, B—bosom, C—caress, D—' she blinked her eyes, 'E—erotic, F—fuck, G—g string, H—hymen, I—inter course, J—jerk, K—kiss, L—lust,' she glanced at him and thought of his age, neither could she giggle not breathe, the frenzy was catching on. Her mouth went dry.

'Hello! Yes, get me another pack . . .' said Alexander over the receiver instructing the security which Laila didn't register. She hurriedly read further with her body still recovering from the mental shock. 'M—mastru . . . .' She barely pronounced and her eyes jumped onto the next alphabet. 'N—negligee, O—orgy, P—penetrate, Q—quickie,', from her mouth her throat had gone dry, such was effect of the alphabets. 'R—romance, S—, T—thrust . . . W—womb,' and as she pronounced 'y'.

'Laila!' called Alex, keeping the receiver down. 'Laila!' He repeated.

'Yes . . .' She replied as though she was watching a horror film in the broad day light. She sat numbing straight.

'Are-you-ok?' he asked, in the way one speaks to a child and kept looking at her. She didn't look up.

She gulped. 'Aahm! yes.' Her words came out like a talking statue with emotionless eyes, which raised an alarm in Alex's mind.

'You will have to . . .' he paused to check if she was listening. 'Are you sure . . . you-are-ok? You . . .' he paused in introspection on seeing Laila sitting with her eyes cast downward. 'Oh I am sorry . . . .' He said. 'My . . . apologies . . . I hope it didn't offend you. I understand . . . .' He was studying her, in a strange apology. 'Your background . . . probably, you didn't expect the sex question from me. You know . . . I understand, small towns people . . . they are sweet, unlike us . . . the big tricksters in life.'

'Yes.' She replied like a robot. In her mind the alphabets were replaying and then she closed her eyes funnily like the lights blinking. 'I mean, no. I am fine. That's absolutely fine. Infact, I was wondering . . .' She resurrected herself, 'about your marriage.' She didn't bother to remind him that she was from Chennai and not a small Towner.

'Oh!' he spoke rubbing his lower lips and breathing in relief. "Aha! . . . I don't know how to put it. Work pressure and then this thing with Laura . . ."

'Laura . . . ?' she squeezed her eyes.' That's a nice name.'

'My wife. Ohhh . . . . I never mentioned. I can be a little lost at times . . . with so much work . . . you know how it is with me. She is my wife. The funny bit is, she is twenty years younger than me.' Said Alexander sounding happy to take her name.

'Can I please get some water?' she requested to which he affirmatively rang the bell asking for a glass of water for her.

'Laura Cannavaro!' he flashed a million dollar smile to flaunt his trophy wife. 'She was a Canavaro before marriage.

'Canna-varo, . . . umm?' she stammered. 'Sounds Italian?'

'Oh yes!' he spoke like an over confident winner. 'My wife is an Italian.'

'I didn't know her sir name was . . .' he paused studying her. 'here's water for you.' She smiled and took a sip of water. 'Laura Chabbra. She is my wife,' to which the water instead of going in Laila's mouth came out like a fountain. Her stomach churned and her fears soared like a high tide, for it was she was the one to advise his boss's wife, Laura to give Alexander a dose of his own drug and that this condition of his was because of her. 'Nice name and better surname.' Said Laila managing to speak and 'm sorry,' she spoke wiping the water with a tissue paper and as for his wife, she was well training her.

Laura got intoaction; she fired her head chef and became the incharge of his food, for the way to the man's heart is by lovingly spoiling him through his stomach. She laid his table perfectly, ranging form Indian curries, to Italian pastas, to Hungarian golash, to American puddings and thus in five months and seven days, Alexander the great became a slave to her culinary expertise.

Tables turned. Now he had the need and she, the talent and supremacy. Her intensive hard work, the killing heat of kitchen and her honest efforts brought her to a day when she tamed the man as unceremoniously, as he had tamed her. One night at the dinner table she requested Alexander.

'Darling!' he responded, 'what is it with you? Everything is so perfect between us and now . . .

you . . . ? I can't stand my wife selling her paintings to some piece of shit or . . . whoever. I can't take it.'

'It's not about merely my paintings, it's about my love and more, for it which I want to reach my buyers.' And this ended their conversation.' Laura broke down with an injured innocence and contempt.

He walked away from his dining room and she, to another country, to another life. He couldn't fathom her free while she didn't want to suffer in silence any longer for her entire life was mocked and left to perish to her unhappiness.

This was Alexander who preferred honesty at work and at home he was bang opposite, going by his convenience. For some men a woman can't satisfy them irrespective of the latters hard work put in for the man's happiness.

'Are you with me . . . I narrated my entire story.' Said Alexander on not getting any response from Laila. She was beginning to sweat. She couldn't look in his eyes all the more not because she was wrong as he was the same man who disgusted her terribly as her friend's butcher husband was turning out to be the same she looked upto as her boss, respecting him for his achievements. And also on one day she wished to share how she was helping her friend Laura get on with life.

'M listening. Please carry on . . .' She forced a smile at him and spoke tenderly. 'Alexander!'

'She calls me Alexi.' He spoke like a child. Laila froze again for it resonated with familiarity.

'Your surname is . . . . Chabbra? . . . don't you call yourself Alexander Ku . . . ? 'she interjected.

'Right. Bang on target. Chabbra is my father's surname.' He said disgustedly.' I don't like using it next to my name.' Her boss, Alexander Kumar's full name was Alexander Kumar Chabbra. She rembered the Cobra incident. As for Laila, neither did she know, Laura's husband's name nor she bothered to enquire about his work. It didn't matter to her as along as her friend was happy. What she remembered from the Spa was that her husband was a photographer working for a magazine who didn't like her photographs and not, that he owned a magazine, as grand as Brazentine. And later she learnt from Laura that Alexander bought pictures from photographers and putting his name in the cover sections he gained applause from people.

'Yep! Kumar is . . .' she paused to pick the adjective and said, 'very crisp. 'She spoke patronizing him for his comfort and not for a selfish gain in the bargain. Though in reality, it didn't matter to her which name he used after Alexander, Kumar or Chabbra and neither did she refer to her boss as, Alex, like her colleagues preferring to maintain a distance from him, from the day one. Also from day one she understood that he loved being patronized and licked, like all successful and egoist men do. So for her, he was Alexander, the winner, the lion and the greatest conqueror she had met in person who courage she admired.

'I gave her every imaginable joy. I loved her so dearly. Yet she is separated by time and land from me.'

To which Laila's eyes rose and met his. In it, it reflected duality, for she knew the truth and how he was covering up the reality before her. He was nonetheless her boss but she didn't lower her gaze. Her work, her dream and her income was at stake. 'No work, no money. No money, no charity. Yet we,' signifying she and Laura, 'will play the other way, Mr. Cobra.' Said

Laila in her mind, to him. 'The truth's way. The way of God.'

'If you love her, then go.' She said looking at him gently. 'Go, get her Alexander. Be as brave as was the great Greek Emperor you are named after. You give a fight each day for your empire, it's time you do the same for your woman. But always remember, if we are bound by soul . . . and not mere relationships . . . we stay together forever.'

He looked in her eyes deeply. 'But what if she doesn't want to be with me.'

'Why so,' she asked tenderly keeping distance.

He fidgeted and said, 'I don't know . . . she wants to be some one else . . .'

'Then let her be,' she spoke objectively. 'This city and this era . . . it makes almost impossible for a man to find love and when he does, he grabs it tight and tighter. Now Alexander, grabbing somebody, so tight leads to bleeding . . . bleeding of the soul. And when soul bleeds happiness ought to be missing.'

'But what else you want me to do,' he asked. 'Wouldn't she run away with some one else . . . wouldn't she . . .'

'Isn't she gone anyhow?' she replied. He looked at her in defence. She didn't move an inch. He lowered his gaze. 'It's the same with women who suffocate their men. So, it's wise to get her back and let her be . . . who she wants to be. Besides as you say about one running away from their partners you would also find a flaw with such men\women who claim to be on the receiving end. Nobody wants a broken life . . . but then it comes about due to lack of unconditional love.'

He thought for a moment. 'I am getting old . . . and I need someone . . .' He touched his wrinkles and pointing at he said, 'these you see Laila, worry me a lot.'

'Everybody gets old, Alexander and the simplest way to cut ageing . . .' said Laila, 'is by acceptance of the universal truth, that we age naturally.'

'Is that a medicine,' he asked.

'It's the cure,' she replied. 'It's called acceptance which also cures many an ailment.' He was stunned. 'You can't beat age . . . and I am aware of the medical advances and the kind of money you can shell out for it. But then . . .'

'It goes to square one,' he sniggered briefly. His head was very full of matters, which's why he sniggered genteelly.

'Yes,' she smiled. 'Which is why there is no and shall be no other, simple and permanent way out than, accepting the beauty, that ageing brings to us.'

He stared in her eyes to cross check her conviction. 'There is this thing I love about women like you . . . you, as I have understood you, never bothered to remain and play sixteen all the time.' He spoke tiredly. 'You know I have known women . . . who are just so soso awful to look at . . . yet so obessed by looking younger and younger and younger . . . .' She smiled. 'Ya,' he said, 'I too belong in that category.' He roared with laughter in acceptance and laughed freely and longer than previously.

'Nobody is awful . . . till their thoughts are clean and clear of jealousy,' she said politely. 'Besides, once our mind is free of the heavy weight of ageing . . . it works like a miracle creams that never work as good as the free mind. And you know, world best skin care products, like Shishedo, talk of protection of skin, because they are wise enough to know that protection is the key word. And I say . . . don't worry about ageing and that's just the perfect protection one can offer to one self.'

'Ahhha . . . Ahhhaa . . .' he was speechless.

'God will bless you for it.' She smiled wider and said, 'God will bless you for it.' You will relieve mankind of one of the most lethal weapon of this age . . . and that's ageing? Isn't it.' he enquired.

'No, the worries that consume people about ageing.' She replied very wisely. He roared with an open laughter affected by the purity of her energy and the wisdom that came from the divine master within her. 'And you know Alexander, when you have suffocated somebody enough . . . stop doing anything about it.'

'About the person?' he asked.

'No, about her being who you want her to be and about the entire issue regarding your relationship. The thoughts of being lonely is like any other thought . . . the more you think, the more complex it shall get." She got up from her chair and before he could have said something, two men in whites escorted by a third one, from the security department of the building, turned up on his office door.

'Sir!' said the man. Alaxander looked up at them, like a brave Roman warrior and then he fizzled in acknowledgement. 'Come in come in.' He roared like a happy lion turning the lights to mild pink. 'What a delight it is to have you both here.' He respectfully got up to greet them as an ambitious and ruthless bends either to love or to power over and above him, in case it was the political might of the two politicians that made him bow before them.

Laila was puzzled, 'polee-t-cians?' she whispered to her boss.

'Yes,' he whispered back, 'to have fire without power is as bad as fighting a war without weapon. Will catch you later.' And saying so, he disconnected from her and she promptly made an exit leaving them for their meet and for him to feed the politician's festive greed.

Power for Alexander was certainly is not just being powerful but also being with the powerful in the society because, wherever there is money, there is cut throat competition. And in competition, there is nasty back stabbing, blood shed and ruination. Even if one thinks of brotherhood, he finds disappointment because the greed of supremacy and jealousy, the brain child of capitalism and ego, is blind to peace. So the wise befriend the powerful wisely, being of help to them whenever need occurs. As for the wise like Laila, God is the only supreme power who always helps the one living with faith in his supremacy and such people need no defense, for the master within them, does the needful for them.

Back to her space in the office, she slumped in her chair exhausted, puzzled and peaceful. It was too much of an exposure, in too less a time; but life can be revealing, because in the adult world, one has to endure and experience more than ordinary people to able to climb the vertical ladder of her career. It gives them endurance and islands; islands as Varun had explained, comes only through volcanic eruptions of life. 'Wait,' she mumbled to herself, her voice echoed mildly, she looked around, there was not a soul in the room, still she lowered her voice and said, 'I will' and she opened her e-mail account, 'shoot a mail.' And she wrote, 'Your "Alexi" is my boss at Brazentine. SOS. Your'sLaila.' And she sat in wait for the reply and anticipated Alexander's response on her photographs. She was nervous and yet calm. She dived backward her chair resting her head on the backrest, her eyes flapped. In another moment, she fell asleep.

'Laila,' somebody poked her with his pen.

'Alex, yes.' She lunged forward. 'I was working on the photographs since morning. God! Lokesh, You scared me. You . . .'

'You have been thinking about Alex a lot, haven't you my pretty face?" he said making it sound like a juicy gossip.

With her eyes wide open she said, 'shut up!' in friendly tone. 'He is our boss and yes, as for your query . . . or whatever that was . . . .'

'You do think about him . . . a lot.' he filled in her sentence for her and held a print out form his mailbox in her face.

"For God sake . . . . you sneak . . . . ," she pounced at the print out. "How did you lay your hands . . . on it. "He swung it above her head. She leaped up and grabbed it. "I am as tall as you . . . got It?"

"Madam Laila, you sent this to me, "he replied. "By the way," he paused to soak in the office gossip. "miss new comer, we call him Alex and not . . . ."

"Well, that was a spelling error. Plus," she looked at him tearing the mail, "this went to you . . . I mean this was sent u as a joke, so that, you would get some gossip handy from me . . . once in your life time." She was amazed at her pace of covering up and appearing relaxed, though inside she was burning like a brick furnace. 'Nice fun? Wasn't it . . . ?'

"Oh! So . . ." he said believing in her words and not wanting to get much into it either, for he didn't want logic from beautiful women, "then I should, take it that . . . you like me."

'Yes, I like you to get up from my table right now and get us some tea, from the canteen. Would't you my dear, Lokesh?' He smiled happily at him. He smiled back. "In turn . . . I will make you happy . . ." she said in gratitude. "Wait, just kidding . . . I will come along with you," she added as Lokesh was turning around to leave for the canteen. He was restless, for she didn't show any romantic interest in him and happy that atleast, she was willing to give him company in the cafeteria. And as he got up, she measured his height and said playfully, "you are short."

'Of what?' he asked.

'Height,' she responded.

'That was very kind reminder from you,' he said. 'That just killed my interest in you and in all the other tall women, I meet.'

'Just meet? Huh! Are you sure Lokesh?' she asked.

'No well . . . not just meet. Flirt too,' he replied like a confession.

'Just flirt? Huh?' she asked.

'No well . . . not just flirt,' he answered.

'RIGHT,' she said with a nice smile.

'You have hit me on the right spot,' he chuckled.

She threw the mail into the dust bin and from being innocent girl, to the James Bond's equal, Laila's life with her soul, was sure to take her places, to begin with, the cafeteria.

After, chilling out with ice tea in canteen, she got back to her desk. Lokesh, the marketing manager for the magazine, stood up five feet eight inches tall, said 'bye! See Ya!' and marched away from her cubicle. It was pleasant to see him confess.

"Lokesh!" she shouted while he was about to make an exit." I have a question." He stopped and turned around holding his laptop bag in his left hand and a blazer in another. "Why does . . . your spectacles have that thick thread attached to it's temple. There, the black one on both sides?" and they looked at each other. 'Well,' she said distracting him, 'that's my only question for you.' And she twisted her revolving chair.

'So that, you,' he paused to grin, it made him look handsome, 'can pull it from behind like a leach and ride on me. I am your horse madam . . . Laila.' Laila burst out in loud laughter, a maddening spell of humour from a straight faced man. She was holding her stomach and laughing harder and louder.

'Is that all?' he asked watching her laugh.

She gave a thumps up sign and said, 'Great. That's it. Now go away. Bye!'

'You have all the men at your mercy. Lucky girl! I liked the last line of your mail . . . yours Laila.' He spoke lovingly enjoying every bit of his time.

"I . . ." she spoke through her laughter, "I liked your entire line, Lokesh. And from tomorrow you better give me a ride from here to boss's chamber." He smiled and drifted away, and her voice faded into oblivion. With him he took the pleasant memory to the elevator through his thoughts. What a delight it was for him to have her all by himself, alone in the three thousand square feet of office space. God was kind to him for reasons unknown and so he waited for the arrival of another such festival, to have a time as good as this one.

Minutes changed into hours and Alexander didn't get back to Laila regarding the C.D. he had handed over to him for his approval, instead the next day he met her in his office like a regular office day.

Seated with the fabulous antiques around him and the dark coloured teak wood furniture, that could well leave one in awe of it, he sat comfortably. The comfort was a gift every child born in a wealthy family has, which Laila inevitably did but with a difference because unlike him, she was not the boss there.

'Ahem!' he coughed, clearing his throat and tapping his finger on his huge wooden table. 'What are you doing over this week end?'

Mentally fatigued and unprepared for his opening line, she said, 'Week end?' She scratched her left arm genteelly mulling over the reply. 'Is this old man asking me out? I rather commit suicide . . . than . . .' she pictured herself wearing a pretty dress in a coffee shop with a fifty-five-year old, rather young and married boss. 'I travel.' She replied. He raised one of his eyebrows.

'I travel to meet . . .' She paused in hesitation.

'A man.' He remarked sarcastically, 'is that true? And on Sundays you must be visiting the Chruch, isn't it?' He looked away in anger. 'The next time you lie, remember to keep the age of the person in mind you are lying to. I must be . . . double your age." he clenched his teeth," I have given thousands such explanations to catch a lie like this one."

'A boy. I . . . visit,' she raised her eyes to meet his, 'a ten year old cancer patient, I meet him every Saturday.'

Alexander's froze. 'His chemotherapy is . . .' she licked her lips, 'it makes him . . . SICK. He . . . vomits chronically and sweats and . . . screams in . . . the pain-of-the-treatment. Chemotherapy is the last resort, if your are aware, to save a patient suffering from leukemia. He . . . has blood cancer. Too young to . . . he has lost all his hair and happiness. Imagine being ten and knowing that . . . anyways, his days are numbered. His name is Sanskrit.'

Alexander was taken aback and still not fully believing her, he asked, 'so you play the nurse?'

'No.' she replied calmly to his sarcasm. 'The doctor and the mentor. And yes, the nurse . . . when his mother is not around. One can't ignore a needy . . . one shouldn't. "she paused with awareness and said, "I pay for his treatment. And if that is not enough," her voice displayed hurt, "and if that is not enough," she said opening her hand bag, "these are the hospital bills for your scrutiny . . . . Alexander."

"Oh I didn't mean . . . it . . ." Said Alexander quickly covering up for venting his frustration on her finding her to be a soft target and because he lied frequently, he assumed so did Laila. A mistake we all commit with people, especially the one younger to us or innocent, whether or not they do wrong we target them with the same presumption, either to ease our frustration or to allege. It feels good, to bring somebody on the same pedestal as us, which unknowingly turns us into a sadist, the one who draws happiness from seeing somebody suffer.

'I know.' She replied, for she knew he was covering up instead of saying a simple sorry but she had faith, that those who knowingly take advantage of innocent, a day arrives when their own life suffers the same battering, as they made others suffer. And for the time being, she stayed serene.

'I had a child too, some twenty years back, when I was . . .' he said with empathy for Sanskrit. 'Around your age. He died.'

"Ooh! M sorry to hear that. What happened? How?" she asked forgetting the hurt of his sarcasm. That's how pure she was in her objective of helping a needy, in the slum or the one around with antiques.

'He had respiratory problem.' He replied with a deep sorrow that he lived with for rest of his life.

'Was it a mal functioning heart or a hole in it.' she enquired on impulse.

"I don't know. The doctors mentioned respiratory problem. It's hereditary. It runs in the family." He answered with confusion in his mind and agitation, in his body.

'Is that why you never had another child?' she asked with concern. He knitted his eyebrows.

'How do you, out of everybody know that I don't have a child?' he probed alarmingly.

"I . . . ." she paused, "umm . . . if you did have one, he/she would have accompanied you to . . . work. Or at least found a mention somewhere by some body . . . around . . . here."

'This,' he said turning a small black and white photograph of a baby, in a silver photo frame that faced him on his desk, 'is him.'

Laila held the frame and looked at it. 'So cute. Was it a boy, Alexander?'

'Yes.' He spoke with much effort. 'Eisher, was his name. He was my child from my first marriage.'

195

'Nice.' She said, 'his smile dimples in the corner like mine.' And she handed back his photograph. He too smiled for he had noticed it during the interview itself, that her smile bore a strong resemblance to her dead son. 'He looks like you.' She added.

'Ya. That is true. I . . . but anyways . . . I want you take out time and come . . . .'

'You fear.' She spoke in between. He avoided eye contact with her and the master of diplomacy went quiet. 'When we fear and not attempt something, we ruin the chances of it's success, completely.' He was listening. 'Are you aware of the advances medical science has made in detecting pre natal, natal and further ailments in a fetus and how easily it can be rectified. It will cost you peanuts for the tests to be conducted on . . .'

'I don't need it for God's sake. I don't.' he trembled. 'Please come along with me . . .' saying so he was about to get up and Laila spoke.

'And Laura?' she asked bluntly. 'What about her? Or is she like one among us, who follows u by the word, out of compulsion or out of fear of facing your wrath? And don't say, you don't want it . . . that's a lie, because you do. You do want a baby, who you can love as much as you love Eisher, till today.'

He was looking up somewhere at the walls and then looked at her, though not in her eyes. 'There is a photograph exhibition in town, at the Taj. Lynn Radheka and Suvo Das will be displaying their work. You may come along. Watching is also learning.' He spelled it all at once and got up from his chair. Suddenly and gently he looked in her eyes and said, 'and I promise, I will get Laura back to my life. 'He took a deep breath and said, 'you may leave now.'

'I wish the best for you and your wife, Alexander. You are a nice person, may God lead you to harmony.' she responded getting up to leave.

'And before I forget,' he said enthusiastically, 'the pictures . . .'

She interjected, 'Do you know why the shore pushed the tide back,' she drew a breath, 'because it tries to engulf her. She needs her own space.' There was a silence.

'The pictures have come out well.' he said and narrowed his eyesbrows, 'You have improved in six month's time.' Laila smiled. 'This is for you.' He said giving her a small teddy bear with a box of choicest sweets, a personal gesture from him. 'Wish you a Happy Diwali. Have a nice time and God bless you.' Laila's spirit soared high. She sprang out of the room on to her desk and from there darted out. On her way back she stopped by a confectionary shop and celebrated the festival, a day in advance and also her success, in her own company, for nobody else would have been as happy as she was for herself, nobody who she knew.

Alexander did not fly to Italy but he did turn up at the exhibition wearing a corn coloured blazer over a stone washed light blue jeans, a leather footwear and a limited edition watch by UlysesNardine, worth a crore. He strolled through the gallery with his square shoulders jutting out like that of a heavy weight boxer, dignified and sturdy. Bystanders gave way like they did to a star with a belief that they were worth nothing before him, why then should they block his way? If they attempted, he could pick them up like a fly form a glass of milk, flicking them aside. Laila was watching how well he knew to sway the crowd and quietly threw his weight around. Sensibly and out of respect, she took a step back letting him lead from the front.' Phenomenal piece of work from a regular camera comes only to the exceptionally talented,' he said complementing Suvo Das shaking hands with him. 'Not many can create the same magic through their lens. Extaraordinary and outstanding, two words that I can use for your creativity.' And, 'divine' he said complementing the other senior photographer Lynn Radheka, 'you are above the rest Lynn.' Generous yet distant, he praised them both, following which he made a quick exit with the entourage of six men, his two body guards and Laila.

'From our shoes, on our wrist, by colours, through our smile, by our walk and through our words, we do leak who we essentially are and how life has treated us,' thought Laila to herself as she sat with him, the chauffer and his body guards on his B.M.W. to be driven home, after dropping him at his residence.

Abruptly he spoke as his car pulled at his residence, 'beautiful women,' and he looked to be in a good mood, 'marry either very early . . . or,' he sniggered while the chauffer opened the door, 'they marry late.'

'Really?' She smiled in wonder thought, he was yet to make a point, of which she was unaware. "This, must be the most happening discovery after that of America?" She remarked politely.

'Thank God,' He said looking up at the sky, 'I caught Laura early,' and he got off the swanky machine that made people drool.' You see! 'he spoke the man with experience, "when they are young they are innocent . . . ."

"You mean, easy to manipulate." She clarified with an agreeable face. "But shouldn't we remember, what goes around comes around."

He laughed. "Don't you leak this secret," he advised her and then said to the chauffer. "Take her home safely. She is a nice girl."

She got his point, that was his frustration and this time for the fact that his money couldn't charm a girl as good as her. 'May God help him get back with her wife,' she said to him in her mind. 'But I am sure she must be born with special stars,' she said to Alexander as the car's wheels rolled, 'to get a man as special as you,' to which he was happier than she had fathomed him to be, as flattery was his favorite dish of all seasons, of his life.

'You remind me of her all the time-' he remarked and waved at her as the car began to drive away.

"M sure, she must be missing you rather longing to be back with you." She replied promptly. There was a purpose to her words, because there was a need for him to be reminded of his marriage and that of his promise, to bring her wife back to his life instead of giving in to charms outside his marriage.

A year later, another exhibition was held, this one was inaugurated by the gorgeous and dimpled bollywood actoress, Preity Zinta, who spared her precious time to stand for the cause. She set the rhythm of the exhibition with her grace and kindness for the humanitarian cause of the exhibition.

Accepting the invite and wearing her electric blue high heels going with a navy blue halter neck dress flowing down to the ground came, another star of the day, Laila. If looks could kill she would have to be put behind bars, for she unleashed genocide at the crowd that had gathered for the exhibition. Standing next to Alexander at the entrance was Alexander and his wife, Laura Chabbra another siren who swung the press, wearing a crimson figure hugging short dress with kitten heels to remain under her husband's height.

The exhibition was of her paintings as an professional artist, making her debut through the exhibition. Laura was showered with compliments and she earned a fair price for it too. The press went bananas writing reviews of her paintings and of her beauty that was as fascinating as was her talent to sell it at a good price. The collection of the money earned went to the treatment of children suffering with cancer and Sanskrit became one of the fortunate beneficiaries. There was a smile on every face present and also on those who weren't, but were to benefit from the charity. Beauty indeed is, as beauty does and this beauty, did her part to being a smile on the faces of those who need her love and financial help, for their treatment.

Addressing the press meet that followed the inauguration of her exhibition, said Alexander, "there was a time when I didn't believe in God and," he said holding a baby girl in his right arm and a blonde baby boy in another, "today I see God in my arms. Ladies and gentlemen, these are my two children Shimmer and Shaurya, a twins born to my ravishing wife, who made me a better man, a man who loves her for who she is and for what she does for her happiness. And behind every successful man is a woman and behind me as you see is this woman," he paused to bring Laila to the front, "she is Laila for the world and for me she is

God." There was a loud buzz in the crowd. "And for me too." announced Laura stepping up to the microphone. "My wife, me and my children will always thank God for her and for this day, when I can give my wife, a life she dreamt of and these special twins. M proud, to be a doting new father, at fifty five years of my age. And the lines that changed my life was, "there is enough for everyone's need; there is not enough for everyone's greed." These famous lines from the IshaUpnishad were recited to me by Laila." The crowd clapped in appreciation as Alexander broke down in tears. The tears of regret were cleansing and healing as Liala smiled over him. And the clapping became louder.

"Thanku all for joining us for a cause and encouraging my work." Laura spoke in between taking her turn to the address the press, 'and thanku Laila, for all the joy, happiness and wisdom you gave us. Thank You for teaching me what Buddha taught, that we should live in moderation in harmony that springs from being in touch with our soul. We love you to death.' Laila bowed to accept their appreciation with her hands joined together in humility. She thanked the divine master within her for the love and respect she was being rained with.

Alexander was shining like a freshly picked apple; plum and full of spiritual passion. And taking his appreciation further, he made Laura the photographer in charge of Brazentine's cover and giving her a good raise. Improving her comfort, he gave her an accommodation on the Carter road facing the crescent bay of Arabian sea, and also a chauffeur driven car, which she cordially refused by her as per the guidance of the divine master within her. Instead she accepted a gift from her father for her achievement; dependable and sporty Honda. The divine master within her took her to yet another level in her life; Laila was now the highly regarded photographer of Brazentine and was looked up by the photographers she regarded as her inspiration, including VarunChawla.

And also from this time on, she got in tune with the divine masters within her.

———◆———

Chapter 7

Selfishness is wisdom, beingignoble and small minded, fatal.

Calling it a night, Laila excused herself from the party that was to go on until morning. Though happy, nonetheless she was exhausted by the sleepless nights she had spent to keep up Alexander's trust in her efficiency alive. He didn't know a word about the file disappearing from her laptop. She said. 'The picture we clicked in Goa was not half as good as this one . . . and certainly not anywhere close to get us distinction for our readers.' Alexander believed her, because this picture boosted the image of the magazine par excellence. Brazentine, set a mark for its quality and style, both of which were close to Alexander's expectations and dreams that he was savoring tonight, for his magazine.

Laila headed towards the driveway. Her driver, Ravinder was on leave that night. She could clearly hear the tic-tac of her heels on the cemented driveway as she made her way to the car. The lights were dim in that area.

'I should never have been born,' said the wailing woman in a miserable voice, wearing a red cocktail dress and shiny black heels laying semiconscious next to Laila's car, that night. 'Never.' She repeated, as Laila bent low to see who she was.

'The only thing that should have never happened,' said Laila bending down to push a lock of her hair behind her ears, gently, 'is an addiction of alcohol.' She opened the door of her car and put the woman in to shelter her from the cold winter wind. 'I will drive you home . . . I think so, but you will have to tell me where to take you.'

'I don't want to go home,' said the woman slumped in the back seat of Laila's car. 'Get me out.' She said giving her hand to Laila. To this Laila shut the door and sat on the driver's seat not heeding her demands. 'Throw me somewhere on the way. It's easy . . . you do it. I shall help you.' She couldn't see Laila's reaction. She was trying to recognize her as Laila was watching, her eyes fluttering lifelessly.

'You need to sleep and so do I.' She told her and then asked her, 'are you carrying any identification . . . your driver's license?'

'You get me out or I will jump . . . . when you drive . . . ,' She said to Laila with a slur in her voice.

'You will what?' Laila smirked and was reconsidering her decision of driving her along with herself as she felt their safety was at risk. She was alone in the driveway and also the only woman in her senses. She could hear a bunch of men from the party smoking in a group, at a hundred feet away from her. But asking for help for a drunken woman didn't seem plausible to her as neither was leaving her alone. 'Taking help from right person is being wise, but here there seems no respite on this line. Where do I take her . . . ?' she asked herself. 'Where do you live . . . . any phone number . . . uum . . . location? Building number or name of your society? Anything?' she asked the woman whose eyes were closed lifelessly and her arms flinging helplessley was dangling from the back seat. 'I know you can't answer but I have to ask you. My mind is tired, it doesn't work. I haven't slept for days so I have to ask you to direct me to where I can drive you to.' There was no reply, so Laila turned back to her position and stared across at the bumper of her car. 'Oh, by the way . . . where is your hand bag? Am sure you must be carrying one, you seem to have a appealing dressing sense, your footwear is perfect with your dress but where is the accessory,' saying this Laila rolled down the window of the adjacent seat and looked down at the tiny pebbles of the driveway. She spotted a red clutch purse, taking off her high heels in her car she got down, and picked it up. 'Got it.' Said Laila rejoicing as she opened it. 'Unbeliveable, I guess that's your style. How did she get in here. Just a red lipstick, a mirror and a comb. No pepper spray, no identity proof. Now this's gonna lead us just one way.' she mumbled and got back to her seat and backed her car.

'What noise was that under my wheels?' She said alarmingly as she heard something crackle, which gave her front wheel a slight bump. She pulled over and got off, the third time with physical aches in her very tired body. 'Good Lord! Her cell phone,' she held her head in her hand along with the woman's dismantled mobile phone that she gripped like sand, 'it's gone.' She drove away from the drive way with the woman sleeping like a log in the back seat of the car. 'The roads are awfully clear at this time of the night. And good she is asleep. Atleast I can drive her to where I want.' She remarked. 'I have less to think about, thank God.'

The next morning with the sunshine galloping in the room, Laila got up an hour before the woman. 'You move very well like the wind, so smooth and agile. What moves,' said Laila breaking the ice, standing at the door as the woman got up and looked around in disbelief. 'Don't be dazed, I got you here.'

'I am not a dancer. I was filling up for the girl who couldn't turn up and you are Laila.' Said the woman mildly cheered to wake up on the celebrity's bed with the celebrity of the last night standing opposite her, leaning against the wall. 'The woman with maximum applause. It was deafening.' She smiled weekly.

Laila smiled and said in a singing mode. 'Yes, I am Laila. By the way what happened to the dancer? You were answering to that while you lay semiconscious.'

'She stopped coming . . . . any how and this is so surreal,' exclaimed the woman in a groggy yet happy voice. 'That was stupendous, marvelous work. I clapped enormously for you. How could you create something that perfect.'

'Thanku!' she replied politely. 'That work was the outcome of pressure and God's grace. Tell me, when you got drunk and what was not working with you because when alcohol mixes in a woman's life it implies that she is looking sadly to her success and sadly to her love.' The woman still not fully awake, didn't reply. 'Taking alcohol is like self immolating oneself in a false hope of being safe somehow. I believe the absent dancer was you . . . and why was there such a ruckus yesterday . . . when you announced to your team about the lead dancer being absent.'

The woman's tired body felt numb, and a somewhat ashamed of being on Laila's bed, like an uninvited guest. She smelled her own breath; it reeked of previous night's innumerable drinks. 'I will clean your bed sheet and the pillow cover . . . it reeks of . . . my lack of wisdom unlike your.' With her head swaying she responded after long. She had big eyes and a chubby face, a clean skin and textured hair to her shoulder level. Her body was lean, unlike her face.

'We can never be as wise as somebody because every life is different and as far as washing is concerned that's very thoughtful of you, but thanks,' said Laila moving ahead in her direction. 'It's not required. Besides my question remains unanswered.'

The woman moved backward, shrinking her legs towards herself in discomfort and shame. Laila realized the woman was giving up on life and was shaken by major trouble of years, in a slow but steady manner. Her smile had an innocent glow which was a clue of whom she was born as and who she was being pushed to become due to lack of support and faith. 'There is nothing to be ashamed of. You were drunk, and that's an habit which one can get rid of provided,' she said gesturing at the woman, 'you decide to get on with life and sort it out. By the way what's your name?'

'Sofia Sharma.' She replied nursing her hangover.

'Sofia was a saint, do you know that?' said Laila softly, to which Sofia looked surprised. 'And if she wasn't, I mean just in case you are not willing to believe me, you can become one. It's never too late to become a seeker of God for all that you have to do is take life positively as a way of God to give you a rich experience of life. Take everything positively and become a seeker of God.' Sofia smiled first time in years, happy to be herself. 'I have kept a set of clothes for you. Take a bath and join me for breakfast. We will eat together,' said Laila to which Sofia dragged herself up, picked up the clothes and did as asked.

On the breakfast table, wearing a bright yellow racer back top and stripped lose pants, she joined Laila. It suited the Mumbai's heat and her carefree personality to the hilt. She pulled the chic matt finished steel chair and was drying her hair in the sunrays dancing in with the breeze from the sea.

'You are comfortable in your clothes?' Laila asked sitting on a chair away from her letting her breathe in peace in her own company.

'Very much,' she answered putting her fingers through her hair in a serpentine movement to drain the water droplets. 'It fits me like a dream.'

'Years back I bought it in a hurry, from Milan.' Laila spoke forwarding acorn, spinach and cheese sandwich with a glass of orange juice, to her. 'It didn't fit me. I wondered why I picked it, but I didn't chuck it. I didn't feel like. And today, I realized it was for you. You can keep it with yourself.' Sofia was pleasantly surprised, then Laila spoke. 'You see, Saint Sofia, it takes time for us to realize the larger picture and it takes patience and nineteen months as in this case, to unravel the mystery of life like that of this garment.'

'Thanku for everything.' Said Sofia, direct from her heart as she accepted her breakfast plate, from Laila's hand into her's. 'And you were right that woman dancer, was me. That's my passion.'

'Thank God instead,' said replied, 'because my dear Sofia, my mother says and I believe, that every time we thank God, He gives us more chances of it. And if you try saying this to your spouse, he would be the happiest man alive on the vast earth,' she whispered, 'atleast for that one moment.'

'Then I thank God for you.' She said sweetly and looking at her sandwich her eyes popped out and she curled her lips inward in thoughts.

'M touched,' said Laila playfully. 'Now, tell me, and of course you can keep eating along side and so will I, what's the issue with you? And before I progress, I would like to mention, that life fails everybody. There's nothing new about it and also that we need to get our act together instead of running away from it . . . you know what I mean. This self mortification will not do you any good. Eat to your heart's content and live life king size, away from alcohol.'

"Hmm . . ." she whispered and pouted, lost in thoughts. Gradually she began to open up, "I am . . . a Salsa dancer to begin with the obvious,' she paused, 'and I am thirty two. And 'm married, with my wedding band missing from my finger.' Her voice had a miserable calmness, as if every breath were weighing heavy on her.

'So among these three, where is the bump in your life?' She asked nibbling her sandwich. Sofia was unsure where to begin explaining, so Laila kept quiet giving her time and her space, for she was new to her as much she was to eating cheese which she was fishing out gradually. 'Are you ok with the cheese?'

'Umm . . .' she gave a wry smile, 'sort of.' She was resting one elbow on the glass table and with the other she was checking if her hair had dried.

'I understand,' said Laila, 'that cheese part, that you aren't very cheesy.' And to this both of them laughed. And come on if your marriage is troubled, we will sort it out. Yours isn't the only marriage that has hit the rock. It happens overtly or covertly to every marriage. It's not unthinkable but what is thinkable is that marriage works on compromise. The more deeply you understand it, the simpler it gets to sort it out on your part."

'Why shall I compromise Laila?' she whined taking her elbow away from the table. 'I have had enough of him. It's a fuckin' pain . . . you know how he treats me . . . He escapes me as if I were a deadly spider on his shoulder. He isn't the man I fell in love with.'

'You mean he looks different now?' Laila chuckled at her expression. 'Yeah men and wine improve with time,' she spoke in a lively and light mood. 'Sofia Sharma, no man remains the same after marriage and neither does the woman, we all take a break from courtship years and thus we try to take rest in marriage, in which we take each other for granted.' She looked calmly at her. 'Cut your expectations and be more of a generous supplier of love than an ugly demander,' and she took a bite out of her sandwich which changed her voice making it sound stuffy. "You know, we all desire happy and satisfying relationship, believing that our friends got luckier than us in terms of the man. When we see a happy couple we are jealous, believing that their marriage is perfect by fluke. My dear, saint Sofia,' and she waited to gulp the chewed sandwich, 'no relationship works without compromise. They all compromise, ranging from accepting their spouse way of talking, to the way he puts his mouth on the bottles from the fridge . . . to the way he ogles at women . . . etc.; accept it. We can't have our way always. We are so full of flaws ourselves that improving it can well take years. It's wiser, if we evolve and accept the way we are, first. Then there would be less of forced acceptance and manipulations from your end. Suppose, I may not love extra cheese in my burger, and my man desires it, so will I throw a rage if he demands it? Be more loving and tending then, you will understand better.'

'No.' she said timidly.

'That's it,' she said, 'ignore it. And work on your flaws. Respect the God in him and get respect in return.'

'Hmm . . . I guess so . . .' she said. 'But what if he doesn't respect me, then too.'

'In that case your soul and the divine master within you shall help you,' said Laila clearly. 'Please keep eating. Why show temper to the food when the real issue is something else. And Sofia, no matter how the world or your spouse is, we need to keep a check over our thoughts and our deeds. And then take my word for it, the divine master within you will help you inevitably for if you develop a sense of gratitude towards God then you will get closer to your soul. Then you wouldn't have to ask for guidance, you shall receive it.'

Sofia smiled like a little girl, 'I . . . sort of don't nag all the time but I do get demanding. It gets on my nerves to stand . . . him.'

'Heay! Heay! Hey!,' said Laila, 'check that line . . . you must be getting on his nerves too . . . somebody has to step back. Why not you? If he is not living in awareness . . . he will suffer. You check your deeds.'

'But, Laila, he doesn't care what I feel.' She answered in irritation. 'I know now that both of us falter. I think I am demanding . . . and thus destroyed.'

'See, believe it or not it's good not to demand and live in peace. And thank you for confessing,' said Laila, as happy as a fresh Tulip. 'Confessions are an easy way to work on our flaws and to improve it. And as for your demands, men feel happy to fulfill our demands, we should let them be. They enjoy it, as long as . . .' her speech slowed, 'as long as they are not compelled for it. You see, otherwise that kind of gift does damage to a marriage. Be happy with what you have.' She flicked her hand and said. 'Come here,' and she pulled her close, 'and dear Sofia trashy lingerie, are also among the biggest killer of a happy and satisfying relationship, my fair lady.'

Sofia giggled. 'So mine are trashy?' she asked controlling her laughter on her plight while accepting in a way. 'And if I may ask, how so?'

'It's . . . not interesting. It doesn't show you are making an effort to please him. Life is about give-and-take, said the Buddha. Where is the give in your case. It's not Karmic just to take,' said Laila in a as a matter-of-fact attitude though keeping the mood light as she was sensitive to Sofia's plight. 'It conveys to your man you are not interested in him. Is that not sad for somebody you love?' she spoke with a composure. 'You see, fun in marriage lasts till the time the man and the woman always apply the wisdom of give-and-take. Be selfish at times and be generous in other times. Give in to the duality.'

'So wearing a pretty lingerie will do him good?' she enquired running her finger around her glass of juice.

'Do him good? umm . . .' said Laila recalling subjects form the family therapy days at St. Allan's, 'and would it not do any good to . . . you. Is that what you are asking me? Grow up!'

'No, but . . .' she said cryptically.

'We shouldn't take love for granted,' said Laila in a way of recalling an anecdote from her past.

'I get it.' She accepted pleasantly. 'I have seen him flipping through my magazines and thoroughly enjoying it. It felt nasty to me."

Laila laughed, 'what's not right with that, there are men who do much more than flipping through the pages of a girl's magazine. That's a stress buster. Let him enjoy. Tell you what, the urban India is living in a dichotomy between what was blasphemous a few decades back and what is the need today, like a pretty lingerie and meditation, one takes care of our exterior appearance and other of inner evolvement. Nobody will tell you, but it's because of stress that one needs to be alert and wise. Prevention is always better than cure, which some people realize it much later, maybe when it's too late in life to do anything about it. Why not we enjoy our way and let them enjoy their way. It just a minor compromise which keeps us karmic. Stress is to a relationship as was the Osama Bin Laden to America—detrimental. But then there are those among us who are wise enough to step back and, irrespective of our daily stress, make the extra effort to love our partners."

Sofia cringed and explained, 'when deadlines are waiting and when the bosses' whip is lurking around, it's hard to think of love. Money and work they consume all our time and life and thus we let stress corrode relationship. We shouldn't carry an unpleasant day at work, into the relationship. He can't lash out on his boss so inevitably, he will unload it on you and you the vice versa. And then you will . . . get drunk. What good will that do to you.' Sofia looked like a statue, hearing every word carefully without any movement. 'Only a wise woman succeeds in saving the relationship as only she knows that, stress has to be dealt wisely, which will enable us to hold on to each other, come what may. That saves the marriage.' Sofia kept absorbing Laila's words and stared at her sandwich and then she spoke.

'Isn't it an out right compromise to stand such tantrums,' she proclaimed coldly. 'It's an endless series, like his test cricket match. And isn't he taking me for granted?'

'When we make honest efforts, our partner feels it.' she explained. 'You were in for love, so stay with it. Do you get my point? Also you have to believe in nurturing the divine master within you through meditation. His power to heal our relationship is immense.'

'Yes,' she said and smiled genteelly. 'I can picture that somewhere . . . . sort of . . . The times when I have been sorted out in love, I was happy. That was when I did as my soul guided me to and that's how we got married.'

'Yes, now you get me right, saint Sofia,' said Laila with a faint smile. 'In the world fraught with ugly disturbances, it's only heeding our soul that will and that does bring respite to us.'

Sofia went back to her husband and a month later she called Laila to thank her for her wise guidance. She and her man, meditated daily and were a happy and cuddled up couple in five months, time. Sofia had pulled her expectations low and let the joy of love go deep in her.

But on the same day, their conversation had proceeded while they were still on their breakfast table, reaching yet another height.

'I will do the dishes.' Said Sofia.

'Dishes?' It startled her, 'you wanted to clean my bed sheets, and now you want to do the dishes . . . .' Laila looked disturbed. 'Who made you feel so unloved?' Sofia began to fidget. 'I hope you don't treat your child the same way.'

'I don't have a child.' She answered in very polite regret, 'I had two miscarriages, right after my marriage . . . ummm . . . one after a year of my marriage and then the next year.'

'You believe in God?' she asked her categorically, 'I know this is an abrupt question, but it's important.'

'Yes.' She said looking at Laila, 'I do . . .'

'So now you have to change your approach because from now on you are wise.' She spoke lovingly as she it was apparent to her that Sofia lacked self love though was a kind soul. 'It means, you have to learn the virtue called detachment and which is why God took away both your unborn children. Hez taken them back. They are safe, don't worry. This world is cruel for them, so they are very safe where ever they are.' Sofia shed some tears and with her eyelids half open she smiled. 'That's the spirit. The wise takes life as learning not as a sad story but as a hurdle racer, they jump and cross the hurdles and then comes the smooth track.' And she gave her throat a break from nonstop talking and spoke after sometime until then Sofia was mulling over her words.

'Do you know somebody . . . ?' Laila asked her.

'Who?' Sofia asked.

'Somebody,' said Laila, with an expression of narrating a ghost's story, 'who has never suffered?'

'No, I don't.' She responded quickly.

She spoke peacefully. 'And yet there are wise people who are never sad, do you know why?" she said looking at her own long fingers." Because, they live with faith. They draw positive messages from life and that's the belief that leads them to eternal happiness.'

'Oh! WoW,' said Sofia clapping without sound, 'I never thought of that. I heard that word, say a thousand times before but, I believed, it was something mystical, you know, something spiritual that's beautiful but unattainable.' She looked away and said, 'I never thought, it was about our approach towards our life.'

'It's is simple,' said Laila with a candid expression, 'It's is about our own approach towards our life and about our faith in God. More the faith the more positive you shall remain.'

Sofia drew a deep and long breath, 'marriages works though compromise and through endless love and lust,' she said agreeably.

'Don't make it sound that dirty, saint Sofia-' said Laila playfully. 'But are you by any chance to give a second thought to it. Are you thinking something else for . . . you still look confused in your head, though less than before.'

'How did you know that?' she asked with her energy dipping again. 'Yes, I am.'

'I will tell you something,' said Laila wisely, 'the people who jump relationships perpetually are cowards. They realize later that there are no such thing as perfect partners, what there is, is compromise and adjustments, being selfish at times and generous at others. And if they don't see this truth, they suffer and keep suffering until they come to the same realization as you do today. Compromise, love and mutual respect, remain the key word of a successful relationship.' They both sat in silence. 'Go saint Sofia, finish your breakfast and call your man. And press the restart button of your relationship,' said Laila.

'Don't you have to go for work?' She enquired relishing her sandwich and opening heart fully to Laila's wisdom.

'Nope,' said Laila, 'it's a Sunday. Vivian, will wake up. I will make his sandwich. And sorry about your cell phone . . .' Laila, unsure of how she would take that loss, said, 'It got crushed under my wheels . . . what I could save was your clutch bag, but I couldn't do much about your cell phone. Your SIM card is kept inside your clutch purse which is laying next to the land line, there in the living room . . . umm.'

'Detachment,' she interjected. 'So it went for my good. I was getting clingy with it, protecting it all the time, as fancy phones are high maintenance. I have more to maintain now, then that phone. Besides, it kept me away from God. I thought more of it and less of God which is a landmine of my spiritual life. So good it's crushed. I will have less to worry about.' She smiled humbly with kind eyes. 'Can I help you make your child's breakfast?'

'Yes, now you can help me with it as you now will be doing it out of happiness and not as a liability,' replied Laila with equal kindness to her. 'But I would be glad if you could please call your husband and tell him you are here. Please.'

"Umm . . . ." she said hurriedly finishing her meal and wiping the cheese on the corner of her mouth, 'Fine. I shall do that.' She felt happy to find love and acceptance in the wild. She did make the call and while Vivian got up and was merrily gulping down his glass of milk, the door bell rang.

'You keep sitting here, finish your meal and go to the bed room. Please, be a good boy as you are.' She said ruffling his hair lovingly as she rushed to attend the door.

'Hi!' said the lanky teenager, wearing a basketball vest and longs shorts with sneakers and he barged in with another man, older than him, chubby and small eyed. Both were tall and looked troubled.

'Where is Sofie?' enquired the elder man. 'I am her brother.'

'I see. Hellow! She is there in the kitchen.' Laila replied pointing at the kitchen.

'I will sit.' And he uncouthly sat on the lounge setter, 'please ask to come over here.' He said and so did the boy though he sat closer to the piano and distant from his father. It a natural human tendency to sit closer to who and what brings them comfort, that's a subconscious decision. Laila didn't approve of her brother's curtness and as she walked to fetch Sofia who on her own came forward, casually.

'Oh! Hi!' she said to her brother. 'Well, she is my friend Laila, a star photographer working with Brazentine and Laila he is . . .'

'I know,' she replied firmly. Sofia understood her mind and sensed that her brother must have displayed rudeness towards her, a perpetual habit of his with her friends too.

'And he is my nephew, Tahir.' She said introducing him to her with grace using her hand. 'Tahir, she is Laila.'

'I heard that.' He replied. Sofia looked at Laila and her eyelids dropped in embarrassment. Both the father and son duo looked here and there as though, they hunted something that was within them.

'We were looking at Sofia's pictures, in the memory card. She is great at her work,' said Laila initiating the conversation, even when she least desired to speak. 'She looked so glamourous and hot in her red outfit . . . and . . . what a talent . . . a typical salsa . . .'

'Ugly women look hot.' Said Tahir, 'they have to for who else will notice them.'

'Shut up. You will need dentures very young if you speak like that again.' yelled his father and he looked at Laila, "Don't mind his mouth. Something come with age . . . only.'

The boy smirked, 'ya they do, like your wrinkle son your face and your gargantuan paunch. They are a gift of your age to you.'

His father got up and slapped him hard. 'First you ate your mother and now you are eating me . . . you should have been done away with at your birth. Bastard.' He said.

Laila froze with contempt towards his reaction and cutting him from his temper she intervened. 'I am sorry, I didn't get your name, sir.' She said looking at his father, 'please sit down. Please calm down. This is an age; teenagers are a confused lot, it requires patience to deal with them.'

'You ate my mother, I didn't. Look at the size of your stomach.' Tahir remarked with hurt. It seemed that father was getting the fruits of the etiquettes he had set forth as an example to his child, to begin with. She could well imagine their plight at their home.

His father half rose from his seat again and said, 'who are you talking to? You unobliged child form a cursed . . . '

'Patience,' said Laila to him, 'it's ok. He is just a kid. He doesn't require all those foul words. Please.' He father mumbled and looked at Sofia with equal disgust.

Tahir left his seat and went to the piano. 'Is this your?' he asked Laila without looking in her direction and excitedly opening the key board cover.

'Yes. That's mine,' she replied overlooking his etiquettes, 'my mother gifted it. She had taught me play the piano, saying we should pursue hobbies that doesn't require people. I tried the guitar too . . . . but . . . '

'It's hurts the finger,' he interjected and turned to look at her. 'I can play the guitar and this, the piano. I want to . . . I can play well.'

'You fuckin don't start with your show off every where, now that's not what we are here for,' said his father. 'Who cares to hear what you play and how you play. You damned creature, wriggle back to your seat. Anybody can play a piano . . . don't you show off here.'

'It isn't easy to play a piano. The keys are very heavy,' said Laila to his father, 'I wonder if you tried your hands at it? It seems a lot easier than it is.'

'I don't have a taste for all this . . . it's rubbish,' he said clutching his left knee in his hands.

'What do you have a taste for?' asked Sofia standing next to Laila against the wall.

'For ruining people. He has a taste for harassing. Anybody good and nice suffers in his hands . . . he compels them to be cruel. His elder brother and you, aunt Sofia . . . didn't he kick you away once he made money," said Tahir openly enraged and blatantly bitter with revolt.

A revolution needs a revolt and a revolt is fed by extreme anger and pain, as in Tahir's case. He was the revolutionary with a voice, like the great, the revered and the very young Bhagat Singh who lost his life, for us to breathe in freedom and happiness.

'He is the one who tormented you, forgetting how you guys were by him in his hard times because for him everybody turns into being a pain once his purpose gets fulfilled. He is a sadist.' He looked at Sofia, 'it must be a disgrace to have a sibling like him . . . sad it's terribly, terribly sad. I know all his moves . . . and don't be surprised if I am killed for being who I am because he, my father wants me to be as nice as he is visually, as capable as he is in tormenting people and as small minded and brute as he is in person. How can I be him?It requires so much negative talent. So death awaits me everyday.' Sofia looked up at the ceiling trying to be strong but the tears of agony from her past began to roll down her cheeks. 'He is full of greed that will eat him the way he ate my mother, Yasir uncle and you.

God will bring us justice, He will. He saved me from him and he will bless us with harmony in our lives.' Her brother got up, gave a dirty smile and left leaving the room in nerve chilling silence like a dry summer afternoon, with hot wind and spiteful stillness. Sofia wept inconsolably.

'He made me feel worthless,' she said bravely wiping her tears, 'and that ate me. My confidence ebbed since then. I didn't want to trouble him . . . but I didn't know how to handle him either. So, I moved away . . .'

'Oh, dear,' said the boy, 'if to such people you show your goodness and kindness, they will keep you under their feet because they don't understand what they put people through and what goodness is. His greed doen't have a soul so he can't sympathize nor can he care unless he sees a need. He can only kill.' Laila in her mind thought how life forced the boy to cope up with so much harshness at home, a place one goes to find peace and love, shelter and care, guidance and grace.

'It's not just greed,' said Laila gesturing to Sofia to sit down, 'it's insecurity. Insecurity is the father of comparison and deceitful greed.' Such a greed is nefarious and so are the people with such greed. A hungry vulture is better, it eats the dead while people with blind greed can kill the dying. That's their temperament and a hunger which gives them the courage to kill the dying and thrive from sucking their life away. 'Tahir, calm down. Hitler conquered through savagery, he gassed people alive, he tore apart lives. He lived with intense fear that savagery begets. What happened to his success. He shot himself in his head, the same head that fed his desire to ruthlessly decide people's fate. He put a bullet through the same head that made people say, "Hail Hitler" (Long live Hitler) neither did Hitler live long nor does treacherous greed because a power higher than them keeps order and puts an end to the victimization by such people. So you calm boy, you have a long way to go. Live with faith and be wise. Be selfish and nurture your soul, then God shall lead you for that is why he gifted you talent of being a creative musician . . . pursue it and gradually you shall see your life being happy.'

'I am ok' ll see you later, I gotta go.' Said Tahir, 'and I will play the piano the next time I meet you.'

'Where are you going to?' asked Sofia through her tears, with concern.

'To become a worthless singer.' He chuckled.

'Priceless not worthless,' said Laila. 'Are you heading to a recording studio?'

'Nope!' came the reply from him. 'I . . . well you guys will . . . laugh.'

'No. We wouldn't,' said Sofia reassuring him.

'It's a date,' he replied with a wink. 'I will go to my friend's home and change into crisp outfit, shave and spray some cologne; I will borrow his and then off to dating. She is cute and tall.' They smiled at the boy's innocence. 'Now don't waste my time, you guys. I wanna be a singer,' he said holding an imaginary mike in his hand, 'and guess what, I went to this music producer, seven times in a week and for months unending,' his face became grim, 'the ninth time I entered his office tipping his guard generously, his daughter, this girl bumped into me . . . rest you can picture. I will leave you guys, here. Oh! Aunt Sofia, come I will drop you home, I guess uncle isn't in town?'

'That would be good,' she said looking at Laila to bid her goodbye and shedding some more tears. 'I shall leave now . . .'

'I will drive you guys, come with me,' said Laila. She went to the bed room and got Vivian to join them for a drive. And they proceeded to the car with Tahir holding Vivian gently and he watched his steps protectively.

In the car Tahir was peeping from the window enjoying the wind rushing through his curly hair and he asked, 'why did the monk sell his Ferrari, he should have gifted it to me.'

'Because,' answered Laila, 'he wanted to experience life without it. He wanted to evolve and experience his higher self, that's why.'

'Nice one,' said Tahir and grinned holding Vivian's hand in the back seat. Vivian smiled at him happy to meet his new friend. They liked each other's company though one had love and a short life, the other had longer life but was searching love. 'You appear sacred to me, I wanna ask you.' Said Tahir.

'Go ahead,' said Laila decreasing the volume of the music player.

'Why do people say one shouldn't sing anywhere, like at home . . . . with friends, guests . . . ?' he said scratching his head. 'They say you lose your voice.' His thoughts were abrupt, though had weight nonetheless in it in parity to a regular seventeen year old of his time.

'Umm . . . because of negativity. You see, not many are born with the talent to sing well.' She said, 'and apart from that one should be humble and wise, not that you are not but . . .' she paused to explain it she required to come down to his understanding, as he was raw and stood a fair chance to get carried away by compliments, 'there is way to go, Tahir. There is so much to learn, which comes with experience with people and observation which in turns calls for working quietly towards realizing our dream.'

'Ya! You are right-' he said, 'man pulls down man. And they probe, how much do you study, your light was on till morning? How much do you practice singing, everyday or on monthly basis. Do you go for special training etc . . . etc.,' he mocked the aunties who hassled him. 'And sometimes they mislead, like suggesting of some music school which is horrible so that I ruin my chances. I know their tricks and I mislead them too,' he chuckled. 'But, where does this wisdom fellow come from?'

'From the soul. Our soul is the seat of wisdom and along with that there is another set of wisdom . . .' she said choosing her words, 'for this world. Ie is called worldly wisdom.'

'Which one is better?' he asked, 'I mean, which among them does greater good to us?'

'Spiritual wisdom. That's the one which links us with the God within us.' She replied in a soft tone of voice because of which her answers had a supernatural aura to it. 'And when we have God with us, we learn better. We can conquer any heights we want to.' The boy and his aunt were looking out of the window pondering over her words.

'Tahir,' said Laila calling for him attention back to her, 'are you familiar with Cuckoo, the jet black bird wit dangerous red eyes who is known to sing well in spring time.'

'Yes, I have heard her sing. She sounds very sweet, like you, Laila.' He replied.

'Ya? Thank you!' she responded, 'The cuckoo sings two ways, one is cohuk-cohuk and the other is cooh-cooh, the milder note which is rare." She said informingly with hidden conclusion.

'Are you kidding me?' asked Sofia from the seat next to her's.

'Take my word, she does and that is why,' she said, 'people value her voice.'

'So, that means we shouldn't be available all the time, ie. in case we want our self to be valued,' said the wise and the worldly wise Tahir.

'Yes, and for your talent to be valued,' came the reply from Laila, 'did you hear me?' she asked glancing at Sofia. She smiled and didn't give a reply. She was wondering and trying to correlate the two.

'Next thing Tahir, is called public relations, which is wise and worldly wise like a potato chips which is salty and sweet,' said Laila.

'Go on, I am all ears,' he said resting his neck on the back rest of the car. His aunt sat up in attention to grab the most of her wisdom.

'The crow,' said Laila.

'Oh, it's so noisy,' remarked Vivian, 'but I feed him every morning from my kitchen window. Laila mummy taught me.'

'Vivian, child.' Said Laila sternly.

'Sorry.' He responded. His apology was for interrupting elder's conversation. Tahir was surprised and he smiled at him in appreciation. 'Serious talks,' he whispered winking at Vivian who smiled ear to ear with his elder friend.

'Ok.' Said Laila, 'crows are scavenger. They clean our surroundings and if I may say it is sweet.'

Tahir jumped form his seat and resented, 'Who is sweet? Crows? Give me a break Laila.'

'Tha's what, people don't see his goodness because it sounds harsh and is always available. What they miss out on is that it's the crow, that as is said raises the cuckoo's baby. Cuckoo are said, never to make their own nest. She lays her eggs in the impulsive but innocent crow's nest. So crow raises her babies.' There was silence in the car and Laila was smiling, looking his reaction from the centre mirror of the car. 'The wise sees the truth that the world cannot because the world prefers to live in the obvious and shallow side of the world.'

'Does that mean we should be like the cuckoo, just appearing good?' he asked seriously, 'wouldn't that be being fake and not being myself because that's what people's pleasers are.'

'That means, one that we should genuinely be kind like the crow and secondly we should be wise like the cuckoo, if we desire to succeed in living our dreams. And in doing so, one has to please people for their own good, that's called worldly wisdom.' She said, 'you have talent and you need to hone your skills to thrive in the grownups' world. Ahem . . . are you listening Sofia? It's for you too.'

'Yes, I am. I need to.' she replied.

'You want success in this world, learn to handle people and be wise to help only yourself and then when you become capable, rising high in life, help the needy but not until you have been sufficient for yourself. And be close to your soul, because that will lead you to God and to your dream to make it big in life,' explained Laila.

'But, tell me who decides what is sufficient for us?' he asked. 'There is so much I want.'

'Your soul,' she replied. 'That will tell you what is blind greed and what is humanity. It will tell you what is corrupt hunger and what is grace of giving and the happiness that it brings.'

'Yeah, said Sofia, 'giving does bring happiness, a kind of satisfying and deep happiness.'

'I am sorry, saint Sofia, but what you practice is senseless generosity to those who don't require it and your confusion to those who do.' Said Laila.

'How do you know that,' she asked full of surprise. 'Yes, I do shop senselessly for my friends and relatives. So much so that some times I run out of money, where as they have a steady income and . . .'

'So will you, work in that direction and save until you have sufficient.' said Laila. 'Do you have your own home?'

'No, I . . . um . . . couldn't afford one, as yet,' she replied. 'But that's because I don't earn that kind of money. Umm . . . better put if I wouldn't have been buying them gifts, I wouldn't have saved lakhs, you know . . .' Laila was about to respond and she heard Tahir shout.

'Heay! Stop! Stop!' Called Tahir loudly and Laila immediately hit the brakes, he opened the door and jumped out, 'aah! That's my friend's apartment. I will go, wait here. I will come back.' And he ran to the near by shop on the other side of the road and saying a friendly hellow to the shop owner he opened a jar, took out what he wanted and pointed at Laila's car to the shop owner to which he nodded in approval.

It seemed he was friends with that man. He crossed the road and reached Laila's car and gave Vivian a bar of chocolate to and another one to Laila. 'She is on diet,' he said gesturing at Sofia, 'I owe you.' He said to Laila.

'You don't. You are a kid-' said Laila, 'M elder, it's my duty to protect you and love you.' For Laila her care was selfless because she was raised with a faith in doing selfless good to people. And with experience, she had acquired the wisdom to help without claiming returns because God gave by far perfect returns.

'Attitude of gratitude,' said Tahir wisely. 'Now come on Laila, accept it. Please.' Attitude of Gratitude, a fast fading element of the cynical world is a way of life to give back to the universe the happiness she gives to us, through people, to people. It's a way of expressing gratefulness towards the one who helps us, \ stands by us\ loves us\protects us.

When Laila was a child she was told a story of two tortoises who were found abandoned by a man in the fields. In confusion, that man put them in a well believing they were aquatic animals, whereas they were amphibians. One tortoise, the older among the two, said. 'How cruel is the man to abandon us in this dark well, with no food and no love.' The younger one replied with an attitude of gratitude. 'He sheltered us, is that not praiseworthy. I thank God for he didn't leave us to be eaten by wild animals. I pray he lives happy.' He ate whatever little he could find in the dark well. Life was very difficult in winters, as the cold water was freezing in the well. Two years passed by, the well ran dry to people's amazement. That well owner, looked for the his two tortoises. He was sad as the elder one of the two had passed away. The younger one who lived with an attitude of gratitude and faith in God, survived to live his dream. The man got him out of the well and he made a tiny pond for him with dry land around and got another a female tortoise to give him company. They both fell in love, and lived happily ever after.

'Ok. That's very sweet of you.' She said, 'and wait, forgive your father Tahir, forgive him. You are wise for your age, act wise.' He looked away squeezing his eyes and biting his lips in anger. 'Forgive him . . . will . . .'

'Why?' he interjected with remorse. 'You have seen him sparsely, I know how I survived . . . with the excruciating pain he unleashes on me. My mother is gone,' his pain was apparent in his moist and honest eyes, 'leaving me with this monster.'

'I understand, but the wise forgives leaving justice in God's hands. I told you about Hitler.' She said empathizing with the boy.

'Yes, I remember,' he spoke with a smile on his face. 'The bullet, I love it.'

'Good. You forgive him and give your energy to living your dream and prove yourself a successful singer. Will you Tahir . . .' She said and she forwarded her hand to him with love. He touched it and smiled through his eyes. Then he turned around and walked away. Laila stared at her car and drove away to drop Sofia.

'You were telling me something about money . . . . umm . . . savings, I guess,' reminded Sofia taking interest to improve her life.

'Oh! Yes,' said Laila letting the boy go past her mind. 'You see, Sofia first you gotta work on your marriage and alongside give your time to doing well for yourself because both are the pillars of our life, love and money. In love comes self love, you have to learn to love yourself, and then you will improve because if you love yourself you will work on your flaws. And when we persistently work on our flaws and strengthen your positive attributes, life turns to favour us. It has to and it does.'

'hmm . . .' she said making a mental note of her wise words. 'I wanted a reason to live and today I have many. It occurs to me how I have been ignorant, unwise and wasted my time. I am responsible for my plight. Neither can I help Tahir,' she said with remorse, 'because, I have been wasting my time in self pity and shame.'

'So self-pity and shame goes out of use from your life,' she replied.

'Yes,' she said, 'I fire them now and in this moment.'

'Be a winner,' said Laila, 'not just a survivor because every improvement that you will make will indicate your win.' Sofia sank in her seat in relief and determination.

'And coming back to money, see if you don't save in thousands,' continued Laila, 'and keep spending it, it will not convert into lakhs because you will never believe that it's thousands that gets converts into lakhs. As going by your belief, spending is better than saving, some for your own good and further, as needs be.'

'True.' She said realizing her wastefulness and her unwise generosity.

'But desires have a price of its own, you gotta work with a resolute mind, like the N.S.G. commandos, who never gives up on their tasks. That's how you will have your dream home.'

'Yes, I have to be selfish and live my dream,' she said filled with hope, 'if I don't want people to walk over me. I have to save. Thank you for, I am the dawn of the day I dream of . . . I am the beginning of my happy life and I am the change I want to see.'

Laila dropped her to her dream home, in her mind and then she drove to her current rented apartment. 'Sofia,' she said, 'having a good partner is destiny, but being a good partner, is a choice.' Sofia smiled and illuminated the dream she had once seen.

'Please come with me to my apartment and have a drink,' she said lovingly.

'Oh! I would love to but, I had promised Vivian his weekly trip to the departmental store. His stack of chocolates is over and he will be sad, if I don't take him there-' replied Laila.

'What drink?' babbled Vivian from the back seat, 'I want . . .' he turned to look at Laila.

'The Spiderman drink!' exclaimed Sofia, 'Come I will get you in a special teddy bear tumbler.'

Vivian was a game. Laila chuckled and said. 'You have raked the wild side of him. I surrender.' She said raising her hands up in the air.

And so, on Sofia's request, she and Vivian had a glass of mocktail, named 'fantasy kisser'. It was a brilliant mix of pineapple juice, raspberry juice, lemon juice and a secret ingredient made by Sofia. Some secrets, are important to be successful, as it gets us valued. And value, Sofia had learnt to command with a vivid mix of her talent, wisdom and an alcohol-free life. She started a dance school named, 'Sparkle—The

Dance Destination,' and a pub without alcohol where her students from different localities would enjoy the popular, 'fantasy kisser' and dance the night away. She taught her students to seek God through the beauty of dance and pray for help when in need and in fulfillment as faith begets miracles, miracles like Laila who rescue and guide us enabling us, to see sweetness in crow, learn gratitude from tortoise and to build up on our public relation, like the cuckoo.

Tahir, went on the date and came back with an experience, which he shared with Laila, later when she met him. In the mean while, Tahir' s father fell off the local train and lost his right leg and broke the other. Tahir the child who rose from pain now became his father's painkiller, looking after him while his friends enjoyed their life. He on Laila's request, sat by his father, as his care giver until the latter could manage his daily affairs, on his own. The wise rises from pain and becomes a healer while the unwise, evoke sufferings and then like Hitler's bullet, they get killed. In between his father's accident and his recovery, Laila met Tahir in a place she least expected.

Sofia visited her brother whenever he was in need of her and whenever, the bond of blood called her back, to him. The bond of blood eases reconciliation and so did her faith in God. It helped him in his recovery and in the recovery of love, she had for him. Life chugged on with smiles and surprises.

CHAPTER 8

*Judgment is the bloodiest wound from one man
to the another's soul.*

Staring out of the large glass windows were a pair of deep brown beautiful eyes, of Laila and in her hand was the white porcelain mug of decaffeinated coffee, with the forethought of one whose mind is momentarily detached from the affairs of this world. A posh neighborhood, glossy life, plush new décor and success, God rewarded her generously for her persistence, endurance and tact with which she was rising high in life and improving as life moved on.

The wise like her learns when to step back and bear the brunt to get our work sorted and when to be humble and when to grab the limelight. She understood, that ego should be handled with care for her good and for the greater good of the world because in doing that she not only get into Alexander's good books, she saved their happiness, too. She gave her best to her work and to the call of her soul to help and save the one whose needs were equal in magnitude like those of Laura's life and life of the children she aided. Thus there was no stopping of her divinity from spreading ahead.

In less than half an hour from then, a sixty years old man one of her old neighbor, a professor of Modern History in the Mumbai University, visited her. A man, who like his subject was modern but living in history and to whom she lovingly referred as Ramesh uncle.

'Aha! Now you are a . . . big girl.' He spoke engulfed with emotions,' you must be enjoying this neighborhood more than living in Andheri.'

His name was Ramesh Manjekar, medium built, bald with little hair on the fringes, round face and a sharp eyes that gave weightage to wealth. He loved wealthy people or rather had deep sense of respect to their wealth though he felt underprivileged before them. And because he felt unprivileged, he took life away from his children, to make his son, an investment banker and his daughter a chartered accountant. If there was anything that mattered to the old man, it was wealth and he amassed it through his children and pranced around like the sensational horse on the Ferrari logo, two legs in the air and his head held high.

'Definitely not.' she replied. 'If this has sea, that had you . . . nice people like you uncle who cared for me and accepted me, a migrant as a family member. And this area,' she said looking low, 'is very quiet . . .' She replied respecting his tender care for her and being humble so that he feels at ease. He treated her no less than his own two children, Deepak and Neelima, both happily married.

He looked at her affectionately and keeping the ambience in mind he said, 'but the rich prefer privacy. Don't they?'

'Ask the rich . . .' she said politely with half a smile, 'not me.' They both chuckled and then, his eyes changed colors frombeing kind to cruel.

'Are you aware,' he informed, 'Deepak is marrying that snake haired . . . lousy female? That good for nothing woman . . .' he squirmed with embarrassment. 'May God damn such women who . . . the contemporary Cleopatras who seduce men for their physical gratification . . . . that woman, that Medusa . . . snake haired soft criminal has got my son. Tell you what,' he fidgeted, 'she is stray.'

'Ouch! That is very harsh . . . .' she grinned pulling herself back, 'not liking a person is one thing, uncle, and stretching it that far . . . is being unreasonably mean. Completely uncalled for a man your age and grace, uncle.'

Shaking with disgust and stubbornness he countered. 'She is poisoning my son. Deepak has filed for a divorce with Jaya. It's because of her . . . that woman . . .'

'Uncle,' said Laila, 'divorce is freedom.' Anger was bubbling even harder within him towards Rihana Saberwal, but Laila continued to talk. 'It means official freedom to end a relationship, one can't do justice to. And, I apologize, but I wouldn't take your word that Rihana is the only one responsible for his divorce. Isn't he a party to it? Just because he is born to you . . . you can't rule out his side of the gratification and the . . .'

'But . . . ,' he interjected blinking, as his eyes welled up with tears and in his defense 'he loves Jaya. She is his priority.'

'HAHA!' She exclaimed laughing in a bid to show mild mockery. 'Leave that to him for his sake and please don't cry. What I want you to understand is,' she spoke lending him solace by keeping her hand on his, 'that your son is right and so are you.' He looked up, bewildered at her words and angry that she was not favoring him despite his love and tender care towards her.' You,' she said referring to him with her hand, 'in your sorrow and he, in his honesty are right and justified.' Laila expressed what she believed to be right like a fair judge in the court of law. 'So, kindly let's end it here.'

'How is he right?' he snarled. 'I put in my years of hard work to give them good education . . .' His feeble body bowed with grief as he wiped his tears which he shed demanding solace and sympathy. 'I worked so, so hard . . .'

'So do all of us, some work through their mind some through their body. That's our duty towards our children.' She replied not giving in to his irrational demands as it would keep him away from inner happiness probably making him a kill joy. She wanted him to realize his mistake which he under cover wanted to escape the blame on himself through his tight defense by reminding her of his efforts, to successfully buffer his mistakes. But Laila could see beyond what he was trying to showcase.

Thinking her to be kind of young to get his point, he looked at her and then looked away, 'you don't know the efforts I and my wife had to put in to raise our children. I gave them the best of education. I gave them, especially him, that sophiscated investment banker, good culture . . . . and good family values.'

'Family values . . . Right? Umm . . .' She said scratching her forehead. 'Family values?' She repeated nodding with a smile, 'definitely, you did impart good values but there is more to a relationship like his, than mere family values. You know uncle . . .' she stopped and looked outside at the calmness of the sea and said, 'tell me, have you ever been in . . . have you ever . . . loved?'

'Yes. I loved . . .' he began to sob soothing his self created misery, 'my bicycle I rode to my school.' He replied politely.

'May be in love with your children? Before waiting him to reply she spoke,' thinking of their happiness without you . . . sometimes fearing for the repercussion if they didn't consult you . . . or may be rejoicing in their happiness for something you didn't like much . . . being sad to see them sad even if the reason could range from not taking your permission . . . to some other issue. This for me is love.' she responded sitting with her head inclined to her left soaked deeply into the matter but relaxed in her physical appearance, which he took as an encouragement.

"I loved the only parrot I had when I was a three . . . , I loved fishing in the sea with my father . . . . and I, I still . . . . love . . . that green chiffon saree on my wife . . . I love" she sensed he got into a narrative mood. 'I shall leave now. This plush job has changed you.'

'Or rather you don't want to buy that this love, is same as Rehana's love for Deepak and vice versa-' said Laila.

'The long list that you recite is your ego that keeps away from your wife to be named amidst the one you loved or still love,' she said with warm firmness.

'Woman?' He completed her line and rubbishing it he said, 'that happens in films. Whereas I,' he stressed on the noun playing in the hands of his ego, 'I a ma family man.'

'Aha!' she said cutting him from his ego, 'then, it isn't your cup of tea uncle to get my . . .'

'Yes, I am useless. You are right. I am very old.' He said resentfully looking away from her. 'I will tell you something, that . . .' he rose his hand half way throwing it behind as a gesture to refer to somebody and said, "that snake haired woman, has cast a love spell on my son.'

'Who do you fear? she asked briskly.' Is it people? Relatives . . . or . . . society . . . who?'

'What have they to do with this?' he said looking feeble and sounding aggressive as previously. Talking of love had calmed him for a while as it does all, but as the conversation drifted he dived back to his temper.

She puffed her cheeks and blew wind from her mouth, 'First thing first. The relatives you fear are no good.' She spoke through experience'. 'And, just in case you can sense their goodness, also remember that if they are good then that's to obligeus now and extract returns later. They will indirectly remind you of their kindness so that you are obliged to them as long as you breathe air into your lungs.' She looked at the sea lost momentarily. 'Now, I will tell you what,' she spoke darting straight in his eyes and 'the relatives you are fearing, they in reality are good only twice, one when they come decked up in a marriage to peep in the camera and picking up material to gossip. And secondly when, they have to raise the flag of kindness in times . . . .' She paused, 'when we are in a crisis, you know a family crisis . . .' she hinted towards him through a mild gesture in the eyes, "so that they remain good in society's eyes and then just when we grip their hands for support to gain strength to rise, they will call for a time to ask returns. We should be wise and not ruin our real happiness for some . . ." she made an ugly face, "some people who in reality are never really happy to see us happy. People love to bitch, don't give them so much weightage, especially in your mind. That's who they are . . . relatives . . . people and together the society."

'But not everybody is cruel . . .' he responded with much difficulty.

'That brings me to my next point. And if you believe them to be nice and evolved,' he squeezed his eyes to the word, 'umm . . . wise, kind and the humane lot then uncle, they would stand by you and your family in ways evolved people do, that is by genuinely accepting you, your son and his divorce as God's will.' He took a deep breath as a sense of realization seeped in the porous old wall of the old fort in his mind. 'Besides, people don't spare God, how then do you expect they would not foul mouth, you and me. They will . . . they do. That's their birthright . . . or so they presume because they are unwise who stick in the rut of life dragging others into it. It makes them feel like the cherries in the same pudding . . . no matter how rotten.'

"But we live in society, don't we?" he asked, knowing she well made a point, which had indisputable truth in it. But he defended again, that's the way he was and wanted to be because unlike Laila, her uncle was also in the group she was making a reference to, the bad and the corrupt, in the society.

'Right.' She said, 'Does that mean you still want to be with them rather than standing by your son's happiness. Go on.' She forced a nasty smile. 'And then, they will turn you very bitter and angry with you son, his lady love and with yourself. Go on . . . .' She said giving way. He didn't reply. He was searching for something on the floor, perhaps his own happiness and wisdom. 'And when you will be that angry . . . remember my words again, that anger is-self harming. It will kill your son's happiness now that he has made choice to be happily remarried and then . . .' she paused nodding her head. 'God forbid, he throws you out of . . . and thrash the wickedness out of your old bones.'

'I get you,' he replied sobbing, 'I always teach my young students that anger kill the God in us. It makes us demons. It makes us pitiless . . .' he narrowed his eyes, 'which we realize when . . . we grow old and . . .'

'We realize it in the old age because we don't have a choice to keep forcing our ways on others. That is why being elder is referred as being wise, but my endeavor is to save you and you future and your son's happiness combined in one. Wise is the mantra, dear uncle. Be wise.' She said. 'Please walk the path of the enlightened mind. Follow your own words because it has experience of years in it. And not every old person is as wise as you. And well if you understand what a love spell is or better put the spell of love, then . . .' she paused to grin, 'I may go on to believe that you know what romantic love is and if Rihanahas cast a spell on Deepak, why don't you make his wife . . .'

'Jaya . . . is what you mean to say.' He asked.

'Yes, Jaya to cast the same spell on him? He will be drawn to her as well . . . may be?' He smirked. 'There is no end to getting into derogatory talks like that. Now he chuckled at her humorous reply and then again, his energy wilted. 'If I may remind you,' said Laila, 'Deepak and Rihana were madly in love with each other and it was you who dragged him to marry Jaya.'

'Yes, I did.' He spoke. 'She is a homely girl not some medusa . . .'

'Not again. Please . . .' she said, stopping him from calling her names, 'and homely . . . huh?'

'Jaya choose not to work. Not my fault.' he clarified taking the easy way out to escape the truth. Laila looked away at the sea and drew a deep breath.

'Nobody can escape real love.' She replied candidly. 'Four years of unhappy marriage, that he chose out of fear and pressure from society and,' she looked at him, 'you. Do you realize how it feels to be in his shoes? And what good did it do to others and to you? 'He was sinking in the lounge chair, growing weak, not just out of disgust for Rihana but also out of self pity. He didn't respond for a while.

'But I got the most eligible woman for him. What went wrong . . . I don't know . . . can't figure it . . .' He said.

'It didn't go wrong. It wasn't right in the first place. There is a difference between the two.' She answered. 'I know, Jaya stood the test of time, she stood pain of rejection, it must be hard on her but Deepak? What about him? He was in two minds. He felt . . .' she went quiet and cleared her throat to reframe her line of thought. 'What was wrong was your choice, uncle. Why did you . . . ?'.

'Why did I what?' he said with casual bitterness.

'Tell me. Did I not get a good match . . . Did I not . . . ?'

'Why did you reject Rihana Sabrewal?' she spoke killing her hesitation, since his conscience was not willing to be awake as yet. Laila became the spokesperson of his soul.

'She is like the Berlin wall . . . which better comes down.' He said. Laila stared in his eyes, a clear indication that she didn't approve his expression.

'Or is it because she is educated, assertive, and successful? People feel threatened. Don't they, uncle?' She probed strongly. 'Anybody with trendy outfit, short hair, a generous dash of fragrance, oozing with confidence, looks defiant to people? Isn't it? Just as defiant as India looked to the developed nations in the Copenhagen summit?'

Her words fell like the first bomb on Hirosima, destroying his old belief like it destroyed the city in war, only here she destroyed beliefs to save innocent Rihana and women like her who put in years of hard work to be successful and to lead a life they desire. A life of freedom, a life of love and a life of work of their choice. The bomb was in response verbal war, between two superpowers in her living room. He had to be bombed because he was opposing his child's happiness causing mass destruction of his love.

He looked away failing to give a reply so Laila lifted the monstrous machine gun and began to fire at him, from zero range. 'I have worked with drug addict in the rehabilitation center. I can vouch they were genuine, only destroyed by disease and habit. I have worked with actresses who are purely karmic and are closer to God within them then are you and I. 'He kept staring hard at her. 'Now, why I am telling you all of this is because, we don't have the right to judge people. We should accept them as they are. Every human being has a reason to become who they are, corrupt or saint. Let's let them live in peace and lets us live in peace too.' The intensity of her words like the steel bullets pierced deep in his head. And then of course was her conviction of the might of right that was giving her the courage to make him accept Rihana the way she was.

He thought for a moment and said weakly, 'Yes. Sometimes . . .'

'Sometimes . . . ? You are judging then again.' She answered. 'Uncle, here I am going to tell you something,' she paused in agitation, 'I have met corrupt professors who bitterly used the P.H.D. students, sexually . . .' she pouted to magnify her disgust at them, 'and otherwise, instead being a genuine guide to them of their degree course. Now . . . does that mean I judge you and show the same disrespect that I show to them? Would you not . . ."

'Please . . .' he checked her. 'That's not true. We are not . . . all the same.'

'No. That's not my point.' She replied. 'M not talking about numbers and probabilities.' She looked at him. 'Do I judge you on my past experiences with professors?'

'No.' He said openly. He couldn't imagine being judged by her for something he never fathomed.

'That's what you should try to do and adapt yourself to doing from now on. Rihana is a nice woman. She is sweet and is to the point because she has had bitter experience of being just sweet.' Said Laila.

'How do you know that?' he asked poignantly.

'I . . . know it.' She replied mysteriously. 'I know it . . .' her voice was now weak, like his. 'So please don't judge. My innocence has been destroyed by people who took advantage of my age and lack of experience, in giving it back to them. They manipulated and churned, I could have died but God pulled me through.' She smiled and said. 'So, I survived. I survived to help those like me. I took it in my stride with faith in God, that someday He will avenge my tears and until that happens, I will go on helping women, children and the weak like me.' She paused, 'So please, uncle,' she spoke with her moist deep brown eyes looking into his, 'don't ruin her life. Be a responsible elder. Genuinely love them for her sake and for yours.' The room felt silent. She was too moved and so was her uncle.

'Can I get you some tea, uncle?' she asked breaking from the emotional web to give him a breather.

'Yes. I . . .' he said taking a deep breath, a very deep breath rather, 'I don't mind having a cup of tea now. I umm . . . feel better and lighter.' He looked at her in affirmation. She give a little smile in comfort and went away from the living room.

Whereas he sat there calm and meditative, lost in deep thoughts and he recalled an incident years back, the day his children brought Madhav to their home. He was a child whose parents, like many other parents were divorced on grounds of incompatibility. Mr. Manjekar had returned from the market and before he kept the groceries in the kitchen, he pulled his children in a corner and mercilessly looking down upon their friend,

245

he yelled in whispers, 'I don't want you both to play with him anymore. He is a nuisance. He will spoil you like himself. His father is gone because of him and his lousy mother. This boy is a the outcome of outcast parent's, society doesn't want them and neither do I. Do you understand, you both?" and he slapped them giving fear. 'And you, Deepak I will lock you in the bathroom and leave you there all night if you are caught playing with him the next time.' His children objected through their eyes, which felt weak before his hatred for divorcees and the child born to such marriages. He grabbed Madhav and separating him form his divine children, he threw him out saying sternly, 'they have to study. You better go home and be there, not here.'

Madhav did go home but his parent's fate returned. It came back to haunt Mr. Manjekar so that when he sheds tears for his son's divorce and when he is devastated with equal magnitude, that child gets justice form God. Madhav wept and became withdrawn from society and social gatherings because as a child that was the best way for him to save himself from more such hurts and the deep scars that some elders and so called educated gave him for the choice he didn't make, for a life he didn't choose. What a pity not for the child but for the men who made the child feel so unwanted, so alone and so weak before his might, that his soul wept. The curse of the soul even in silence is very cruel.

He drummed around loudly, 'divorcees are hi-fi people setting a wrong example to our children. They are away from their culture and are result of bad parenting,' and here, he sat in tears in a similar plight requiring the same support that, he as an elder should have had rendered to Madhav. Life was with him then though not now. He was brought on the pedestal as that child he mistreated for this was his time to understand that divorcees are in as much a human beings as is his son, today and as were Madhav's parents. And that they were made of same blood and flesh and not worthy of ill treatment because like Deepak, Madhav's parents had their reasons, in marriage that lead to their divorce for which destiny and choice, both were responsible.

Their destiny came to his family to force him to realize that no matter how rich, how civilized or how well educated we may be, we don't have the right to judge others or disgrace an innocent, in anbid to prove ourselves better because everybody has their own reasons of leading life the way they do. If we can't understand, we should ask God to be by them in their crisis and do our part in making their life worthwhile through our kindness and love.

'Life is fair; it waits for the perfect timing to give us an equalizer,' said Mr. Manjekar to Laila as she lowered the tray on to the glass table to serve him tea.

She smiled at his wisdom. 'That's the most perfect line I have heard in ages. I like it.'

'Age?' he remarked relating to what he was thinking prior to her entry in the room. There was an aura of silent sadness, the one that comes from a sudden tragedy or from a realization of how brutally we have lived away from our soul.

'Years, that's a better word.' She informed. 'It's years that heals, years that we call age that adds experiences and make us humble.'

'Years. Yes, it does make us humble,' he said in support.

'Because some of us realize only with time that there is a power working over and above us which can never be superseded although is attianable.' Her word sent him to another world, a world from where comes truth and love, in this world. She stirred the sugar free tablet in his tea and filled with peace she forwarded it to him and got back to her seat beside him.

'Thanku.' He said stirring the tea absent mindedly, he didn't look her in the eyes as the injustice meted out to Madhav by him began to haunt him. It had to haunt him because that was the truth that brought that child hurt and deprivation. He raised his eyesbrows, 'Your cup of tea?' he asked her, very gently. 'Sorry, I got into thinking something.'

'Ohh! I just had a cup of coffee.' She replied, to which he didn't react pleasantly. 'I was neck deep into work . . .' she reiterated not giving in to pseudo socialization that he demanded because more important than sharing a cup of tea, It was to help him to align his life and correct his approach towards life and God for blames from the unwise does come on God. 'It's quite demanding to keep abreast of the latest collection at the International level . . .' she said, 'it's funny, you know uncle. One winter purple eyes shadow is supposedly hot whereas in another season it goes in the trash. The world of hi fashion is . . . aaah . . . tiring . . . hahaha . . . for fashionists are that finicky. I could never imagine an eyes shadow can be of such importance, but that the way it is . . . to the fashion wolves.' She laughed at her demanding work schedule at the same time underplaying it. She loved her work but she was aware of how he viewed her work, as if she enjoyed a good life doing not much beyond holding the camera and clicking a few times.

'Hmm . . . you are a big shot why would you join me for tea?' he replied with his manipulative mind at work.

'When I can join you in your sorrow, what so untouchable about having a cup of tea with you, uncle?' She responded not giving in to his manipulation to which he was left with no more queries.

'You have become an archer.' He said taking a shot at her. She knitted her eyesbrows, 'so to the point, Laila. You weren't this way. I . . .' He said.

'Umm . . .' she raised her ten fingers in air and smiled, 'hands up. I can't answer that.' She very well could have, but she didn't because she knew he was trying to dig in her success and the problem was, he was doing it to destress. 'Cheer up uncle. Just stay together as a family and what come may don't let an outsider intrude in your family's affair. That is,' she said, looking angry in the eyes, 'very very poisonous and obnoxious.' He got her point. 'Uncle, in the end it's your family who will belong to you in good times and bad. As for people, they just look around for fun, please don't give them a chance. And what good are your family values when you can't stand by your own son in dark hours because that darkness is very dark which doesn't have our parents, supports in it. And heaven forbid, he pounces back on you when you would need him the most. Karma, ie. Our deeds never forsakes us.' He was humbled and checked.

'Hey! Who's this?' he asked demurely pointing at the child with his week arms, who came to the room awake from sleep and rolling a big exercise ball which was larger than his body size. 'Laila mummy, exercises on this . . .' he babbled.

'Yes, my love I do.' She said getting up from the setter to lift the child in her arms. 'He is Vivian,' and she kissed him. 'Say hello to uncle.' The child playfully turned his head away refusing to acknowledge him. 'Now come on, you are a good boy. Aren't you?' she coaxed him lovingly.

'No.' He replied rubbing his fingers over his eyes and smiling.

'Yes, you are.' Said Laila patiently.

'No,' replied the child again.

'Yes.' She replied quickly.

'No.' he said. 'Yes,' she replied tickling him.

'Yes,' said the little boy. 'Hellow!' he said to Mr. Ramesh who was pleased to hear him babble.

'Hellow!' he replied. 'Come here. Come quick.' Laila got him down to the floor.

'He is a good boy, he greets people.' Said Laila and the child went ahead.

He held the child in his arms and complimented him saying, 'That's a nice bandana. Who got you that.' Laila got alarmed as the child looked at her suggesting she made him wear the bandana.

'Ahhh! Uncle do you know Vivian can tell you stories. And he is good at sports. Show us how you roll the ball.' The child was more awake at the mention of sports than Mr. Manjekar could imagine him to be. Vivian rushed towards the ball and kicked it against the wall. 'That's nice' said Laila. They clapped with joy for him. He was even happier, he kicked harder and got busy with the ball.

'How is Sanskrit?' Enquired Mr. Manjekar.

'He is dead. Replied Laila. 'This is Vivian and the bandana is to cover his bald head. He too is also a cancer patient losing his hair in chemotherapy.' Mr. Manjekar was stunned.' I picked him form the railway track and he will survive. I will take care of him on my own.'

'I don't believe you are doing it all over again. I can't believe it . . . I can't . . .' He remarked shocked as to how this girl was bravely handling her emotions and not only that, she was helping him cope up. She was cheering him up, making him happy while she had a lot more to deal with. He felt belittle and ashamed before her. How wrong is a wrong man, this only he can judge the best.

'I have to, that's the purpose of my life.' She said numbly. He broke down in tears. He had held Sanskrit in his arms when Laila got him home when he was recovering form the fatal disease. He couldn't reckon he lived no more. 'We can't deny God and nor can I question him.' She said, pacifying him. He wept.

In the meanwhile, Vivian was hitting the ball calling for her attention. 'Come here,' she said lovingly calling him back to her, 'not that hard my boy, you will get tired.' She had to check his pace because for Vivian, getting tired could have meant death. He could pass away with his weak body giving way to fatigue and loss to breath to his lungs. No air, no life. People judge, it's easy for them, than to show love and to care.

'You still believe in God?' he asked bitterly like an atheist.

'I will tell you what, the day he passed away . . . .' She paused as the memory came alive.

'Do you still believe in God? He killed that child . . . God damn it.' he interjected.

'Yes I do and I always will.' She answered with conviction though she did moan his death. 'See you are still calling him. 'God . . . damn it that is because, nobody can run away from God and nobody can run away form death. Who is alive without dying, uncle. There is no life without death and there never will be. There should be no questioning on what is universal. The water will remain wet and the sky will be blue, whereas you and I will come, live and go back to where we come from.' She replied. 'It depends when one's time is up. You know . . . anytime can be one's time to bid goodbye to the world. Your tears will dry but life and death will continue.'

'So that was the message the child gave . . . to . . . you.' He asked gathering courage.

'And to you too.' she replied still holding Vivian close to her. 'We lose time and then life is up. And what good is that life which has only pain and disgust, regret and misery, jealousy and hoarding. Try this life uncle. It's more satisfying and it has eternal happiness to it because every time we serve a soul, we experience God.' To this he held his face in his hand and behind him the noon sun was setting in the Arabian sea, and he in the dawn of enlightenment of his soul.

'Oh! I was telling you about this day when, you know Sanskrit was no more with us as he was,' she looked at Vivian, 'with God. It was hard for me, so Alexander suggested I leave Mumbai and take a short road trip to Pune." Suddenly she looked at him. 'Are you with me?' she asked.

'Yes.' He spoke feebly, 'I am and I always will be.' He replied humbly.

'That's kind of you, uncle.' She answered. 'How much does it cost you to pay for his,' he said pointing at Vivian, 'medicines Laila?' he asked. She didn't reply. 'I will pay for him.'

'Oh! Aaah . . .' she said, 'that's very . . . . aaahh . . . kind of you but thanku uncle. Laura's charitable organization pays for him.' He looked bemused because her eyes were hideous. 'Laura. Oh I didn't mention, she is Alexander's wife. We run this organization together. It's for children suffering from cancer, like this boy.' She replied jittery.

'I am H.I.V positive.' said the boy dropping the other atomic bomb on Nagasaki of Mr. Manjekar's head.

'Yeah! Ammm . . .' answered Laila looking away from Mr. Manjekar who was still not believing his ears.

'But you said, cancer.' Babbled the boy. 'Yes . . .' said Laila wiping her mouth unable to hide the truth successfully form her uncle.

'Umm . . . there was a confusion.' said Laila trying to hide behind the child.

'So that's how dirty I am-'said Mr. Manjekar. 'I judge. I pass painful remarks. I hate successful people and I mock the one's in need. I am the new synonym for hurt.'

'No, I didn't mean to hurt you.' Laila chipped in. 'I thought it would cause you inconvenience to accept the boy as he is. And since there is not much I can do to chance his diagnosis, I altered it for which . . .'

He held the child's hand and gently pulled away from Laila and made him sit on his lap 'I am sorry too,' he said to the boy holding his tiny palm against his cheeks, 'to you and to Rihana Sabrewal and to the rest.' He wept. 'May God and may you, forgive me for my corruption and for my sins.'

Vivian, the little boy said wiping his tears for him. 'Laila says, God forgives everybody. So he will forgive you. Don't cry.' And he shyly turned to look at Laila for her approval. She smiled and the evening set in. Her uncle the new man, the one as young and tiny as Vivian, finished his cup of tea and went home as a new man, in his latest evolved version. His life changed. He began to experience God by accepting Deepak, his son's decisions and his new daughter in law, Rihana Sabrewal Manjekar. He also found a new match for Jaya on the website and attended her wedding to her new groom in Canada, a doctor by profession and an issueless divorcee. Life became soothing and so was he. Evolved and as loving as was towards his parrot he had, when he was three.

As for Laila, life flowed on. It was the usual day at work except that from the cubicle she had been shifted to a cabin, a symbol of an upward movement an and success at work. Laila was operating her laptop.

'Laila, Alexandar has asked for the copy of the shoot we had in Goa . . .' said her assistant Deepa, a slim girl who like Laila worshipped work and unlike her, wore her hair short as it required low maintenance. But she was fond of clothes and of chewing gums, her favorite being the green apple flavor from Lotto.

'Where?' said Laila with an obvious firm face.

'In Goa.' She replied clutching a writing pad in her arms. 'My God Laila, is that . . . you don't remember last week we went to Goa . . .' she was getting hysterical, 'on the sandy beach . . . the white sandy beach there with that Brazillian guy in a brief . . . with Noorie, that . . . that talk . . . talkative model . . . in a bikini?'

Laila lifted her eyes, 'where is the file containing those pictures, Deepa?'

'In there.' She said pointing at the laptop.

'In where?' she growled, searching for suspects in her mind, 'my laptop has been hacked. Somebody out there . . .' she clenched her teeth gently, 'did it.' Then she looked at Deepa who had disappeared. Laila got up from her chair to look for her and Deepa was lying on the floor. She had fainted. 'Deepa . . .' said Laila, 'Deepa . . .' she sprinkled some water over her face and calming herself in the crisis they had been pushed in. 'She couldn't take the pressure.' Said Laila to herself, 'poor girl.' Alexander's temper got the good of her, even though he hadn't said a word on the matter. In two days time that photograph was to mark the third anniversary of the magazine and was meant to be on the cover of Brazentine. 'It's ok. We will find . . .' Laila simultaneously rubbed her own forehead while talking to Deepa., 'ummh . . ., we will find the way out.' To which she saw Deepa opening her eyes and regaining consciousness.

'Alexander will kill us all.' She replied in whispers with abated breath. 'Laila our Roman emperor is pitiless like a hungry alligator. Laila . . . he will kill us.'

'Don't scare me girl.' Said Laila taking control of her nerves and raising Deepa head slightly upward form the floor resting it on her palm. 'I will be back,' said Laila comforting her assistant. 'Baby, you need sugar, have this candy and stay put. I will be back ok?' and she was about to get up. 'Oh! M so sorry. M hasty.' She remarked realizing that Deepa was still laying on the floor while she was about to walk out to find an option that would bail them out of the crisis. 'Let me help you get up, you can't manage right, can you Deepa?' And she smiled at her.

'Ahhh! . . .' she moaned, 'ammm . . . I can . . . gimme your hand . . . Lai-Laila.'

'Ya sure,' replied Laila raising her head higher to give her momentum to get up. 'come on, come on, come on,' and as the she rose up and sat on the chair Laila gave her the candy and she disappearing leaving Deepa regain strength while she herself took control of the situation. She rang up Alexander to check if he was available for a chat, an emergency one given the crisis they had been hit by and he was not available. She came back to her cabin and called up Laura asking her for a favor. 'Hi Laura. There is an emergency. Please, can you send me a painting of your's the three dimensional one with the Japanese man laying down facing up, in the painting. Please Laura. I need it.'

'Yes, there are no two ways about it. I will get it sent,' she replied as humble as ever.

'Good,' Said Laila breaking into sweat. 'Thanku. I will get back to you. M a bit in hurry. Ohhh . . . just another favour, do you have somebody who can print that picture on a silk cloth . . . I know I am asking for too much but please Laura . . . please anybody . . . anyone you know . . . ?' Laura was humming and recalling her contacts.

'Rohit. Rohit can do it,' butted in Deepa like a spark.

'Who? Rohit Bal?' asked Laila, 'tell me quick . . . come on girl.'

'Rohit Verma . . . that designer that short and swaying one.' She replied explaining his profile.

'Oh all of them sway . . .' said Laila. 'Can he do us the favor . . . I mean of course we will pay for it . . . but still?' said Laila still holding Laura on line. 'Listen Laura can you recall somebody, coz . . . I need it. My neck is on the line. I . . . we have a designer name but just one is . . . not dependable, though I am yet to check on him.'

'Hey! I will get back to you on that my angel. Just give me some time.' Said Laura.

'Some time. Laura, in some time I . . .' she sighed, 'I may not be . . .'

'Heay! Don't finish the line.' Said Laura sweetly. 'I can kind of understand the kind of pressure my man can put on you, but the thing is . . .'

'There is just one thing, you send me the painting and the contact number of the man who can possibly help us get the work done. Please Laura.' She pleaded saving every possible second that she could have.

'Oh! Give Eisher and . . .' she fumbled.

'Shaurya.' Said Laura in her heavy Italian accent giggling at her angel's memory loss.

'Ya . . . yes, umm . . . Shaurya, my love and you take care. M pressed for time Laura. We will catch up later.' She said as she was about to put the receiver down, 'and this shouldn't go to Alexaneder's ears for God's sake, please. I will explain all this later, when we meet.'

'I love secrets. It's gonna be with me. Take Care Laila.' And both hung up on each other.

The big day came three days later. The day to mark the third anniversary of the magazine that spelt and defined glamour, 'Brazentine!' said the M.C. over the micro phone unraveling a huge poster that cascaded from the high ceiling to the floor with a close up shot of a naked model resting backward on her elbow, on a beach. She was facing the camera three fourth and the Japanese man, that three dimensional painting printed on a cloth, lay on her bust covering her till her upper thigh, exposing her legs as long as river Nile to the glitterati dressed in the finest and the chic. It fell marvelously on her body as though the man was laying on her and her tousled dark brown hair flew in the air. The crowd loudly gasped for air, in amazement at the out of the world creativity that Laila had captured through her lens. 'Ladies and gentlemen, lets join our hands to welcome the gifted sensation of the year, the one and only, the blessed and the obsessed . . . with the camera, the one who created this beauty, 'he said gesturing at the poster behind him,' the eighth wonder of the world . . . the gorgeous Laila.' The crowd clapped like a thunder and the room echoed with adulation. 'And she herself is the ninth wonder of the world, the Michaelangelo of India.' Said Alexander with Laura seated next to him, raising a toast to her a glass of Champagne from his round table covered with a white lacy table cloth, which was one among the many tables to seat the guests for the evening.

Laila stood there humbled by the crowd's appreciation and one person who was clapping the loudest she could, was Deepa. 'There couldn't be and isn't a photographer better than my boss.' She proclaimed with pride joining the crow giving Laila a standing ovation for her unparalleled creativity. 'Everything beautiful is mysterious. And if that mystery is trapped in the camera, it's creativity.' said Laila with humility to the crowd. 'Thanku for joining us tonight. May God grant you your wish like he granted me mine.' The crowd was overwhelmed by her acceptance speech, and so the room buzzed with appreciation and applause. The party continued as the happy evening slipped into a beautiful night.

———⬦———

CHAPTER 9

The one, who forgives,
can surmount the universe.

Laila was returning from a client meeting, on one evening. She got down at Luster located in Colaba, a sizzler cum bar, which had two entrances, one from the bar and the other from the restaurants' side. Like it's name, Luster was shining and doing well for itself. Now that was Laila's favourite sizzler bar for it had good food and a fascinating fish aquariums surrounding the three walls of the eatery, which satiated her appetite and rested her mind. In a knee length black skirt with a lilac top and black heels she entered Luster from the bar side of the entrance.

She rested on the tiny stool by the bar and flipped the pages of the drinks menu.

'What shall I serve you mam, flat water or sparkling?' asked the jovial bartender.

'Gimme blue lagoon and a veg grilled sandwich,' she said taking a deep breath.

'Sure,' he said and went to the kitchen and came back in a nick of time, 'here we go,' he said with a clown like smile presenting her with her order.

'Oh! . . .' she uttered in confusion. 'Thanku.' She was mentally occupied thinking about the coming photo shoot, with an Indian designer selling her collection like hot cakes in New York. Laila wanted the shoot to be in sync with the image she had created for the magazine, chic and soft, whereas the designer wanted it to be loud and yelling. To get her to cut down on the chunky accessories on the model was becoming a pain for her so much so that she was carrying it everyhere.

'I will get back to you madam,' replied the bartender and dashed to another customer, next to her, two chairs away. He asked for a drink and was playing with the ice cubes in the glass already in front of him. She didn't care to take a look at him, as she was building on the concept of the shoot. Then, a woman in her late thirties sitting on the either side of Laila, got up and went to him.

'Hey choco pie!' She said seductively in a volume audible clearly to Laila, 'how are you? Can I buy you a drink? . . . . aaah,' she moaned, 'tell me . . . or you want to get started without it.' The boy smirked. 'Five thousand for an hour . . .' she said running her finger on his shirts collar.

'Nothing for now!' replied the boy. Laila now turned to her right as his voice sounded very young and familiar. She looked at him and he looked back at her. He sank in his stool and her heart sank with it.

'Stay away,' she said nastily, getting down the chair, to the woman. 'This boy is with me.' And she looked at him again with disappointment.

The woman snarled, 'I don't care who he is with, as long as he gives me company tonight.' Her depravity had propelled her lust, as depravity does to those, whose soul runs away from them, leaving them to find solace in lust. And lust doesn't have any solace because lust propels lust, not faith.

Respecting Laila, the boy got up from his stool and said to the woman. 'Hey you fatty!' He flicked her hands away, 'lay eggs on your seat. Get that? M not available . . . tonight. Go away.' Laila's sinking heart sank deeper on hearing his second last line.

Acceping the reality, she said, 'Tahir,' it was difficult for her to look at him but she did it with her cosmic might, 'what are you doing here?' Her tiredness was merging with sadness and pulling her energy further down. 'I . . . I thought, you wanted to be . . . a singer. Is this . . . ?'

'I . . .' he said moving towards her from three stools away from her, with loss of words, 'I gave up . . . I can't afford it.' He looked at her with a look that said he loved her dearly and was sad to fail her. The other woman stood watching. He looked at her and changed his voice into a sweet irritation, 'You want me to make an omlete out of you? Fuck off.'

A bartender passing by objected and was to call the bouncer and just then that woman walked away. She turned back and said, 'fuck you, choco pie.'

'I have been asking for you but in vain. What about your father?' asked Laila in whispers. 'Do you have any idea what will . . .'

'Don't talk about him. He is fuckin' my life.' He replied with utter repulsion and pain. 'He fuckin'doesn't give me money. He fucking doesn't care what happens to me and to my music.'

She stood up quietly for him and then she looked at the bartender and asked him to transfer her order to a table towards the end where she intended to sit with Tahir in peace and talk him out of toeing a wrong path.

'Remember what I told you long time back, that in living our dreams with clean deeds troubles does come as a test of time and in that time we should pray and seek God? Remember? Then troubles find its way out.' Her conversation sounded out of place at that hip eatery yet she had the courage and the conviction to talk in that boy's benefit, leaving behind all the distraction. 'What do you want money for?' She asked and patted him genteelly on his shoulders gesturing at him to walk ahead and have a seat opposite her.

He sat. 'I wanted to record some songs at the local studio in Andheri.' He said, 'I have to pay them for their services. They don't give a damn to me, without money. And yes, I remember what you had said at that time and also that help does come sooner or later by that time we should pray for it's easy to fall apart then to stand by truth which is rewarding for later years. I waited but nothing came by.'

'But there are other options to make money? Being a . . .' she said looking downwards unable to use the word gigolo. 'This is . . . a waste of you and your precious life. And as for your wait I am sure you didin't wait for appropriate time. You must have done in a hurry . . . then it's difficult to wait.'

'I don't care,' he said in an impulse, 'that bloody man doesn't let me work and I get free from college in the first half of the day and then I . . .'

'Are you done with your drink? We will move out, I will get my stuff packed,' she spoke forgetting her hunger. Accepting the boy was something that only somebody highly evolved or divine can do.' And Tahir, one can never justify what is not right. If you want money, you convince your father. I will pay for you. But this is not going to lead you right. You are very young Tahir, I don't want you to get lost in this malicious world for there is no end to stooping low there.'

Laila knew that the power of a dream can be compelling for young mind, to take a wrong path and a path which is not right leads the wrong destination as well when we have victory at the cost of inner happiness. In such a time one needs to realize that there is always a key to unlock the lock on our path which lies with our soul.

'No,' he said lifting his drink placed by the steward previously, 'you don't pay. I haven't really used my skills to convince my father . . . umm . . . like you said,' and he looked at a woman who was staring hard at him. Laila, worryingly understood that he was a popular boy with the women crowd for his innocent face, a cute grin with intensely curly locks of hair falling from his forehead. He was also regular to the gym which was apparent by his bulging biceps and a broad shoulder. 'It's exhausting to talk to him . . . he is like aaa . . . moving a mountain. One can't do it. Atleast I fuckin can't.'

'Tahir, if you can put so much efforts in . . . all this,' she said hinting at his biceps and the women who he charmed through it, 'why not in your work, in your dream? Why not work at a studio, . . . you know . . . all this will lead to nowhere . . . . what world are you living in, you don't even know . . . you are too young to know the repercussions of your acts.'

'But there are impediments, too,' he replied.

'So, find ways to negate it,' she said.' Besides what has happened until this day take it positively as God's way of telling you about the ways of the world. Take it as learning and change your way, my boy. Be a wise boy . . . don't be disillusioned. Don't lose hope. If success was so easy, it wouldn't be valued.' Tahir looked awake in the eye. 'Nobody gets success as painlessly as one thinks. You are like a child to me . . . I would be glad to see you happy.' Then calling the waiter she asked him to do the needful.

After getting her food packed, she got up and so did he, from the table. They were about to head out of the eatery, from the restaurant's side, came the steward, 'mam, your bill.'

'Oh!' said Laila embarrassedly, 'I am so sorry. Get it please . . . m in rush. Get me the bill for this boy too.' Her head was heaped with her work but she couldn't let the boy sink deeper into troubles.

'Why do you pay? I will,' said Tahir stubbornly but with love and respect.

'Because I am elder than you, that's why. Put your money, into something sacred if you want to get where you've stopped living your dream,' she replied. 'All this,' she said pained, 'is leading you, to a fallacy. Every one of us who lived a dream, has been through trials because that hones our skills and polishes us, which you need to understand and to put your soul into that, into progress and not into . . ." She paused as the steward came with the bill. Clearing the bill she left him a generous tip. 'I will pay for your recordings, get five good songs and meet me at my office the coming week.' She said looking at Tahir.

'Five songs?' he shrieked bending low in wait grabbing the shirt falling on his stomach, 'in the next week? . . . I can't do that Laila. I have just three.' He replied bowing before her. 'I can't.'

'And forgive your father Tahir,' she replied politely, 'please forgive him. Forgiveness is a power. It will cleanse our soul.' He looked in her eyes looking for a conviction and found it. 'And once your soul will be clean, it will lead you to the right path. It will bring you creativity in abundance and an enigma to the way you sing. You see child, forgiving will make you lighter and stronger from within and then your talent will rise to a new height. Right now your soul is wearing a veil and that is why you are more yes to the wrongs and more no, to the right. That's what a soul in veil does. It drains away the goodness and empowers the evil, so that you keep suffering without meaning, without progress making us mean and painful. And such a suffering just adds to more dilemmas and obstacles. Your talent is suffering, do you agree with me? Be a man who is happy and satisfied. And not just one of it.'

After a pondering pause he said, 'Yes, I am . . . I have been away from making good music . . . . I don't feel like.'

'Acceptance is a first change. You don't feel like, because,' she said, 'you are distracted. Such distractions will eat you up and your creativity. Who will care what happens to you, if you don't care to save yourself? Have you heard a saying, no guts, no glory?'

The boy looked up and said, 'Yes. I have.'

'So follow it.' She replied crisply,' your father is not the kind one would desire, or rather he is very unkind to you, which has . . . pained you. I can feel your pain. But, his life is depleting, it's gone. Why do you want to waste your life in self harming activities.' She kept looking at him with hope and faith.

'I will forgive my father,' he said after pondering over it. 'But can I ask you something?'

'Ask.' She replied.

'Why in my life I have no mother and a beastly father? Why me Laila?' He asked.

'So that you give more time to your music and less in getting spoiled by your parents.' She replied. 'Never question God and gradually you shall become a seeker of God helping new talents in your field.'

He smiled with his locks of hair swaying by the cool breeze from the sea near by, 'you are a genius.'

And forgive yourself too.' she said earnestly. 'Walk on the right path, the path of our soul and then God will conspire my child,' she smiled, 'to get Tahir, what he dreams of. It's a simple, give and take Tahir. You forgive yourself and your father, and nourish your soul. Which in turn will get you . . ."

'It has got me,' he interjected deeply looking away, 'what I was looking for,' and he looked at her, 'I will meet you the coming week. I sure will.'

'That's . . .' she replied. 'That's the spirit with which I wanted to see you work. Here,' she said taking out some money from her bag, 'five thousand will do for your song's recording.'

'No,' he replied, 'thanku, just give me three. It's kinda expensive, so I put saved some of my money . . .'

'This money . . .' she asked, 'no.' She rubbed her face with both her hands in disappointment and disapproval, 'no.' They walked slowly after clearing the bill. 'Do you know that everything is energy?' He looked at her in amazement and grinned somberly. 'Our thoughts, our deeds, our money and everything visible and invisible is energy. Our emotions, our dreams, our disgust, our anger, our creativity, and our love . . . it's nothing but energy. If you hate, hatred will get energy and it will grow. If you love, love will grow.'

'Is that why people say, watch your thoughts . . . ?' he asked walking along side, by her.

'Yes, that is true.' She replied. 'Thoughts are also energy. That's why also we should think positive, always. Then not only positive will happen, we will also learn to weed away negative thoughts and thus would progress. Do you pray?'

'umm . . . sometimes . . .' he replied, 'umm . . . ya sometimes.'

'Pray every day, because prayers are energy. The more you pray the easier your road to success becomes because God's power is supreme and to draw his power you have to forgive your father and clear your soul. Then God will reside in you and not hatred with even lower self confidence. We are made complete, so preached Osho.' She replied affirmatively. 'And like a wise, never give up either on your dreams or on faith in God. Pray each day unfailingly and you will see the miracles God will show you. He will hold your hand and lead you ahead.'

The boy was overwhelmed and he held his face in his hand, 'Thanku for your guidance. You are a miracle in yourself in a . . . world where nobody cares for each other. You are a miracle and I can't thank you and God enough for that.'

'We should avoid seeing what others do for us, that's unwise,' she said tenderly, 'we should see what we can do for them. Expect only from God and not from people. Our universal father is very rich, expect only from him and along side thank Him for what He has given you. Never take Him for granted. Keep thanking Him.' Laila was wise to believe that God has abundance to give provided we learn to ask with the purity of our soul and with unshakable faith in the Almighty. Our soul gets cleansed by our good deeds. He watches us always and caters to our needs and fulfils our dreams. The clearer our soul is from the worldly dirt, the closer we remain to God and then help, love, guidance, care, fulfillment and success is inevitable in our life.

The boy was suffocated by the lack of family support which for any human is important on their path to success. Fortunately, he was saved and was compelled to forgive him wisely, and walk the path of the wise. Or else, he would have diverted his energy on reciprocating the hurt and avenging the wrongs committed by his father on him. His innocence was and would be destroyed earlier than his time.

A week later, on a Monday morning Laila was at her office and was sorting out the stack of designer garments dangling from the bar.

'What kind of shoes will go with this Laila?' asked Deepa restlessly.

'Bare feet,' she replied, 'let it be natural. You see,' she said moving her hands over the garments, 'the colors are so bright, the designer didn't heed me. So . . . so be it. I kept quite, why to put her off. Instead, I thought

269

I will do the styling and cut the scream. I can't stand a crowded picture. And Deepa my dear, stop worrying. You have to figure the way out. You have head, use it. Churn it.'

'Yes boss!' she smiled, 'I worry less since I last fainted.' They chuckled. 'What if she the designer disapproves of the shoot, the bare feet girl?'

'Hmm . . . good question,' said Laila, 'but this time you . . . give me the answer Deepa.'

She hesitated, 'aaah! I . . .' she said and then made up her mind, 'I would say, the garment was strikingly pretty, so we thought we shall not take away the attention from it and so we left her feet bare. Natural is in, all seasons.'

'Brilliant!' Said Laila as proud as a big bloomed pink and white lotus, 'not many I know can give such an honest yet a fabricated reply. Keep it up. I owe you a treat, for this one.' She smiled with composure and Deepa's, eyes glowed with her sense of achievement.

'So we should fix the shoot for Thursday?' asked Deepa confident of handling it well.

'No,' replied Laila, 'we will shoot over the week end.' And she picked up a loud leaf green short kurti covered with Swarovski crystal in beautiful patterns, form the international collection of garments. 'Hmm . . . India is hawt and Sunday, the designer is leaving for New York.' They chuckled. 'It's better to avoid fuss as I am aware of her demands. I mean, Brazentine has built a repute, and we will not stake our honor.'

'Yes,' she replied, 'we will keep it for Sunday and as an option we will consider Saturday.' She saw Laila's face, it wasn't in agreement. 'We will keep it for Sunday. Will that be ok?'

'Better.' She replied. 'And the model will have to do a trial on Saturday, a dry run of the shoot. Call the girl directly and pay her on time.'

'You don't want them through the agency?' Deepa asked.

'Not all the time.' She replied. 'Pay the girl on time.' She reiterated. 'No fussing with it.' In that moment, Tahir entered her office with his guitar and a sling bag. 'Heay!' Said Laila, 'walk in . . . walk in.'

'Um . . . shall I wrap up and fix it for this Sunday?' Deepa spoke confirmingly, wanting to move out of the room. 'I will send something to drink for you guys?'

'Yes. Please do so. Thanku. And I will see in you in some time.' Replied Laila. 'Keep your guitar there,' she said to Tahir, pointing at one of the empty chairs, 'not on the floor. You have to earn through it, so please respect the instrument. Oh by the way, welcome,' she said now looking at Deepa who was about to make an exit, 'welcome the new rising star of India, Tahir Sinha.' And they clapped. Tahir blushed, 'and meet Deepa, my assistant and my friend.' They smiled at each other, in acknowledgement and Deepa then made an exit from the cabin. 'It seems we got meet over drinks, since our last meet.' Said Laila to Tahir and both smiled.

Every talent needs support from people, from elders, responsible and sensitive because what may seem unimportant to others, is a matter of great significance to an artist. It gives them self-confidence and assurance of their talent which is very meaningful for them. It helps them and encourages them to perform better.

'Here,' he said, forwarding the C.D.

'Thanku,' said Laila, 'given your capability, I am sure you must have done a great job. Now, Tahir . . . I am going to introduce you to my boss.'

'Alexander . . . ?' he asked, 'don't tell me. I had a hunch, an intuition . . . oh . . . m . . . ok ok . . .' he checked his negative words. 'Fine. We will go.'

'Use your head.' She said, 'he is kind though a little pompous. And take this,' she said, taking out a pack of world's best cigar.

'Hmm . . .' he hummed in surprise.

'Give this as a gift to him,' she said, 'as an appreciation and as a mark of love.'

'To that old man? You are doing so much for me, I can't thank you enough,' he asked and chuckled covering his mouth shyly with his long artistic thin fingers.' Her kindness is unbelievable,' so thought the boy.

'Oh! Tahir . . .' she whispered, 'never tell that man, that he is old. He is very sensitive . . . about the issue of his age.'

'I got it,' he chuckled again. 'He is Immortal . . . ahhh . . . Yahoo! I am to meet the world's youngest old man,' and he chuckled loud. 'I got it. Don't panic, I kinda know what you wanna covey. I will be careful.' Laila smiled in relief though she knew how he knows about such, 'immortal' peopleie. By his past job at the bar. 'I will be good; debonair and polite.' he said and regained his composure. 'My shirt is ok?' he asked.

'It's perfectly fine,' she said reaching out for the intercom, 'nice color. Ok, now, I will check his availability over the phone and then we shall proceed.'

They were both nervous and he out of his anxiety was laughing nervously looking at Laila and her reaction to him. She appeared different at work, serious and composed. 'Lets go, he is there.' She said and went silent for a moment. She prayed for his success. They got and she walked before him, keeping him in her protection.

'Hi Alexander!' she said standing by the door, 'may we come in.' She was seeing his mood. He was on his laptop.

'Ah! Come in,' he said taking his eyes partially off the lap top. And Tahir started to giggle at the sight of Alexander's eternal youth with his dyed hair showing whites at the roots. He was right behind Laila and so she could hear him giggle. It made her recall her first day, how she had entered his office like a small ant meeting a spider.

'Alexander this is Tahir,' said Laila introducing him to the boy, as he was elder, 'and Tahir, this is the ever so powerful and famous, Alexander Kumar.' Alexander got and gave his hand, Tahir gave his too and very humble he did a Namaste post the handshake. Alexander seemed pleased.

'Please have a seat, young boy,' he said looking at Tahir. 'You can keep your guitar with you, no problems with that.' Tahir controlled his giggling and sat resting the guitar on his lap. 'It's all tuned?' he asked playfully, to make him comfortable.

'Um . . . yes!' he smiled.

'I hear you are quite a talent,' he said encouraging him through is remark. 'So tell me of your achievements.' Laila panicked. For a couple minutes there was this silence, not unhappy one but that of uncertain one. Tahir was not prepared for his answer as he came very casually prepared.

'I once, caught a rat,' Tahir spoke taking out his guitar form it's case. Laila was calm and Alexander settled his hair on his head displaying his expression that meant he found him not that big a talent as Laila had mentioned, 'and then I poured some whiskey over it, my father's,' and another silence engulfed the room, 'and then Sir Alexander,' he spoke anointing him with knighthood, in the presence of queen Laila. Alexander was aghast but he didn't interrupt. 'I lighted a matchstick and threw over it. It ran for it's life . . . . round and round and round. It got roasted.'

Alexander stared in silence and chuckled. 'How is that related to your music?' He asked staying surprisingly clam. Laila opened his mouth in an apology on his behalf for his nonsense noticing her Alexander waved at her with a slight raise of his finger, to stay quite.

'Sir Alexander,' he said, 'while the rat was getting roasted I was singing a song,' and he struck his guitar, 'may I?' He asked for his approval and he stringed his guitar and played it. It was followed by Robbie Williams' popular song, 'Lord, I am trying to be a better man.'

'What a boy!' exclaimed Alexander clapping at the his narration and the song. 'What an entertainer . . . I must say. 'Laila breathed in relief and forced a smile. 'God bless you child. You are tempting or so shall I say, pleasing to the ears. One in a million come with this kind of talent. You are praise worthy. 'Tahir bent in a bow to him and to Laila. 'Perfect setting.' Said Alexander and bowed slightly as a mark of acceptance and respect for the boy's creativity.

'Sir Alexander, while I was singing this song,' he said, 'there was an awakening. A voice that shook me. And I rushed to aid the rat. I poured water over it charred flesh and then I ran . . . what we do to others, as they say, comes back to us.' Laila looked at him. 'I ran and reached a hospital to save the rat. I met a beautiful nurse . . . who had beautiful eyes.' Alexander smiled. 'I sang another song,' and he asked, 'may I Sir?'

'Play on,' he replied enjoying every bit of it.

'Aankheen teri,' he began and took the note very high, Alexander was impressed, 'ittni hasseen . . . ki unkaashiq mai bann gaya hun . . . .' The depth of his song was enchanting. He sang a part of it, and said, 'It's a Sufi song.'

'M aware. They are mystics, they,' he said looking at Laila, 'sing in search of God and live in union with Him. Sufi songs are about one's relationship with God.' He looked away.

'True and Sir, so a nurse agreed to help.' He said in a flow. They smiled in enjoyment. She sent me to a healer,' he looked at Laila. 'She, sir, is a very wise woman. A faith healer. She asked me to leave the rat in her care and to pursue my talent. And thus I met you, Sir Alexander. May I?"

Alexander loved the importance the boy was showering on him, 'sure,' he roared.

'Wise men say . . . only fools fall in love . . . but I can't help . . .' he began singing. Alexander was charmed and sang along, 'falling in love with you . . . like the river flows . . .'

'Deep into the sea, darling . . .' Tahir sang the entire song seeing Alexnader enjoy it with memories from the past. Laila and Alexander clapped at the boy's clever talent. He stood up, bent and bowed. 'And Sir!' he said, 'the rat is recovering. It's safe with Laila.' They smiled.

'That was a quick and witty.' He replied and sat back on his chair rattling his mind to volley Alexander's words, which could be anything, from a query to a mere compliment.

'What shall I say . . .' said Alexander and paused with a sudden loss of words, 'stupendous. Tahir my boy, you deserve a break. How come you have not been signed?'

'Sir, Alexander . . . the world talks of supporting underdogs, "he answered naively, 'but the reality bites.' He was compelled to talk well because Alexander had good contacts, and that extra push from Tahir could get him to live his dreams. We all have to put that extra effort even when, we are tired of doing it, because luck takes over hard work.

'Hmm . . . I get that.' He said nodding his head. 'Your voice has depth . . . it rings of pain . . .' Laila looked at Tahir, who sat calm as that pretty much answered his question as to why God give him an unloving father and a dead mother. Alexander kept studying him. 'Give me your guitar,' he said in an impulse.

It sent a fright to Tahir because he loved his instrument and couldn't afford it being damaged as he didn't know what trick the rich man was about to pull on him and his dear guitar. 'Here,' he said, faintly, 'my guitar.' Alexander took it and he touched the string and struck a few notes. 'It's 'Take my breath away,' . . . yelled Tahir surprised at the man's talent. And Alexander rolled his eyes up an played some more. He was immersed in it . . . like floating in another world. Laila was quietly looking at him. He was in sync with his soul.

'Wonderful.' She said keeping in pace with the slow tempo of the song. Alexander genteelly opened his eyes.

'I forgive my father,' he said very calmly.

'Sir Alexander,' said Tahir, 'that was good.'

'I loved playing the guitar,' he said, 'but one day, my father banged it, broke it and threw it on the floor. Like a baby chick with broken legs and twisted wings, it lay there. I, from that day, didn't touch a guitar. It gave me a sense of a perennial fear . . . . because that day rang in my head. And it was from that day, I was a changed boy and a degraded man. A man who hated his father's guts and feared his wrath.' he said, looking at Tahir, 'In doing so, I transformed into a sadist, inflicting pain on people and gaining pleasure form it. The pain that my father gave me and taught, me was being passed on. I was happy, as though life will happen to me again,' he paused, Tahir was looking at him and in his mind he felt for that man's suffering, 'I became a happy tormentor.' He smirked calmly but his eyes were red. Laila, didn't utter a word for she wanted his bitterness to be out of him. 'That pain,' he said, 'I saw in you. But you my boy, are fortunate, you live in, today and you have her, the messiah with you, to save you and to help you. Never let her down.'

Tears welled up in Tahir's eyes, he licked his lips to cease it from falling down in public, but pain found it's path of solace and the strength to cry. 'Yes,' said Tahir, 'I am aware of it. She is my savior.'

'And mine too,' said Alexander, 'because through her I evolved. I learnt to give love and today, I learnt to forgive. And though you don't know, you inspired me to forgive my father and to let go of that pain . . . of the years of depravity form my soul because,' he said, as Tahir smiled, 'you, one fourth of my age, or so I may presume, have forgiven your father.'

'Is that why you were studying me?' he asked innocently, 'yes, Sir Alexander, I have forgiven my father. And Sir, Alexander, 'he said sweetly, 'you are an achiever.' Alexander looked up with his square shoulders upright. 'So, forgive your father and rule your empire, Brazentine.' Alexander smiled bravely. And you are wise, because only the wise can forgive.' Laila smiled looking at him.

'Yes,' she said, 'only the wise can forgive.'

'And here's your guitar,' he spoke like an angry child, 'take it my boy, before the devil in me . . .'

'It wouldn't rise Alexander,' confirmed Laila, 'because, you have forgiven your father. You are reborn and you are rising on the steps of evolvement. There is no devil in you who will destroy the lovely guitar because when we forgive, we give up the pain inflicted on us by others and in doing that, the devil dies. The soul takes over. The soul is love. And love is truth. And truth is God. And God, never victimizes. He fills us with His love.'

'Unless, we call for it,' he replied interrogatively.

'Yes,' she said with a broad smile. 'That, God's advocate and the chief justice, both in one.'

They felt quite for a moment.

Tahir looking at them said, "Sir Alexander! "and he got up from his seat and forwarding him, the C.D. of his original compositions recorded at the local studio, he asked courteously, "may I give you my original songs?"

'Is it as original, as the rat story?' Alex, asked with a clean smile. 'Well then, I have to hear it, once.'

'Once will be more than satisfying for me, 'he answered patronizing him, Laila looked at Tahir, 'You are a very busy man, so once will be satisfying for me. Please accept this.'

'Very well,' he said, 'young man I shall hear it, for you and for your talent.'

'There is a story running behind this, too,' he chuckled. Laila twitched, for the mouse was playing with the lion, though the spiritually awakened, he was scary. 'God,' she prayed, 'please take care', in her mind.

'Let's hear that, young man.' He said serenely.

'The rat, went to God and he pleaded for my brute act to be punished,' he said with pressure on the last word, 'so God said, 'don't shed a tear dear rat, I shall ask a messiah,' he said gesturing at Laila, but keeping his attention to Alexander, 'to punish him. She in turn, like an awakened soul, asked me to record not one, not two but five original tracks, for her. I died . . . almost, and then she said, that since you are genuinely guilty, it was an honest act, so, I today will introduce you the an Emperor who conquers any land he walks.' Alexnader smiled the at the fascinating way of his narration. 'I thought, how could I meet such a worthy man empty handed,' Laila froze and made a gulping sound. Tahir got up and said, 'Sir Alexander, this is my token of love. Please don't say no to it.' Alexander, was touched by his gesture, flawless and naïve and accepted the pack of cigar, form Tahir.

'Sir,' said Laila, 'I mean, Alexander . . . amm,'

'That's very sweet of you,' he said too Tahir. 'I appreciate it.' Alexander spoke with kindness and grace. 'You know, young man, talent that survives pressure is worthy of trust.' Laila twitched and went silent. She felt unease.

'That's very kind of you, Alexander,' she spoke peacefully, 'to appreciate this young talent. I shall leave with him?'

'Oh no,' he said stopping her from vacating the room. 'I have some news for you. Your photograph has been nominated one among the five pictures for the Indian association of photography. Congratulations for that.'

'Haa-n . . . ?' She looked in his eyes and said, 'thanks.'

'But, the thing is, we need to go to that podium as a winner,' he said pushing in the air with his palm, 'some push. Lobbying, as they call it at the Oscars. I need to do that for you.' He looked at Tahir and nobody spoke as he was thinking something important. 'I would be organizing a small get together, inviting the biggies, the contacts and the lens, the camera people from news media.'

'You mean the media?' she asked convulse. 'Ya, that would be good. More over, you are my boss and the boss is always wise.' She concluded not believing his words and not making a big scene out of it either.

'It's a benchmark for our magazine,' he said, 'no less than an achievement to look forward to . . . we will make it loud and clear, as clear as crystal that you will sweep the awards. The judges will have to be greased . . .' he said confidently and with a will.

'Greased?' said Tahir, 'but I heard . . . it was out of the world creation . . . isn't that . . .

'I wish, it was.' He replied, 'You will play there. I will ask my wife to arrange for it.' Laila was now cheered up and gay. She smiled at Tahir who was blushing at his victory. It meant a lot to him. 'If I wouldn't grease them, somebody else will. Somebody, less creative but more smart will sweep it. I will do my best to claw him down. I have heard, the rest are elder to you and very well connected. No defeat for Brazentine because,' he said with passion, 'success has to be claimed.' Laila, couldn't object, for it was he who ran the magazine, not her. It was not wise on her behalf to check his pace. She left the room gracefully, with his permission and with Tahir.

The event was organized amidst the judges and the media. The party was held at Alexander's gigantic bungalow. Like the man, the well rounded pillars of the bungalow, were old and strong, wise and polished. It was humid night. People glowed in the moisture of the nature with a drizzle form heaven, as the party began. It was a sing on God' blessing for, Alexander, Laila and Tahir, the young boy who was now engulfing the limelight standing with his guitar on the stage that was erected in Laura's supervision. A crowd of about hundred guest were present around the stage.

'She asked me,' said the boy in an American accent, 'who are you?' Then he paused and grinned, 'I said, a lover.'

'She asked, what is it that you are stairing at,' he smiled, 'I said, your pretty face." He replied pointing at an old woman in the front row.

'She asked, what is it that you want? Lovers as you see, have to answer a lot,' he spoke and looked at the end of the crowd. 'I replied, your love.' The crowded giggled.

'She asked, you may regret your move?' He said playfully, 'women,' he brought some pain in his voice naturally, 'they always test us, so I said, let regret be my destiny . . .' The crowd roared with laughter and in appreciation. 'Ladies and gentlemen,' he struck a chord of his guitar, 'some sing for love, some for the lack of it,

I,' he said, pointing at the crowd holding the guitar in his left hand, 'sing for you.' And he began with a grin that stole many a female hearts, 'I just called to say I love you.' Women drooled; the boy sang even higher notes and called for cheers, from the small gathering. 'Once more, once more, 'shouted the oldies hiding behind the young ones. 'We want more . . . .' cheered the young and clapped like deafening pitter patter of the rain. He raised his hand giving in to the crowd and presented another song and two more in a row.

At the end, Mr. Darshan Kedia, approached him and hired him on the spot for his international event management company. Tahir soaked in disbelief, ran to announce it to Laila, who was serious faced that evening and hugged her crazily. He pulled her away from the man, a judge of the future's awards event, she was interacting with, on Alexander's request. She patted him on his achievement and congratulated him for being his own sponsor. He ran and thanked Alexander who was having his dinner with a guest. Alexander smiled and said, "this is just the beginning . . . By the way great work from you, tonight. Get your passport handy young man." The night was delightful for two talents were climbing their way up to set a new horizon for themselves and the world around them.

Tahir came back to Laila, 'you don't seem . . .' he said, unable to tread her thoughts, 'there's something missing from the usual . . . you.'

'The night has set in, Tahir we have to wait for the sunrise,' she replied toying with her glasses stem. 'Have your dinner.'

'Hey!' he said, 'tell me, why we call this, a mock tail?' he giggled.

She understood, he was trying to pump up her serotonin level, the happiness hormone for he was a kind and sensitive boy. She replied, 'because it mocks the cocktail and says, 'hey! you give people a fake high. You throw them out of balance whereas I, give them a nice time and keep them sober.' Tahir began to bubble with laughter throwing his head backward. He was crazily happy.

'You, beat me always!' he remarked.

'So can you,' she said, he was perplexed, 'you can and shall, beat your own achievements, Tahir.' He laughed louder. 'Come'on stand straight, you are a celebrity now . . . some poise is expected out of you.'

'Give me your glass,' he said giggling, 'I will keep it there.' And he took the empty glass form her hand.

'Oh! No.' she said, 'you are star.' She chuckled at his sweet gesture, 'and stars don't hold other's glasses.'

He chuckled, 'yeah!,' he said, 'm a star who's yet to like shine like you and for that, I gotta multi task,' and he crazily took her glass and leapt, to keep it away. 'You know, Laila . . .'

'Ok. Hold on,' she said cutting his conversation. 'What all do you thank God for?'

He jerked his body and looked away. 'For you, for Sir Alexander,' he said, 'and for this . . . it's like a dream not a penny less. A local street boy singing for the elite . . . I sincerely thank God for . . . it. What is luck, if not God's grace.'

'Tahir,' she said, 'there are only,' she glanced at him, 'four seasons in life. Don't lose your life to meet God in the fifth season.' He was taken aback. 'Don't let your grave be more fortunate than you, you become more fortunate than it. Be wise and seek God. Tahir, for there is no life as beautiful, than the one lived, as a seeker of God.'

It was imperative for Laila, to brief him about the beauty of the life in search of God because, he was successful and success is a strong detonator as strong, it is a creator. The polarities, always exists in the same energy, except in that of the purity of God. And the one who chases success as a seeker of God, he remains sober in the highest high of life because only, he knows, the universal truth, that nothing last forever and what does last is the energy, called love. The energy, which created us and the energy that, caters us. The energy that is, God.

'I will never fail you,' he said making solemn promise for Laila love was as pure as the God she was referring to.

She raised her head at the universe, above her and said, 'don't fail your own soul, Tahir and never fail God. Be right and be strong. As for me . . .' He was beginning to comprehend her forth coming words and did not want to hear it, 'I may not be with you . . . God will.' He gripped her hand and began to weep at the thought of, her death. Like a child he cling to her fearing getting lost in a huge fair, called life. 'If you seek God, you will never need me, child.' By then it began to drizzle. She said, 'see Tahir, even God is shedding a tear, moved by your's. This is how powerful the life is, in sync with God, nothing and nobody can break you . . . for nobody is more powerful than, the creator.'

'Our universal father.' He said wiping his tears and the rain drops from his face. She smiled, this time, from her soul. She felt a peace, in guiding the boy into the Almighty's, guidance.

Laila won the award, as the photographer of the year from the Photography association of India and was nominated for an International award, the same season. Wearing an evening gown, as when she graced the stage to collect the award, Tahir and Alexander were cheering up and clapping like a thunder. Tahir was the star performer for the evening and he put half of the money he earned into and an old age home. The boy had well learnt the attitude of gratitude as a seeker of God. He was clapping and stood up with respect as she collected the award. She said, 'I forgive,' she said, 'and I thank the man who made this award possible for me.' There was a grim silence in the huge hall. 'He is and will remain my inspiration and may God,' she smiled, 'bless him always.' In that function, the ovation had a different tune to it. It had adulation, and a suspense, which thankfully didn't overpower the success of Brazentine and that of her first award night, it did leave the press buzzing. The media turned her into a star and a phenomena that comes once in a lifetime. Champaign popped and appetizers did rounds, celebration flowed and Alexander inevitably was a happy man. But there prevailed was a grim silence: the silence of deceit and the power of forgiveness, for Alexander was the man, who had her laptop hacked, to test her talent in pressure. It had turned out to surpass his imagination and his expectations from Laila and won allocades, taking his Brazentine empire, to a new height.

CHAPTER 10

*A lover chases love in pursuit of a paradise
and what he gets is even superior.*

It was the month of February, mild sun, clear blue sky and slight cold. It was cozy and lazy. Laila wearing a floral snug fit dress up to her knees and a covered toe stilettos, walked out of the elevator of her apartment. A man wearing a simple t-shirt without collars and jeans, handed her a large bouquet of flowers. "It's sent for you." He said and gave her the white oriental lilies wrapped with a thick red ribbon. Unsure if it was for her she half held it and the rest half the man was supporting it with his hands.

"Excuse me," she said as though he was giving her the plot to carry out a bank robbery, 'who is it for?'

"You." He said and began to pace away.

She held the bouquet and said, "hang on. My name isn't Laila and who is this for? I mean my name is Laila."

The man marched back, took out a small card from in between the flowers and held it to her, "it reads your name, "Dear Laila," the watchman told me it was you."

Laila was aghast. She reread it and holding the bouquet she delved into reading the next line. The script had a foreign origin, like sticks put here and there. 'It seems, it's written in Chinese. Who knows me from China?' She smiled and looked up with chaotic energy. As they both disembarked from the elevator, the delivery boy was soon gone, thus no availability for further questioning.

She walked ahead and Ravinder greeted her, "Good Morning Madam. May I help you," he said gesturing to help her with the bouquet, "Nice flowers madam," he remarked. She clutched it tight as if she were a prisoner heading for trials holding the shackles and not a bouquet. Newness has an unease to it and unease in the morning was new to her. "This is for you," he said giving her a rolled gift, with a red ribbon and a note, that read, "Dear Laila," and she said, trying to read the next line, "it's Persian."

She blinked her eyes, "I can't read this. But I will unwrap it."

"Oh, MY! . . . this is so beautiful," she said with disbelief, as he unrolled it before her eyes. It was an intricate and exquisite hand made Persian prayer carpet. "Who gave and why did you take it? You shouldn't have accepted it . . . . God knows who . . . she said enraged, "you should have acted responsible."

"The watchman gave me," he said sheepishly pointing at the gate where Tulsiram, the watchman of the building, stood.

"You mean . . . he bought this for me?" she asked him and commanded, "call the watchman. I would like to have a word with him." The watchman was a man tired of watching the same faces everyday, came forward to meet her. He was a man in his late fifties and wore a khaki shirt and pants.

"Madam," he said, "this is for you." And he gave her a rectangular gift.

Laila almost got close to fainting in confusion. She smirked looking at his age and what he was up to. "It's his kindness," she murmured in relief. "May be he is grown very fond of me . . ."

"That's very kind of you, Tulsiramji." she said soaked in mystification and clutching the flowers, "where did you manage to buy this form . . . . it's beautiful?" She said pointing at the carpet hanging from the car's roof.

"My entire life's income," he said with a pitiful smile, "can't afford this, madam. A man gave it early morning, today, saying it's your anniversary."

"Anniee . . . Haan!" she said breaking into amusement, "Tulsiram ji, how could you believe such a thing? What about security . . . any man walks in and . . ." He stood there speechless cutting a sorry figure to which she checked her mouth. "Thanku anyway, I will handle it."

And he forwarded the gift saying, "that man said, that I should give this one, to you as I am your lucky charm."

Laila broke into a puzzled laughter and said. "He said you are my luck charm? Ok then I too believe the same for today."

"Yes," replied Tulsiram. "I will open the gate for you, madam, otherwise you would get late."

"Right," she said, "right . . ." and she put her left hand on her forehead in disbelief, "let's go." Her driver carried the flowers and kept it genteelly on the back seat next to her, while Laila unwrapped the rectangular gift handed to her by Tulsiram. It was a bottle of fragrance with a similar card with a silver background and the rest engraved in gold. It read, "Dear Laila," and line the next line in French, which she tried hard to pronounce. She tossed the cover and smelt the fragrance. It smelt of love, with the sweetness of apple and refreshment of jasmine flowers. She sprayed some.

On reaching her office she got off her car holding the lilies in her arms. A boy came forward, with mysterious eyes. "Are you Laila?" he asked with a grin. She was looking at him trying to solve the riddle, "this is for you." He said and gave her a bigger rectangular gift. It contained a pair of passionate red stilettos, with glass heels, an absolute delight form Italy. It had her name and a message in Italian. "Why don't I get something from England," she mumbled, that would be less labyrinth to walk by.

The breeze blew more mystery and love with it, that morning. Somebody patted on her back. Laila turned around, there stood a teenaged girl, and she gave her a box.

"My God," she thought to herself, "what is some one upto and how perfect is he . . . what a beautiful mind . . ." she wondered. It was a girl's dream come true to own a make up box as complete as this, it was from Switzerland. The girl and the boy, both disappeared.

"I can't resist the footwear," she said looking at her neck piece and taking the shoes out from the box, "it will go with this red garnet neckpiece, if not with my dress." Overjoyed and out of patience, she wore the footwear,' How did he know my size . . . the man has some taste . . . hmm.' She rang on her driver's mobile and said. 'Please take the gifts to the car. I can't carry it to the office. They will die of a shock.' Shyly she sent it away. 'Oh! Ravinder, umm . . . take this bouquet too.' and she freed herself of all the token of somebody's love apart from the stilettos and his heart.

As free as the waves of the Arabian sea, Laila swung and staggered like a marathon winner, who comes to a stop after a long run to the victory podium. Celebrating the success of hiding her invisible lover's all visible sign of love.

But love is not easy to escape when destiny carves it, mentally we always remain close to our lover. That's why it's lucky to find love and remain with it.

On her way to the elevator, she, to her surprise, felt the youth and her child like charm reappearing. Oh! She was blossoming and transcending in a fluid state of mind, that weightlessness, that dreamy cloudiness in the head, that vitality to go out and have fun. The cheerful mystery made her sway from end to end. A little coy and a little lightened up than her usual reserved demeanor she entered her office. Laila by now was already an enlightened mind and yet the mystery loomed for some suspense is revealed with real person in sight.

"You look . . . ammh . . ." said the deep eyed Deepa, catching her unaware, "um . . ."

Laila looked at herself and clarified," I kind of didn't dress up really well, my boy Vivian . . ."

"If there somebody who can look strikingly gorgeous in a crisis . . . it has to be you. My boss! You!" she replied.

"I see, thanku," said Laila walking faster to cover her soft beaming youth before Deepa could guess something more. She dashed into her cabin, flicked her bag on the chair perpetually looking out of the window, giggling and gushing in her own company. She wanted to see glow in the mirror to figure out how remarkable was difference. Happily she sat on her table resting her passionate high heels on the glistening floor. She wanted to swing, and laze. She was floating and Lokesh, her colleague entered her room.

"Hi dear! This is for you," he said holding a huge bouquet of Tulips and red roses, "and now come give me a hug . . ."

"Lokesh! I didn't know you had . . ." she said going moist in the eyes, "umm . . . this is the first time . . . um . . ." she spoke sensing the mystery man was finally in front of her. "I never . . ."

"You never," he said with love in his eyes, "mentioned that 6th February is your birthday."

Winding up her emotions she responded, "what? I . . . Oh! I am . . . ya, yes I forgot it's my parent's anniversary today, I am not February born. So, that pretty much, ahem . . .' she said coughing, "solves the riddle."

"Oh! I was," he said, "planning to ask for a treat . . . we could . . . umm . . . but anyway, congratulations to your parents. They live in Chennai I believe. The receptionist gave this gift along with the . . ."

"Bouquet . . ." she said wanting to get rid of him and of the mystery and get back to work, "bouquet . . .

give me . . . and the gift, thank you dear. Why didn't you ask the bell boy . . ."

"Oh why bother him . . ." he said looking at her from top to bottom, "I was coming up anyway. Besides your sight early in the morning is always welcome." He smiled.

"Ya, right. Kind as ever," she said playfully, "and now Mr. Lokesh . . ."

"I know, I know . . ." He replied. "M going to my cubicle." And they chuckled.

"I didn't mean it like that," she said, "but anyway, have a nice day."

"Nice dress and . . ." he complimented, "how do you look without it?"

"Ahem!" she said narrowing her eyes, "thanks."

"I mean, without your high heels," he clarified with lust dripping from his eyes behind the spectacles.

"The cubicle awaits you my dear, grace it," she spoke diverting his attention back to his word, sternly. "See you."

Lokesh nodded his head, "see you. Bye," and walked out. Laila stood in a stupor stage and looked at the flowers. She touched the rose first, it was velvety and fresh. She opened the gift, which was a sterling silver mirror from Holland and the tag remained the same, maintaining the link of the mastermind. She held the mirror and fulfilled her desire of seeing herself in it. Her oval innocent face and her deep brown eyes, her supple lips and her delicate porcelain skin, they were glowing and vibrating with excitement and youth. 'Who is it?' she murmured. 'God . . . end the mystery . . . ,' she prayed.

The most important element of love is love itself, but the most important thing about mystery is, the plot. And when there is plot in love, it sets in a desperation to conquer that love, and to remove the blindfold that caresses our mind. And mind they allege isn't required in love. So less one uses their mind the deeper forms the bond between the lovers because mind is love's enemy and who requires an enemy in love, who but the fool and the unwise. The wise, the one who follow their souls, follow their heart, soaking in the magical charm of love.

Her phone rings drawing Laila back to office. "Mam, Miss Tara Shah would like to talk to you. Shall I connect her? She is on hold."

Laila recalled the date, "oh, ya, yes you certainly can put her on the line."

"Laila?" said the woman in a husky voice from the other end of the lines.

"Tara?" replied Laila sweetly.

"Yes," she confirmed. "You are coming for my wedding? You can't miss it . . . it's my wedding."

Laila held her head in her hands in disappointment, "Why do you say that, of course I would be coming. I mean it's your wedding tonight"

"Tonight?" yelled the woman, "come" on Laila, you have to be here now. It's my wedding . . . I mean can there be something more important in life than wedding?'

Laila went quiet. "Is aunty with you?" she asked. "The end to the mystery man," a voice came to her mind that lowered her energy.

"What about her now? I . . . this is . . . you can't do this . . . you have to be here, in five minutes flat." And she hung up.

"God," said Laila, with the receiver in her hand touching her forehead, 'for once you forgive me. I hate attending weddings . . . the pressure . . . and the aunties . . . they come on me like hungry hyenas on deer. God," she said innocently, 'the theme is constellation and I am burning like the sun right now. And did you hear her, "what is more important in life than marriage . . . ?" She chortled. The phone rang again, "I want to see you here in five minutes." Said Tara Shah, a pediatrician friend of hers and Vivian was found abandoned by his parent's in her clinic in Pune. She was to getting married to a pilot, Dev Shrivastav, a tall and elegant man with high lighted self grooming and polished social grace. He was the man on the move.

In thirty minutes, Laila was at Tara's apartment which was crammed with guests, children running here and there, half opened suitcases, beauticians at work and men ogling at women ; who is the slimmest, who has gained weight from the previous wedding she was seen, whose blouse has the thinnest strap, who's lingerie is standing out from the fabric, to who is the available one.

Preparation were at its peak at the Shah's residence. And Tara, was shying away from the public eye as her make artist had not turned up. "No problem," said Laila, 'I will call Shenna Hussain, she is the best in the industry. Please don't panic, sweat will damage your skin. And to this, Tara began fanning herself with anything handy, from a comb to a plate. 'I can't take a chance with my skin, it's . . .'

'The most important event of your life,' said Laila with a poise.

'It's not funny Laila, I am . . . .' She said panicked, "what will Dev say . . ."

'What will he say,' said Laila, what more did he expect from a doctor?' and she broke into a spell of loud laughter. 'You guys . . ." she said calming her, 'ok . . . fine . . . chill it . . .'

'Laila,' called Shenna Hussain standing by the door, 'hi!' as Laila got up to usher her in and she hugged her. Her fragrance was exotic and loud like the kajal in her eyes. 'This is for you,' she said handing her a gift.

From the corner of her eyes Laila looked at Tara, that was the most cunning expression ever, from her to her. 'umm . . . tha . . . thanks. Have a seat, here's the mirror,' she said calmly, 'and you give my Miss Tara Shah, the bestest glow on her skin. Come'on Sheena . . . she is all your's.'

'Just my skin haan!' corrected Tara, 'Not me.'

'Take it easy.' Said the make up artist, 'Laila make our work fun. She doesn't mean hurt.' As Tara cooled down and the heat turned on for that night, celebration. Laila opened the gift and gasped, it was a hand crafted jewelry box made form ivory, and the language as the box suggested was of, Tanzania. It read, 'made in Tanzania.'

'Lovely. I wish I could . . . ,' said Laila in bid to keep the mystery under cover. She opened the box and found a pair of chandelier earrings sparkling like white sand in the sun. "Thank you, but nice gift. Thanks a ton. M gonna wear this tonight, with my saree."

'No, it's given to me . . .' replied Sheena. 'This, the watchman . . .'

Tara, looked at her and shrieked, without hearing what Shenna said previously 'Oh my God . . . that is so sweet of her.' She remarked and said, 'what's in the box? Get it here . . .'

'Ya it is,' she said hiding the earring to pretend it was Sheena who gave the gift not the mystery man which Laila had figured out by the silver card attached to it. 'It had to be him.' She whispered. 'Listen,' she said, 'you focus on your make up and your man. It adds to the charm of the day . . . okahy? Let this box be . . . I will go home and come back,' she said.

Her friend calmed her excitement, 'You?' she asked, 'You will come back? Who are fooling you escapist?'

'Escapist?' said the makeup artist, 'I haven't heard of a woman braver than her.'

'Ya?' asked Tara and then she recalled Laila's transformation from a psychiatrist to a very successful fashion photographer, paying the price well with time. 'Yes,' she said, 'my Laila is brave.' They smiled and Laila realized she was sweating.

'I will take a shower and get dressed after you just in case you aren't wanting me to go away to my place.' She said.

'I am already dressed . . . it's just the make up and the jewelry that I am to adorn.' Said Tara. 'Please hurry up Laila . . . I don't wanna be late.'

'Chill,' she said, 'it's not a hospital and calm down or your skin you see . . .' and she chuckled. 'My head, "she said to herself, 'it's swinging. I will take a shower and get normal." She headed to the shower while Sheena sculpted a exuberant and pretty bride out of Tara, who was exulted to look at herself in the mirror.

'Gee!' she remarked, 'this can't be me.' And the evening knocked. She headed towards the venue with her kith and kin who were swinging with happiness.

It was a clear night sky, alike the morning the breeze blew slightly cold, the huge fire light were blazing up towards the night sky at the entrance of a posh five star hotel, J.W. Marriot, the venue of the wedding. Cars rolled in one after another and guest dressed in shimmer and shine, were welcomed at the wedding hall.

Then came, the lady of the night draped in black chiffon with tiny silver stars on it, black high heels, the diamond earring hanging in her ears and her long black hair cascading like the black clouds in the sky. She looked like a star fallen from the constellation, so passionate and stunningly attractive and through her garment was visible her porcelain skin and her perfect curves, as full as the moon on that night.

Her, elegance personified and her untouched beauty was cynosure of eyes, as she stepped out of her car and entered the hotel's lobby. People turned in awe and broke into whispers . . . 'that's Laila . . . the star photographer . . .' said a lady to her man. 'AHA! She is as pristine as her pictures,' complimented the man on the couch. 'Awesome,' said a woman banging into another man while her eyes were fixed at her. 'Sensational,' said another man standing near the reception. Photographers clicked and steps of people lost movement, stewards delayed turning up on the table to catch to look of her to their heart's content as Laila, confident and graceful in her chiffon walked toward the marriage hall. In there history repeated itself, in next to no time. As Laila walked to wish the couple seated on the stage decorated with flowers; yellow, red and white, the guest soaked their eyes in the delightful creation of the God, the powerful yet delicate, the successful and the humble, the kind and the beautiful, the one and only, Laila.

When a woman walks by a crowd what catches people's eyes is her beauty, but what remains in people's heart forever, is her soul. And Laila had a soul with the beauty of faith, and faith in turn soothed the parched eyes of the guests in the hall who may be had seen a better face than hers in their lifetime but not a better woman than her. For she was a woman with a mystical aura of love and grace which reflected through her deep brown thoughtful eyes as she glanced at people with honesty and loveliness that comes to one through God's grace only.

Extending her good wishes to the couple, she was walking back and the steward offered her a mocktail and said, 'mam, this scroll is for you.' Laila took a drink and without looking at who's looking her way she moved ahead and with opened the scroll feeling a calming energy around her. It read, 'I am waiting in the terrace of this hotel.' She froze and looked down at the marble floor.

A child wearing a blazer held her hand and said, 'come with me.' He was tiny and he babbled, his fingers were very tender and had sparkling witty eyes. Laila gave in to his charm and couldn't say a no to him. He walked outside the hall and towards the elevator. 'Don't fear,' he said as she began to retreat.

'Where do you want to take me?' she asked.

'I don't know,' he said with a warm smile. 'Come.' And he asked her to press the button for the elevator and as she did it, the elevator's door opened and they both stepped in. He took her to the terrace.

The terrace looked empty and a man began to play the saxophone, in a intoxicating tune under the full moon of the night sky. The breeze was blowing her through her hair, she looked at the child who had escorted her, he was smiling at her and freed his tiny hand of her grip. And suddenly, the man stopped playing the saxophone and the silence was bewildering. There was a loud noise and Laila looked up at the sky. Two choppers were flying side by side with a huge banner and then there was fire work and huge light from below, to light up what the banner read.

It read the three magical words, 'You are beautiful.'

Laila was as amazed as she, all one could be are in the effect of the magical words. The choppers came closer and dropped rose petals on her. "AHA . . . ." She went breathless . . . and amazed. 'I don't believe this . . .' she said bathing in the red petals of the flower of love, roses. They dropped more and more and then they flew away.

'Ten years of my life, 'said the mystery man, 'ten years,' he repeated and emphasized, 'I waited for this night,' Laila turned back and the light turned on without revealing much,' the night that would have completed my life and my soul's quest, Laila.' And he walked closer to her.

'Who are you?' she asked and stood still with the wind touching her genteelly.

'Who are you, Laila?' he asked like a night in the shining armor.

She smiled, 'God, psychic, saint, messiah . . . the greater the experience the bigger the designation 'm given. I am born to make the world believe in the good and God.'

'I am a Zen monk. How good is life without me,' and then Laila saw his face and her eyes welled up in tears of the love she had lost from the man who loved her and had set her free for her happiness.

'Tears,' said the man, 'are for rituals. For you my love, is only happiness.' Laila was over whelmed and gave a unforgettable smile which comes from the soul, when the soul finds it mate, a soul mate. That rare was the magical connection between them tonight.

'How have you been . . . ?' She asked wiping her tear drops.

He looked in her eyes and said, 'your tears says, my love that," and he wanted to wipe her tears, but as a monk he refrained. 'I have not been very well . . . and that, you will take better care of me.' And his eyes went moist with affection. 'As a zen monk I shall love you for your thoughts . . . I have been doing well under my master's guidance.'

'You have changed,' she said.

'I had to, you told me on one night, life is about welcoming changes,' and he genteelly gave her a peck on her cheeks.

'Zen monk!!!!!!,' she whispered warmly like the girl she was ten years back, 'I missed you . . .' and so the mystery began to clear up and what remained was love and the strength of it.

'That's why,' he replied looking deeply in her eyes, 'I had, let you go.' And he embraced her in a warm hug in amidst the cold breeze form the sea. She felt a peace like a ship being harboured after years of standing the rough weather and the wild storms, in the sea. The silence of the night was the serenading silence of deep love, a love that that find love in a way as beautiful as it could be.

'I didn't know, you were such a talented lover under cover,' she said breaking into a sigh and a smile.

'How special is special, if there is no specialty in it, my love,' he said tenderly clapsing his hand, 'and what love is from a lover which is not special.'

'Where have you been for so long, so many years . . . almost a life time . . . I never heard from you.' She spoke softly and the breeze blew.

He pulled himself back and said, 'I moved to the U.S., in the city of angles, Los Angeles.' He smiled, 'because after losing my angle what I thought of was of money and her.'

'Who?' she asked like a girl.

"You, you and God," he said. 'I missed you Laila, I missed you a hell lot but that stopped bothering me under ever since I was under my Zen master who said I shall meet you in a beautifully bizzare way.' Shyly she looked away and looked back. 'You have turned by far more beautiful than you were . . . is it because you wanted to flatter me or it's your habit to look good?' he whispered.

'I was wrong,' she chuckled, 'you haven't changed.'

'Well,' he said taking his face away from her, 'that reminds me to mention that I am . . . also a part time Salsa instructor.' Laila eyes lighted up.

'Hmm . . . that's quite a passionate dance, is that why you chose it?' she said politely.'

'You are judging me,' he said with a grin, 'my Tai-Chi master says, judgment is only God's prerogative . . . as everybody has our own reasons to be who we are.'

'Oh! My,' she said, 'that's quite a line from you, no wonder you are so calm in the eyes.'

'You see Laila,' he replied, 'he taught me a line,' a man's character is in his eyes which is why what he sees, he becomes."

She said, 'that makes you a complete man . . . I am . . .'

'You are impressed, my royal highness. But the chalice of your eyes are getting me drunk . . .' he said and moved close her. "You are an angel, victory of good over bad. There can't be another you and that's why my love, I followed you through your friend, Tara.'

Her eyes narrowed in surprise and she held his hand very genteelly. 'So you were the man, in the bus . . . who got off with me on my first day at work? You were the man, in the spa where I had left my keys? You were the man who stood away clapping for me . . . on Brazentine's third anniversary?'

'Yes,' he replied sweetly. 'I was the man. I was the man . . . Laila . . . I was failing the strength to keep myself away from you . . . but I couldn't approach you.'

'But why?' she asked. 'We were such good friends.'

'Yes, we were,' he replied, 'but . . . I wanted more and my master suggested . . . not to block your path . . . and that's why, I never called.' His eyes went moist and he covered it with his fingers. 'I was in love with you and I love you, more than I love myself. And he said, 'no man is a man who doesn't surrender his love to the one he loves.'

'Yes, Dr. sandeep. You win,' she said and he forwarded his open palm to her. She slipped her hand into it and glowed by that touch, the touch of love.

'Congrats!' And the fire crackers burned high and beautiful behind her.

"You win too!' Said the Zen monk, Dr. Sandeep. 'For, we had a word as to who among us becomes a seeker of God first {thereby attaining Nirvan}. You win Laila you win and I am still a monk. But I knew, deep within me, that one day, the storm with pass by and that, I will meet you . . . . thereby living my dream and . . .'

'And so did I . . . .' said Laila pleased by his words.

A life that touches other's, a heart that conquers hearts, a soul that gives solace, belonged to a woman, evolved, contemporary, successful and high heeled. A woman who lived with faith and endurance, innocence and simplicity, tenderness and strength, the woman who lives her dreams and added to the joy of the world. A beauty so pristine and powerful was that woman who was loved and respected by everybody. The woman born out of love, to love was Laila Mallya.

———❖———